Tamarack River Ghost

Books by Jerry Apps

Fiction:

The Travels of Increase Joseph
In a Pickle
Blue Shadows Farm
Cranberry Red
Tamarack River Ghost

Nonfiction:

The Land Still Lives
Cabin in the Country
Barns of Wisconsin
Mills of Wisconsin and the Midwest
Breweries of Wisconsin
One-Room Country Schools
Wisconsin Traveler's Companion
Country Wisdom
Cheese: The Making of a Wisconsin Tradition
When Chores Were Done
Country Ways and Country Days
Humor from the Country
The People Came First: A History of Cooperative Extension
Ringlingville USA
Every Farm Tells a Story
Living a Country Year
Old Farm: A History
Horse Drawn Days
Campfires and Loon Calls
Garden Wisdom
Rural Wit and Wisdom

Children's Books:

Eat Rutabagas
Stormy
Tents, Tigers, and the Ringling Brothers
Casper Jaggi: Master Swiss Cheese Maker

Tamarack River Ghost

A Novel

Jerry Apps

Terrace Books
A trade imprint of the University of Wisconsin Press

Terrace Books, a trade imprint of the University of Wisconsin Press, takes its name from the Memorial Union Terrace, located at the University of Wisconsin–Madison. Since its inception in 1907, the Wisconsin Union has provided a venue for students, faculty, staff, and alumni to debate art, music, politics, and the issues of the day. It is a place where theater, music, drama, literature, dance, outdoor activities, and major speakers are made available to the campus and the community. To learn more about the Union, visit www.union.wisc.edu.

Terrace Books
A trade imprint of the University of Wisconsin Press
1930 Monroe Street, 3rd Floor
Madison, Wisconsin 53711–2059
uwpress.wisc.edu

3 Henrietta Street
London WCE 8LU, England
eurospanbookstore.com

Printed in the United States of America

Library of Congress Cataloging-in-Publication Data

Apps, Jerold W., 1934–
Tamarack River ghost : a novel / Jerry Apps.
p.   cm.
ISBN 978-0-299-28880-8 (cloth: alk. paper)
ISBN 978-0-299-28883-9 (e-book)
1. Swine—Wisconsin—Fiction.
2. Factory farms—Wisconsin—Fiction.
3. Farm life—Wisconsin—Fiction.
4. Reporters and reporting—Wisconsin—Fiction.
I. Title.
PS3601.P67T36   2012
813'.6—dc23
2012009944

To
Sue, Kate, and Natasha

Contents

Acknowledgments   **ix**

Prologue   **3**

1. Josh Wittmore   **9**
2. Lazy Z Feedlot   **15**
3. Fishing on the Millpond   **21**
4. Natalie Karlsen   **24**
5. Tamarack River Valley   **29**
6. *Farm Country News*   **38**
7. Tamarack River Ghost   **46**
8. Nathan West Industries   **50**
9. Dr. William Willard Evans   **56**
10. Dr. Randy Oakfield   **61**
11. Research Proposal   **67**
12. Big Hog Farm Coming   **72**
13. Dinner Date   **77**
14. Ice Fishing   **86**
15. Valley History   **94**
16. Fred and Oscar   **97**
17. Skiing in the Park   **100**
18. Informational Meeting   **105**
19. Opposing Positions   **116**
20. Fred and Oscar   **118**
21. Yes or No to Factory Farms   **122**
22. Winter Festival   **126**

Contents

23. Fred and Oscar   137

24. Paper Problems   141

25. Smear Tournament   145

26. Nathan West 435   152

27. Decision Time   161

28. Tamarack Museum   165

29. Zoning Committee Meeting   168

30. Newspaper Demise   177

31. New Journalism   182

32. Fred and Oscar   187

33. Different Results   190

34. Spring Snowstorm   201

35. Confession   204

36. Opening Day   211

37. Electronic News   216

38. Surprise Present   224

39. New Hog House   228

40. Outrage   234

41. Department Decisions   238

42. Fourth of Seventh-Month   241

43. Truce   249

44. Disaster   254

45. Blame   260

46. A New Beginning   268

Epilogue   273

Acknowledgments

I began this novel while in the Boundary Waters Canoe Wilderness Area of northern Minnesota. It was in early September 2009 that my son and canoe partner, Steve, and I were staying in Moose Cabin at Hungry Jack Lodge and day-tripping into the famous canoe area. On a rainy afternoon, when we appreciated having a roof over our heads, I posed a "what if" question to Steve, who is chief photographer at the *Wisconsin State Journal*. (My novels always begin with "what if?") I asked, "What if an agricultural reporter is caught up in the potential demise of his newspaper and at the same time faces one of the biggest stories of his career, a potential large-scale hog farm coming to central Wisconsin?" Being a newspaperman, Steve was intrigued with the idea. When we weren't paddling or fishing, we began fleshing out the main characters, and the basic elements of the plot. A year later and once more in the Boundary Waters, we worked on the drafts I had been writing since the last time we were there. This time we discussed subplots, further character development, dialogue, and a host of other matters, including the ghost. Many thanks to Steve, for his knowledge of the newspaper industry, as well as his always honest appraisal of my musings.

All of my writing, novels included, requires a considerable amount of research. Even though I grew up on a farm and had a professional career in agriculture, there is much I don't know. Emeritus Professor Gerald Campbell, Department of Agricultural and Applied Economics, University of Wisconsin–Madison, College of Agricultural and Life Sciences, helped me understand some of the nuances of integrated agricultural firms as well as insights into confined animal feeding operations (CAFOs). I appreciate his knowledge and insight.

A big thank you to my friend and fellow historian Elmer Marting, Monona, Iowa. Elmer introduced me to Steve Kregel. The Kregel family operates a well-run hog-producing operation near Guttenberg, Iowa. Steve not only took time to answer my many questions about large-scale hog-producing operations, but he also gave me a tour of one of the buildings so I could see their very modern system firsthand.

Discussions with my brother, Donald, helped me to recall how we cared for hogs on the home farm when we were growing up and raised as many as fifty hogs during the war years of the early 1940s. I also want to thank Wisconsin Department of Natural Resources conservation warden Todd Schaller for information about firearms and equipment DNR conservation wardens have at their disposal.

Several people took time to read various drafts of the material. My wife, Ruth, read sections of the manuscript and offered helpful comments. My daughter, Sue, elementary teacher, author, and reading specialist, read parts of the manuscript several times. Her eye for character development and plot sensibility was greatly appreciated. Natasha Kassulke, editor of *Wisconsin Natural Resources Magazine*, read the entire manuscript and offered several valuable suggestions for its improvement. I can't say enough about Kate Thompson's contributions. She digs into my stories, looks around to find out if they make sense, and then makes suggestions both large and small to make the story a better one. Thank you, Kate.

A special thank you to Raphael Kadushin, senior acquisitions editor at the University of Wisconsin Press, for believing in my work and supporting me every step of the way. Many others have helped and encouraged me, as I worked my way through the development and writing of my several novels. A big thanks to everyone who in one way or another helped me with this one.

Tamarack River Ghost

Prologue

April 1900
Tamarack River Valley, Central Wisconsin

"Daylight in the swamp!" yelled the log-driver foreman as he pounded a stick on the bottom of a cooking pot. "Daylight in the swamp!" A hint of pink showed above the pine trees to the east, but it would be another half hour before sunrise. The night temperature had dropped into the low thirties, and white frost covered everything, not unusual for April in Wisconsin. The mighty Tamarack River roared as it tumbled over rocks and raced south. Logs, thousands of them, filled the river, which was just below flood stage. Huge chunks of blue ice also floated on the water, some breaking apart when they crashed into the rocks, sending up plumes of frigid spray.

"Hell, it's still dark," mumbled Mortimer Dunn, one of a dozen log drivers sleeping in the big white tent the crew of sturdy men had pitched on the banks of the river the previous night, just before the sun went down. Dunn's big, brown German shepherd slept beside him. Prince was his constant companion in the woods and on the river. The dog wore a leather collar with a little brass bell attached, so Mortimer could keep track of him while he was hustling logs caught in an eddy or hung up on rocks, something that happened often on river drives. Mortimer also carried a wooden whistle in his pocket, one he had carved. He used it to call Prince when they became separated, as sometimes happened when they moved down the river.

Dunn, only five feet seven and 165 pounds, was part of an elite crew in charge of guiding logs down the Tamarack River when the ice went out in the spring. They moved the logs from the pine forests north and east of Stevens Point to Lake Poygan, then on to Lake Winnebago and the sawmills in Oshkosh.

"Doin' you men a favor. Worked you kinda late last night, so thought we'd get an early start today so we can knock off a little earlier this evening," the foreman said in a too loud voice.

Most log drivers also worked as lumberjacks during the long winter. They earned twice the money as log drivers as they did as lumberjacks; riding the logs on the river was a far more dangerous job. As lumberjacks, they sawed down giant pine trees and, with teams of oxen and bobsleds, toted the logs to the river's edge, where they stacked them in huge piles, waiting for the spring breakup, when they rolled the logs into the Tamarack's cold, brown, swirling waters.

The men, cursing and scratching themselves, crawled out of their bedrolls, dressed, and prepared for breakfast. With breakfast finished, several greased their legs and waists with lard to protect them a bit from the icy cold water. The cook prepared lunch for them and placed it in nose bags, canvas sacks they took with them so they could eat without leaving the river and the thousands of logs they shepherded south. The men climbed into their bateaus, double-bowed boats, and began their day's work.

Mortimer Dunn and Prince, riding in their bateau, brought up the rear of the crew, ready for any emergency the log drivers might face as they kept the big pine logs, some of them four feet and more in diameter and twenty feet long, moving in the rapid current of the river. Mortimer's specialty was undoing logjams, which meant first locating the key log that must be dislodged before the logs in a pile-up could begin moving. Though a small man, he was all muscle, with the agility of a cat, a characteristic that served him well on the river drives.

The men used long pike poles with metal spikes on the ends to nudge the logs along. Occasionally, when several logs were hung up in a rapids or in a sharp turn in the river, the men climbed out of their boats and rode them, often falling into the bone-chilling water. The work was not only uncomfortable, it was also exceedingly dangerous. Every river had its "dead-man bends" where a log driver had lost his footing, drowned, and was buried on a little knoll overlooking the water.

But this day was going well. The logs moved straight and true, with few hang-ups. So far no one had to leave his bateau to dislodge a log stuck on the river bank or caught on a rock.

Mortimer saw the floating cook shack, the "wanigan," coming down the river a half mile behind them. It was a barge made of logs chained together with a small, unpainted, rustic wooden building riding on it. In addition to being a floating kitchen, it also carried supplies such as axes and extra pike poles.

From the pocket in his thick red-and-white-checkered wool shirt, Mortimer retrieved his ever-present pipe and tobacco. He filled the pipe's bowl, struck a match to the tamped-down tobacco, and tasted the sweet-smelling stuff.

The sun had come up and quickly melted the white frost on the river bank with a promise of making it a warm day—perhaps the warmest the crew had experienced this spring. Long *V*s of Canada geese flew over, winging their way north, and calling loudly. A sure sign of spring. Mortimer heard the log drivers singing, something they did when things were going well and they were enjoying being on the river.

> Ho Ho, Ho Hay, keep the logs a-going.
> Keep 'em rolling and twisting.
> Keep 'em moving, keep 'em straight.
> On the way to the lake called Poygan.
> Ho Ho, Ho Hay,
> What a day, what a day.

Mortimer joined in the song as his big dog looked up at him. He felt good, much better than yesterday, when he and the crew had gotten soaked trying to dislodge a minor logjam. It took them more than two hours to loosen up the logs and get things moving again.

Prologue

Mortimer thought of his wife, Amelia, and their five children who spent the winter on their farm in Ames County, in the Tamarack River Valley some forty miles south of where he was now. In November, when the farm work was completed, he traveled to the Northwoods and the logging camps where he had worked for the last several winters. His sandy Ames County farm did not produce enough for him to pay his taxes and otherwise make ends meet with his large family. The lumberjack income, and especially the extra money he made as a log driver, made all the difference. Mortimer missed his wife and family and thought of them every day.

A few days ago, he'd written his wife a letter and mailed it at one of the trading posts along the river.

> Dear Amelia,
>
> Oh, how I miss you and the children. Tell them I am doing well and have had some exciting experiences here on the great Tamarack River. Just yesterday, I spent most of a morning breaking up an enormous logjam that backed the logs up on the river for nearly a mile. We finally got it loose, and the logs started moving again.
>
> It won't be long now and I'll be home with all of you, and we can begin putting in the spring crops. Working in the woods is not a bad job, but I sure miss working on the farm. Nothing beats the smell of freshly turned soil in the spring, not even the smell of fresh pine sawdust.
>
> I have a special surprise for you, something I made during the long winter nights in the Northwoods. I can't wait to see your reaction to it. A hint of what it is—something I carved.
>
> From somewhere on the Tamarack River.
>
> Love,
> Mort

Dunn heard the singing abruptly stop, a sign of trouble ahead. Most of the crew had moved around a bend in the river, so Mortimer could not see what happened. He poled his bateau into the main current so he could catch up with the rest of the log drivers. As he rounded the bend, he saw the problem, another logjam. It didn't look as serious as the one the previous day.

"Over here, Mort," one of the drivers yelled. "The problem is over here." Mortimer poled his bateau close to the jam and climbed out, the calks on his boots digging into the soft pine as he jumped from log to floating log, with pike pole in hand. Prince stayed behind, watching his master's every move.

Mortimer bent over to see if he could spot the key log. When he did so, the entire jam broke loose of its own accord, with several huge logs falling on him and tossing him into the deep and treacherous Tamarack. The other drivers heard a scream like none they had ever heard before as they saw Mortimer Dunn disappear into the mass of logs that once more hurried down the river.

Prince heard the scream as well and jumped into the churning water, leaping over logs, the little bell on his collar ringing. The dog disappeared into the river, and neither Mortimer nor his dog was ever seen again.

Heartbroken when she got word of her husband's death several days later, Amelia Dunn erected a tombstone in the family cemetery on the far corner of their farm, within sight of the Tamarack River. The words on the tombstone said:

Mortimer Dunn
Father, Log Driver, Farmer, Woodcarver
May 15, 1865
April 15, 1900

Mortimer Dunn's tombstone stood next to that of his son, Albert, their firstborn, who had died on his third birthday.

On foggy nights in spring, just after the river ice goes out, people say they've seen Mortimer's ghost on the river, rising above the water. Others say they've heard the tinkle of the little bell his dog always wore and smelled his tobacco smoke. And still others claim to have heard the song of the log drivers on still nights in spring, when the night is dark and there is no moon:

> Ho Ho, Ho Hay, keep the logs a-going.
> Keep 'em rolling and twisting.
> Keep 'em moving, keep 'em straight.
> On the way to the lake called Poygan.
> Ho Ho, Ho Hay,
> What a day, what a day.

Josh Wittmore

Josh Wittmore wondered how long his charade would last, how long he could continue until they found him out. He was reclining on his lumpy bed in front of the flickering TV in his dreary motel room in Crumpet, Missouri, when his question was answered.

The Sleepy Rest Motel's sign on the highway proudly proclaimed, "American-owned, clean, restful, all on one level." When Josh parked in front of the motel a few days ago, he followed the little path to the door that was marked "Office." Inside, a deeply tanned man with a Missouri accent greeted him. When he got to the room, it was one of the smallest he'd ever seen, maybe twelve feet by twelve feet. It included one hard-backed chair; a narrow desk; a tiny TV perched precariously on a metal shelf in the corner, its power cord stretched across the window air-conditioner to an outlet shared with an underpowered table light; and a bed with a reasonable mattress. The bathroom, not to be outdone by the rest of the accommodation, was tiny and sparsely furnished, with a shower made for those tall and skinny and not prone to turning around when showering. But the room was clean, as advertised.

The motel, like so many built in the late 1940s, allowed a motorist to drive right up to the door, as if the room was to be shared by a vehicle. Josh was in room 18, his truck parked so close he could nearly reach it by stretching an arm out the room's tiny window, which faced the highway.

It was Friday night, and Josh was bone tired. He wondered why he should be exhausted; he was only thirty-two years old and in reasonably good shape. He was thin and tall, a little over six feet. Soon he was dozing, thinking about what he had been doing the past few weeks and at the same time trying to drive the job from his mind.

The brick that crashed through the motel window landed at his feet with a thud, missing him by a few inches. Broken glass scattered throughout the room—a rush of warm September night air poured through the jagged hole. The red brick had a grimy piece of white paper held around it with a thick rubber band. Fully awake, Josh jumped out of his chair and picked up the brick, removed the rubber band, and unfolded the paper:

Nobody takes pictures at the Lazy Z.

The words were written in bold, black strokes. Josh put the brick and the paper on the only table in the room. He could feel the hair on the back of his neck standing on end. Were the culprits who tossed the brick still in the parking lot? Would they next be pounding on his door? He began to perspire. He ran his hands through his thick hair, which he had dyed from its natural brown to blond to help with his disguise. He also wore dark-rimmed glasses to complete his makeover—the glasses, all dusty and dirty, sat on the little desk.

A few weeks earlier, Josh's boss, Bert Schmid, the editor of the Midwest's *Farm Country News*, had phoned him from the paper's main office in Willow River, Wisconsin. Josh, a reporter for this popular agricultural weekly newspaper, worked out of the paper's regional office in Springfield, Illinois. He'd been there since Bert hired him in 2000, when Josh graduated from the University of Wisconsin's agricultural journalism program.

"I've got an assignment for you, Josh," Bert said when he called.

"What have you got?"

"You ever hear of the Lazy Z operation? They've got huge cattle feedlots scattered in three states. Got a big one over in Crumpet, Missouri."

"Yeah, who hasn't heard of the Lazy Z?"

"Some rumors flying around that they're cutting a few corners, fudging some of the environmental rules, and lots more."

"I heard about that," said Josh.

"It's more than a rumor. I was wondering if you could do a little digging around. Find out what's going on there."

"Think I could. Should be kind of interesting."

"There's a little more to it—might as well tell you right up front. A reporter from St. Louis spent some time out there trying to put a story together. She spent a couple of weeks working on a story that she never wrote. Shortly afterward she quit the paper and moved to Maine. Some said the reporter had been threatened—never any proof of it though. She did file a complaint."

"Really?"

"The police stopped out at the feedlot. They talked to the manager, some guy named Tex Rampart, or Rapport, something like that—anyway this Tex guy said the reporter had been out there a couple of times, nosing around. He said he'd never threatened any reporter, male or female.

"So you want me to just sashay on over there and ask a few questions and snap a couple pictures?"

"Hardly," said Bert. "The woman didn't get the story; I have a better idea for you."

"And that would be?"

"I want you to go undercover. It's a helluva place to work, I'm told. Cow manure everywhere. Mud when it rains. Dirty dust when it doesn't. Somebody is always quitting—or getting hurt or sick. Nearby stream is polluted."

"And you want me to find a job there, to go undercover?"

"Seems like one way to get the story. Get an inside look at what goes on. You know how to ride a horse, don't you?"

"I do," said Josh. "We had horses on the home farm—but I haven't done much riding in the ten years I've been working for the paper."

"Here's what I want you to do," said Bert. "You figure out some kind of disguise, then you go over there and see if they'll hire you. A cold beer says they will. You rent yourself a room at a motel in town—we'll pay for it—and you are on your way."

Josh called the Lazy Z the next morning and asked if they had any job openings. He talked to a Tex Ramport, who said he was the feedlot manager.

"Yeah, we always need help. You come on over here tomorrow, and we'll have a little chat," Ramport said. "See if we got anything that'd interest you. Be here around 1:30 or so."

Josh made a trip to the local Wal-Mart, where he bought hair dye and some dark-rimmed sunglasses. He checked the Maps Online website and learned that Crumpet, Missouri, was a little more than a three-hour drive from Springfield. He didn't sleep well that night, wondering what he was getting into. This would be his first undercover reporting job. *How dangerous could it be?* he thought. He went to sleep with visions of being paid for riding a horse.

The next morning, he pulled on his blue jeans, a faded yellow shirt, and a cowboy hat he bought when he visited Texas a couple of years ago. He fired up his Ford Ranger pickup and was soon headed south on Interstate 55. He tuned his radio to a country western station to get in the mood for his interview. He listened to Willie Nelson belt out "On the Road Again." Next he headed west on Interstate 70, rolling into Missouri just north of St. Louis. Waylon Jennings was singing "Good Hearted Woman."

When he found State Highway 940, he turned toward Crumpet, some twenty miles south of the interstate, but even before he reached the town he could smell cow manure; the stench of a large feedlot told of its presence long before it came into sight. He drove through the town; Crumpet was but a couple thousand people. He spotted the Sleepy Rest Motel on the south side of town and tucked the information away in his memory. About a mile out of town, as he topped a little ridge, he spotted the feedlot stretching out in the valley in front of him on both sides of the highway. A cloud of brown dust hung over its many pens, all filled with cattle. The stench had become more intense; the ammonia burned his eyes. He spotted the entrance to the Lazy Z feedlot and a sign pointing to the office in a double-wide trailer. He glanced at his watch; he was right on time. When he climbed out of his pickup, he saw men on horseback, working the alleys between the pens, driving cattle and stirring up even more dust. Sounds of cattle bellowing and men yelling filled the air along with the yellow dust.

"Hi-yah!" he heard a man yell as he pushed his horse alongside a steer that moved too slowly. "Hi-yah!" he yelled again. He poked the steer with a metal prod; it jumped and quickly moved on.

Josh pushed open the door to the office and saw three women working at computers.

"Can I help you?" an attractive young blonde asked as she looked up from her work.

"I have an interview with Mr. Ramport," he said.

"And your name?" she asked. Josh wondered why such a good-looking young woman would work at a place like this.

"It's Wittmore, Josh Wittmore," he said as he removed his hat.

"Have a chair. I'll tell him you're here."

Josh sat down and picked up a copy of the *American Cattleman* and began paging through it.

"Mr. Ramport will see you now," the young woman said, smiling broadly. She pointed to the door to the left. Josh hesitated for a moment.

"Just go right in," she said. She had a pleasant accent, a soft way of speaking, different from the folks up in Wisconsin, where he was born and raised.

Inside, he saw a middle-aged man dressed in a business suit and wearing a bolo tie with a longhorn head. They exchanged names and shook hands.

"So, you're looking for work?" Mr. Ramport asked. He was all business. No small talk.

"Yes, I am," Josh said.

"And why is that?"

"Fellow's got to eat," Josh answered.

"Good answer. You know anything about cattle?"

"Some. I grew up on a farm in Wisconsin."

"Hell, they aren't cattle you got up there. They're cows. Out here we got cattle, about ten thousand of 'em, last count. And every damn one of them is better eatin' then those skinny milkers you got up there in Wisconsin."

Josh laughed. "I expect you're right about that."

"You know how to ride a horse?"

"Been a while, but I do."

"You're probably wonderin' why I'm not asking about your previous work. Tell you the truth, I don't wanna know. I don't care if you just got out of jail, your wife kicked you out, or your last boss fired you. Don't matter. If you can do the work, that's all we ask."

"Well, I do need the job," Josh said.

"OK. If you're willing to work for $7.50 an hour, you're hired. You'll be on probation for six months, and then we'll talk about stuff like benefits. No benefits while you're on probation. Check with Stephanie when you go out; she'll have you sign a couple of things to get you on the payroll."

As it turned out, Stephanie was the young woman he'd met earlier. She pushed a couple of pieces of paper in front of Josh and watched while he signed them. "Don't forget to print your name under your signature," she said. She had the nicest smile. Josh wondered if she was married, checking for a wedding ring on her left hand. Just as quickly, he removed the thought of starting anything with Stephanie. He had other reasons for finding work at the Lazy Z.

"When you go outside, you'll want to look for Amos," she said. "He rides a big white horse, and he'll show you the ropes, so to speak." She lowered her voice. "It's Amos that really runs this place—and, by the way, you don't wanna get on the wrong side of him.

Lazy Z Feedlot

*O*utside the headquarters office, the smell and the dust rolled over Josh again. He pulled on his hat, adjusted his glasses, and glanced around. Through the dirty haze he saw a skinny, weathered cowboy astride a big white horse. Josh held up his arm. The rider slowly moved the horse closer to Josh.

"Name is Josh Wittmore," Josh said when he reached up to shake the rider's hand.

"Amos," the man said. His voice was rather high pitched, almost feminine. "I'm foreman of this operation. You get hired?"

"I did." Josh was taken aback for a moment by the foreman's less-than-bosslike voice.

"Know anything about feedlots?"

"Nope."

"Can you ride a horse?"

"Yup."

"Good. Let's find you something to ride, then."

Amos swung around in his saddle and yelled, "Charlie, go fetch this guy a horse, and slip a saddle on it. Pick out an easy one—don't wanna put him in the hospital his first day of work." Amos laughed at his idea of a joke.

In a few minutes, Josh was astride a little bay mare, name of Daisy.

"Tell you what," Amos said. "You just follow behind me and keep your eyes and ears open, probably the best way to learn how this operation works."

"What all goes on here?" Josh asked.

"Well, it's pretty simple. We haul in a bunch of feeder cattle, heifers and steers that have been weaned from their mothers and maybe grass fed for a season. Some of 'em weigh six to eight hundred pounds when they git here. We feed 'em for six months or so and send 'em on to market. Most of 'em will be twelve to fourteen hundred pounds when they leave."

Josh was making mental notes, trying to be careful to ask questions a new worker would want to know, but not so many questions that he might arouse suspicion. Amos kept on talking without any prodding from Josh as they slowly rode down one of the dusty, manure-strewn lanes.

"We feed a mixture of corn, grain byproducts, and hay. Feed them critters quickly take a likin' to. Got a lot of crossbreds these days—they seem to put on the pounds faster than, say, your Angus or Hereford. Some of these critters even got a little Holstein blood in 'em. Folks eatin' their steaks and hamburgers don't much care what the critter looked like, as long as their steaks are tender and juicy." Amos laughed; it came out as almost a cackle.

Josh saw men on horseback, emptying pens and driving cattle to waiting semitrucks backed up at loading docks. Other men were driving tractors with feed trailers behind, augering feed into the troughs alongside the pens.

As Josh made his way with his new boss through the feedlot, he learned it covered some seventy-five acres. His eyes burned from the dust, and the smell of cow manure was almost overwhelming. When he arrived at the lot's far end, he noticed a lazy little river running but a few hundred yards from the last pen. He could see its dirty brown water from where he sat on his horse, and could also see little gulleys, now dry, from where feedlot runoff had entered the stream.

They came up to the riders moving cattle from pens to the loading dock, where a cattle truck was parked.

"Wittmore, you work with these guys. They'll show you what to do," Amos said. He introduced Josh to the men and told them Josh was new and they should show him the ropes. Before he rode off, he eased his big horse in close to the little bay Josh was riding.

"If I hear one damn word from anybody that you're screwin' up or goofin' off, you are outta here. You got that?" He looked Josh square in the eye. Amos had small, intense black eyes, sunk deep in his tanned, wrinkled face.

"I got it," Josh said, trying to keep his voice level and unafraid.

With that, Amos turned his big horse and trotted off. That was the only conversation Josh had with the foreman that entire first week, so he assumed he was doing OK. Each evening, he returned to his little motel room covered with dust and grime and smelling more like the feedlot than the feedlot itself. After the first couple of days in the saddle, his behind was so raw in the evenings that he could hardly sit in the chair to work at his little Toshiba laptop, where he jotted down facts and impressions.

Scarcely a day went by as he worked that he didn't think about the young reporter who had been doing a story on the Lazy Z operation. He knew he'd better be careful and not ask any questions that went beyond what an employee needed to know to do his job and not go nosing around in places where he shouldn't be.

At the end of his first week, he filed a story for the *Farm Country News* using the name Jed Walker. He hoped that the folks at the Lazy Z would never put Jed Walker and Josh Wittmore together and figure out they were one and the same.

Josh's first story introduced his planned series, titled "Cattle Feedlot Situation USA." He wrote: "American consumers like their beef tender and juicy—the kind of beef that is corn-fattened in a cattle feedlot where thousands of animals are crowded together, not a spear of grass in sight. One-third of the country's beef is produced in feedlots like this, some of them with a capacity for more than a hundred thousand animals. If more people saw a feedlot, they wouldn't enjoy their steaks so much."

A week later, when he stopped in the Lazy Z office to pick up his paycheck, he noticed a copy of the *Farm Country News* on the counter. His story, with a generic photo of some other feedlot, ran on the first page and was topped with a big bold headline: "Is This What American Consumers Want?"

When Stephanie handed him his check, she pointed to the newspaper. "You see that article?"

"Don't do much reading," Josh replied.

"Well, you ought to read it. This guy, Jed Walker, ought to be strung up."

"Why's that?"

"He's out to do places like this in, close us down. Look at all the people who'd lose their jobs."

Josh nodded in agreement and went back to work. His next week's story was considerably edgier. He asked the occasional question around the feedlot, always carefully and never seeming to be nosey. And he had learned much. His article ran:

The Long-Term Dangers of Consuming Feedlot Beef
By Jed Walker

That juicy steak sizzling on your grill can be the worst thing you can feed your family, if it comes from an animal fattened at one of the nation's major feedlots. Owners lace their cattle feed with antibiotics to prevent disease in the animals, something nearly inevitable when so many animals are crowded together in an outdoor environment where they wallow in mud and manure.

Numerous medical studies warn that antibiotic residue remains in the meat that people consume. Over time, people with various infectious diseases no longer respond to standard antibiotic treatment. Medical doctors are increasingly seeing "super bugs," requiring new, more powerful antibiotics to control them.

Some feedlot owners also regularly feed anabolic steroids as growth promoters to their feedlot animals. Steroid residue has also been found in the muscle, fat, liver, kidneys, and other organ meats of treated animals. Studies are beginning to show links between these steroid residues and human reproductive problems. Knowing all of this, the European Union has banned the use of animal growth promoters since 1988.

Next week's story will examine in some detail the operation of the Lazy Z feedlot operation in Crumpet, Missouri, one of several feedlots operated by the Lazy Z corporation.

Bert Schmid sent Josh an e-mail after the second story. "Great story. Now we need some specifics about what goes on at the Lazy Z," he wrote. "And we need some photos."

For his third week's story, Josh's headline read: "Missouri's Lazy Z Feedlot Cutting Corners." This time he described conditions at the feedlot after a recent rain. "Cattle wallow in manure and mud, many with mud caked on their bellies and up their sides. The smell is nearly unbearable." He described in detail how workers regularly used electric prods to move cattle and how each employee was required to carry one at all times. He wrote about water troughs contaminated with manure.

Josh managed to take several photos of manure pouring out of the feedlot and running into the dirty brown stream that overflowed its banks. One of the workers saw him and asked, "What in hell are you doing?"

"Just taking a few photos to send to my mother back home. She doesn't know anything about cattle feedlots."

"Well you'd better knock it off. Amos told me, 'You take a picture around here, and you're fired,'" his coworker said.

"Thanks for telling me. I didn't know that."

Now fully awake, after deciding that no one lurked in the motel parking lot with further intentions of doing him harm, he packed his bags, told the motel clerk that there was an illness in the family, and checked out. He didn't bother to say that the window in his room needed a bit of repair. He also didn't bother to tell anyone at the Lazy Z that they wouldn't be seeing him anymore.

He tossed the brick into the back of his pickup, and he was soon on his way back to Springfield. When he passed St. Louis and entered Illinois, he quit checking his rearview mirror. For a time, he was sure someone was following him, but he finally concluded it was his imagination getting the best of him. Not until he entered his Springfield apartment did he finally relax. He got on his cell phone and called his boss at home, waking him up.

"Slow down," Bert said in a sleepy voice. "Take a deep breath, and tell me what happened."

Lazy Z Feedlot

When Josh finished telling his story about the brick and the broken window, and the message written on the dirty sheet of paper, he paused for a moment.

"Sounds like you did the right thing to get out of there. Imagine the guy who saw you taking pictures ratted you out," Bert said.

"I suppose," Josh said. "Glad to be outta there. I'm gonna stink like a feedlot for weeks. Gonna throw my clothes away. Can't get the stench out of them."

"It was a helluva good story you wrote," Bert said. "And pretty fair pictures, too. We're running the whole thing on the front page of our new edition. Jed Walker's made quite a name for himself."

"Yeah, right," Josh said. "I left Jed Walker at the Lazy Z."

Fishing on the Millpond

Oscar, you been hearin' what I've been hearin'?" asked Fred Russo, Oscar Anderson's neighbor and longtime friend.

"How in hell am I supposed to know what you've been hearin'?"

"Well I was just wonderin'."

Oscar had a puzzled look on his face as he reeled in his fishing line and tossed the bobber and hook baited with a small minnow back into the quiet waters of the Willow River Millpond.

"So, what have you been hearin'?" A soft September breeze riffled the millpond waters.

"What did you say?"

"I said, 'What you been hearin'?'" Oscar said, louder this time.

"About what?"

"What you said a little while ago."

Oscar and Fred, both in their eighties and retired farmers, often fished together. The Tamarack River had long been their favorite fishing spot, but for the sake of variety, they chose other places as well. The Willow River Millpond was one of them. Here, they could fish from shore for native brook trout, talk about the issues of the day, and reminisce about earlier times.

"What I said was 'Have you been hearin' what I've been hearin'?'"

"About all I hear is the wind blowing through the willow trees, kind of a nice sound too. One of the sounds of early fall. I kinda like the sounds of fall. Easy to hear. Not like winter. Winter sounds are harsh on the ears."

"Are you through talking about sounds?" said Fred.

"I could say more. Tell you about the sounds of summer, sounds of spring. I could tell you about them sounds, Fred," Oscar said, a big smile spreading across his wrinkled face.

"Hell, I ain't talkin' about the sounds of the seasons. I'm talking about the gossip goin' around the Tamarack River Valley," said Fred.

"What gossip is that? Old Shotgun Slogum shootin' off his mouth about something? The cranberry growers in trouble? Some new rumor about the fancy golf course? Somebody see the Tamarack River Ghost again?"

"Nah, ain't none of that," said Fred. He reeled in his line and tossed it out again. The big red-and-white plastic bobber bumped up and down as the wind played across the millpond's surface.

"Well, what the hell is it? You gonna tell me or not?" asked Oscar, looking his friend in the eye.

"Well, I am gonna tell you. I was just wonderin' if you've heard it yourself," said Fred.

"How in hell am I supposed to know what you heard if you don't tell me what it is?"

"Well, I'll tell you. Then you don't have to get all huffy on me."

"I ain't gettin' huffy, just curious, that's all."

"Well, here's what I heard," Fred began.

"I'm all ears."

"You know about our conservation warden, Natalie Karlsen?"

"Yeah, I know about her. Never met her. Don't wanna meet her either. Heard she's a tough cookie. Arrest her grandmother if she had one too many bluegills in her bucket."

"Yup, that's Natalie Karlsen."

"Well, what about her?"

"Heard she's payin' particular attention to the Tamarack River Valley this fall," said Fred.

"What's that mean—payin' particular attention?"

"Means she's spending lots of time in our neighborhood."

"So?"

"Oscar, do I gotta spell it out for you?"

"Guess you do, 'cause I ain't heard nothin' about what Warden Karlsen is doin' in our neighborhood."

"She's lookin' for poachers," said Fred.

"Lookin' for what?"

"Poachers," said Fred, raising his voice a bit.

"Thought that's what you said. Why's she lookin' for poachers?"

"'Cause poaching is against the law."

"I know that. Also know that now and again some of our neighbors take a deer or two out of season to feed their families. I wouldn't call that poaching," said Oscar. He reeled in his line and tossed it out again.

"Still against the law," said Fred.

"Shouldn't be; folks have to live. Have to feed their kids. Like as not, the deer they take are ones they've fed all summer on their own land. Deer that ate their corn and alfalfa."

"Doesn't matter to the warden. If she catches somebody, she's gonna fine 'em, take their guns away. Raise hell with 'em."

"Ain't that lady warden got something better to do than arrest these poor folks trying to make a livin' off the land?"

"Yup, agree with you there, Oscar, you'd think she'd be doing something better with her time. Maybe she should go lookin' for that old Tamarack River Ghost," said Fred.

Both men laughed.

Natalie Karlsen

*T*wo rifle shots echoed through the Tamarack River Valley and rolled into the low hills surrounding the slow-moving river. The spotlight coming from an old Chevy pickup parked on a field road caught in its sharp beam a six-point buck and doe fattened on Ames County corn and soybeans. With two rapid shots, the deer dropped dead. A .30–30 soft-point bullet struck each in the neck and severed its spinal cord.

"We got ourselves some good ones, Pa," the sixteen-year-old boy holding the light said. "Got ourselves a nice buck and a fat doe."

"Looks that way, Joey. We better get them gutted out quick and into the pickup 'fore somebody comes snoopin' by. Heard that nosey lady warden has been on the prowl in the valley. Don't know why the hell the DNR and their wardens spend so much time trying to pinch us poor folks. Don't understand it a bit."

With the freshly killed deer in the back of their old pickup, they slowly drove home, with their lights out, but a half mile from the field where they shot the deer.

*N*atalie Karlsen, Ames County conservation warden, sat in her four-wheel-drive, Ford F-150 extended-cab pickup with the windows down, listening. Twenty-eight years old and single, she had served a couple of years in the U.S. Army Military Police before becoming a warden. She was not a big woman, only five feet six, but she kept in excellent condition. The one thing people noticed immediately when they talked with her were her big, expressive brown eyes. She kept her long blonde hair tied back in a ponytail. After only two years on the job, she had gained a reputation for being tough. She had earned considerable respect, especially from other law-enforcement officers in the county, including the county sheriff. Of course, she also had her share of enemies—it goes with being in law enforcement.

Natalie carried a .40 caliber Glock on her duty belt. In her truck she also had a .308 Remington rifle and a Remington 12-gauge shotgun—all standard firearms for a Wisconsin warden. A laptop computer in the pickup allowed her ready access to both the Internet and the mobile data computer radio system so she could do an immediate check on license-plate numbers and other necessary information and keep in close contact with the sheriff and local police networks. The computer screen glowed in the darkness.

Earlier in the week, Natalie had gotten a tip that game poachers were at work in this part of Ames County, where the deer population was heaviest. A woman had called the ranger station in Willow River and left a curt message.

"I heard rifle shots last night. Somebody is shooting my deer. I think Dan Burman is one of them. Look into it." She didn't leave her name, only said that she lived in the Tamarack River Valley and that the warden should do her job. "Our taxes pay the warden's salary. Why isn't she doing something about this?"

Lately, game poachers had become Natalie's biggest headache. She'd parked her pickup on a little hill overlooking the Tamarack River Valley where she had a view of the valley in two directions. Though small in stature, she had a way about her that few people challenged—maybe it was the badge, perhaps the gun at her belt, or, more likely, her way of staring down a game violator without so much as a blink. As a result, she'd had few problems apprehending everyday violators—fishermen with more than their limit, boaters without life jackets, those sorts of folks. Poachers were different, a tougher bunch, more difficult to catch in the act, and more dangerous, too. Some would just as soon shoot a conservation warden as an illegal deer.

Natalie remembered the story her father told about a conservation warden in Adams County back in the 1930s. The warden heard about game poachers and had apparently run into an outfit that was shooting deer and selling the meat in Chicago. The poachers jumped the warden, stripped off all his clothes, tied him to a tree deep in the woods, and left him. This happened on a Saturday. Some kids walking to school Monday morning heard the warden's yells. He had nearly died of exposure and was covered with ant bites, as an anthill was near the tree where he had been tied.

The moon was just coming up, and Natalie could see steam rising from the river in the distance, little horsetail clouds that formed when the cool early fall air collided with the warmer water. It was a typical evening in late September. The temperature had climbed into the high fifties during the day but had dropped rapidly with the sunset, as had the wind. The only sound Natalie heard was an owl's call, eerie yet pleasing, far off in the hills. Otherwise it was dead still. The smells of fall were all around, dead leaves that had fallen from the aspen and birch trees and dead grass alongside the country road where she parked.

Natalie heard many stories about the Tamarack River Valley and wondered how many were true. She'd heard that a ghost and his dog roamed through this valley, especially on cool, quiet nights like this one. People claim to have heard the tinkle of the dog's little bell on still nights when the moon was down and the wind was up. Some even said they heard the log driver's song, "Ho Ho, Ho Hay, keep the logs a-going." Natalie didn't believe in ghosts, yet she still listened for these sounds. She'd heard the Tamarack River Ghost story several times; she'd like to run into him and his dog.

Natalie thought about all she had learned about the people living here in the valley in the two years that she'd been conservation warden. She'd learned that some of the farmers, now third and fourth generation, lived on the same property as their pioneer ancestors. Many were dirt poor, yet they stayed on because something more than money kept them on the land.

She thought about the dozen or so younger farmers, members of the Ames County Fruit and Vegetable Growers Cooperative, who were doing reasonably well on their farms, growing vegetables for the Willow River Farmers Market, and selling their produce directly to restaurants and grocery stores. She knew many of them and considered them some of her strongest allies in the county, because they were, as she was, committed to taking care of the environment.

The cranberry growers in the southern part of the valley also came to mind as she sat waiting. Here was another group of families who had lived on the same land since the 1870s, but, different from some of their hard-scrabble neighbors, these farmers were making money as the cranberry market was growing and expanding, even internationally.

Natalie wondered how such different people managed to get along with each other; yet they did, living side by side year after year. Sure, some had left, moved off to the cities to find work, especially in the 1950s and 1960s, when agriculture changed dramatically here in the valley and across the United States. Some of the valley farmers sold their farms to city folk in Madison and Milwaukee who wanted second homes in the country or land for hunting. So the part-time city person became a part of the mix of people in the valley. Additionally, several people who had grown up in the valley returned there to retire.

Natalie had backed her vehicle into a driveway to a cornfield that had yet to be harvested. If she heard or saw anything, she could fire up her pickup and be on her way in a matter of seconds. She poured a cup of coffee from the thermos she'd filled when she left her cabin just after dark. These deer poaching cases took time and lots of lost sleep. Last year, she had spent fifteen September and October evenings looking for poachers. All she found was a young couple looking to get better acquainted. She had scared the wits out of them when she shined her flashlight into the window of their car and discovered both of them stark naked.

"Better get your clothes on and get out of here," she told them.

"You're not gonna tell anybody, are you?" the embarrassed young woman pleaded. She was holding up a blanket to cover herself.

"Just get yourself decent and be on your way," Natalie said, more sternly than she had intended.

Natalie sipped her steaming coffee, taking a moment to inhale the smell of the brew. She liked coffee. It had become her partner on many a long, lonely night on guard duty in the army and now as a warden.

Some parts of waiting out poachers she enjoyed, when the quiet of the night surrounded her and the never-ending phone calls, reports to complete, and meetings to attend were for another day. On these quiet nights, she had time to think, to organize her ideas, and even scribble down a few notes in a brown, leather-covered journal she always had with her in the truck.

*K*A-BOOM," and a few seconds later, another "KA-BOOM." Natalie nearly spilled her coffee when she heard the rifle shots. Quickly, she threw the rest of the coffee out the open window, started up her pickup, and headed down the country road in the direction she thought the sound had come from. It was difficult to locate the source of sounds as they echoed through the valley. Perhaps this night she might be lucky and find the poacher in the act, field-dressing the deer or dragging it to his vehicle.

*F*ather and son turned their pickup into their driveway and parked behind the barn, out of sight from the road. They each grabbed one of the buck's legs and hauled the animal into the barn, where they tied a rope around its neck, tossed the rope over a small beam, and hauled the deer up so its back feet were just off the barn floor. They did the same with the doe. The father held a small flashlight in his mouth so he could see what he was doing yet not cast enough light to raise suspicion from anyone driving along the road this time of night.

"Nice pair of deer," said the son.

"Yup, nice deer. I'd say the buck would be about 180 pounds, the doe around 150." The two deer hung side by side.

"Looks like this oughta do it for a while," the father said. "All we gotta do now is skin 'em and cut up and freeze the meat. Yup, we're not gonna go hungry this winter."

*W*arden Karlsen drove slowly along the road, watching and listening, looking for a light, listening for another shot. But the countryside was once again quiet, eerily so.

She drove by a rather run-down-looking farm and didn't see the sliver of light coming from the old, unpainted gray barn, so she kept driving.

Tamarack River Valley

*J*osh parked his Ford Ranger in the Ames County Courthouse parking lot. He had an appointment with the county agricultural agent, Ben Wesley, whom he hadn't seen since he graduated from college. Now that *Farm Country News* had given him a promotion and transferred him from the Illinois bureau to the home office in Willow River, he was reacquainting himself with his home county. Josh grew up on a small farm west of Link Lake, twelve miles from Willow River; his folks, now retired, still lived on the home farm. He would now have an opportunity to occasionally visit them. As a 4-H member, Josh had gotten to know the agricultural agent well. He had fond memories of showing cattle at the Ames County Fair and attending the end-of-the-year 4-H achievement program, always held in the courtroom.

When Josh arrived in Willow River a week earlier, he drove down Main Street and noted the changes that had taken place since he'd left the county. He saw that the population had increased a little, to 3,010, but it was still a small place when compared to cities like Green Bay, Oshkosh, Madison, and Milwaukee. The first thing he spotted was the new Willow River High School, on the west end of town. He noticed a second stoplight as well. For years, Willow River had the only stoplight in all of Ames County. Driving slowly down Main Street, he saw what had been a clothing store and now housed All Such and More, a place that sold used stuff, everything from clothes to books, flower vases to dishes. He stopped there and bought an almost-new leather jacket for five dollars—he'd seen one like it in a Madison store for two hundred dollars.

As he slowly drove down Main Street he saw the offices of Jensen, Jensen and O'Malley, a law firm that had been in Willow River since the

1920s. He drove past the two taverns on Main Street, there since he came to Willow River as a kid with his folks: Joe's Bar and Johnny J's Saloon. He remembered walking by them and smelling stale beer and secondhand tobacco smoke. Several of the once thriving businesses on Main Street had closed their doors since he left after college—a pharmacy, an office supply store, a big grocery store, a bakery—all gone, the buildings vacant with For Sale signs in their windows.

At the stoplight, he turned north toward Link Lake and spotted the Willow River Hospital and Clinic. The clinic was new. So was a dental office next to it.

Back on Main Street, he traveled east, past the new McDonald's and Culver's restaurants, and past the big Buy It Here grocery store with a statue of a life-size Angus steer standing out front. He saw the *Ames County Argus*'s new building. The weekly *Argus* was a newspaper nearly as old as *Farm Country News*. Its handful of reporters, several of them stringers, covered all corners of Ames County; its circulation was primarily households in Ames County and thus was not a competitor of *Farm Country News*, which covered much of the Midwest and concentrated on agricultural stories.

Josh looked for the Lone Pine Restaurant that he remembered standing on the far east side of Willow River. He found it, but now it was a part of the Willow River Plaza—a strip mall with an Ace Hardware store, an Amish furniture place, and a small-engine repair shop, all scrunched together with no attempt at architectural aesthetics.

He swung south, off Main Street and past what had been cucumber receiving and salting stations, now warehouses or mostly old abandoned and graying buildings. He drove past the new Farmers Co-op Feed Store, and then past the Ames County Fairgrounds, where he saw a couple of new metal buildings, but it mostly looked the same as it had when he was a kid in 4-H, showing calves there.

Josh pulled open the courthouse door and walked down the long hall to the agricultural agent's office, past the register of deeds office and the county clerk's office.

Brittani Martin, office manager, smiled when Josh entered the ag agent's office.

"What can I do for you?" she asked pleasantly.

"I have an appointment with Ben Wesley," Josh said, smiling.

"Your name, please."

"Josh Wittmore, with *Farm Country News*."

"He's expecting you, Mr. Wittmore. Go right in."

"Josh, it's been awhile," said Ben as he walked around from behind his desk and shook Josh's hand. "I remember when you were in 4-H and helped out at the Ames County Fair."

"Those were good days," said Josh. "Fun days."

"How're your folks doing? Heard they sold their cows a couple years ago."

"Yeah, dad's knees were giving out. Besides, it's time for both of them to take it a little easy."

"Yup, there comes a time. What brings you to town?"

"You probably haven't heard that I'm working out of the main office for *Farm Country News* now, right here in Willow River. Moved back here last week. Found myself an apartment here in town."

"Well, good for you, Josh. Welcome back. Always good to have one of our best and brightest return."

"I don't know about the best and brightest part, but it feels good to be back home. I've been living in Springfield, Illinois—worked out of the Illinois bureau until last week."

"You're with a good paper; it's done a lot for midwestern farming, no question about it. I've been reading the series on cattle feedlots. Let's see, I got the last issue right here. You know this guy, Jed Walker?"

"I do," Josh said.

"He's a good writer. Your paper get in any trouble for telling the Lazy Z story?"

"Made some people pretty mad," Josh said. He didn't want to get into the details of just how mad a few of them had gotten.

"Well, what can I do for you?" Ben asked as he folded the paper and put it back on his desk.

"I'm looking for an update on what's going on in Ames County. I know a lot has changed since I left. And, of course, I'm looking for a good story."

"You might want to spend a little time in the Tamarack River Valley, lots going on there these days—and in some ways nothing going on."

"You lost me there, Ben."

"Some of the old timers out there aren't about to change; they're farming just like their grandfathers farmed. Then we've got a half dozen or so younger farmers and their families trying to make a go of it with vegetables and fruits—doing pretty well too, especially with the public's increasing interest in buying locally. Our Wednesday farmers market here on the courthouse square started a few years ago has also helped their sales considerably."

"Had several of these kinds of farmers around Springfield too. Interesting group," Josh said.

"That they are. Something else, too. A couple years ago, a developer out of Chicago came in here waving dollar bills and tried to impress the locals with his fancy talk and big ideas. Wilson Johnson was his name. He bought out three retired farmers, got himself 480 acres, some of it right along the Tamarack River. He built a golf course and a bunch of log condos."

"How's it working out?

"Been a struggle for Johnson," said Ben. "Guess there aren't as many condo buyers out there as he thought."

"Sounds like some good stories out there in the valley."

"Yup there are. Even a whopper of a ghost story."

"You wouldn't be talking about the Tamarack River Ghost?"

"That's the one."

"My dad told me the story when I was a kid. Scared the bejeebers out of me at the time."

"Yup, it's quite a story. Lots of people believe it, too."

"What about these guys farming like their grandfathers? You have a name of someone I could interview?"

Ben sat back in his chair for a minute and ran a hand through his thinning hair.

"I'd suggest Dan Burman. He doesn't have anything to do with my office, but I've heard he's an interesting fellow. He's one of those 'keep the government away from me' guys. He's got a point of view worth hearing—even though I probably wouldn't agree with him very much."

"I'll go see him," Josh said, getting up from his chair. "You got an extra hour to talk later today, when I finish out at Burman's, assuming he's home?"

"Sure, I'll be here. I plan on being in the office all afternoon."

Ben gave Josh detailed directions to the Burman farm, located along a little traveled gravel road not far from the Tamarack River and about fifteen miles from Willow River. This was a part of Ames County that Josh did not know well. He'd fished the Tamarack with his dad when he was a kid, but he didn't know any of the people living there. Josh's dad had a low opinion of the farmers in this part of the county. "Swamp angels," he called them. "They take a bath and get a haircut in the spring, and that's about it. Mostly live off the land. Hunt, fish, pick berries and wild apples." Of course, Josh's father was remembering farmers who lived in the valley two generations ago. Josh imagined those living there today did considerably better than their ancestors.

Josh slowed his pickup, looking for the fire number that would tell him he'd found the right place. The driveway was almost overgrown with brush—box elder and the dreaded buckthorn that seemed to grow everywhere these days. He turned in and drove about fifty yards to the farmstead, a gray, forlorn-looking farmhouse with tall grass growing around it, a couple of sheds, a corncrib, and a barn that had once been painted red and was now a dreary gray.

A big mixed-breed dog bounded out from in back of the house to meet him, barking and not wagging its tail. Not a friendly looking animal. Josh grabbed up his clipboard and cautiously opened the pickup door. The big dog, a dirty, short-haired brown animal that Josh figured was a cross between a rottweiler and a hound of some kind, stood a few yards off, still barking loudly.

"Good dog," Josh said. "Good dog." Josh had met many dogs over the years, some of them friendly, some of them ready to chew his leg, and the rest somewhere in between—unknowns and unpredictable. He put this one in the third category. One of the reasons he always carried a clipboard was that if a dog decided to bite him, he would slam the edge of the clipboard against its nose. That generally worked, although it did not put him in the good graces of those he visited.

A thin woman wearing an apron and holding a broom appeared on the porch of the farmhouse. No doubt she'd heard the dog barking.

"Shut up, Ralphy. Shut up that damn barking," she scolded.

"What was it you wanted?" the woman said to Josh. "Ralphy, you shut up that barking or I'll bust your ribs with this broom." She swung the broom at the dog, but she obviously had not intended to hit it. The dog slunk away, its tail between its legs.

"I'm from the *Farm Country News*," Josh said. "I'd like to talk with you folks."

"What newspaper?" the woman asked.

"*Farm Country News.*"

"Never heard of it. Only paper we know about is the *Ames County Argus*. What'd you want to talk about?"

"Want to talk about farming."

"Talk about farming." She paused for a minute. "You wanna talk about farming, you gotta talk to the mister."

"Where would I find him?"

"I expect he's out in the barn. That's where he usually is this time of day."

"Thank you," Josh said as he turned toward the barn. The woman disappeared into the house. The dog remained out of sight.

"Hello?" Josh called when he pulled open the barn door. "Mr. Burman?"

"Yeah, who wants to know?"

"My name is Josh Wittmore, and I'm with the *Farm Country News.*"

In the dim interior of the barn, Josh saw a short, thin man wearing bib overalls and working at something spread out on some boards over a couple of sawhorses. The man had about a five-day growth of whiskers and hair that stuck out from under a dirty John Deere cap in every direction.

"Whatever you're sellin', I don't want none of it."

"I'm not selling anything," Josh said. "I just want to talk to you for a few minutes."

"Talk about what?"

"I'm doing a story on farmers like yourself, how you're doin', how things are goin'."

"Nobody cares how I'm doin'. I don't think nobody gives a damn about me and my family."

"Well, I'm one of those who does. I'm writing a story about people like yourself, farmers who are trying to make a go of it."

Josh, with his eyes adjusted to the dimly lit interior of the barn, noticed that Burman held a big butcher knife and was carving up two skinned animals. He cut off a chunk of meat and tossed it into a big tub.

"What kind of meat is that?" Josh asked, curious.

"These here are goats. We raise a few goats, eat a couple of them every year. Not the best meat in the world, but we don't go hungry."

"So what can you tell me about farming here in the Tamarack River Valley?"

"You really want to know?" He waved the big butcher knife in the air.

"Yeah, I do."

"Well, in a couple of words, it's a bitch."

"How so?"

"First problem is the damn government. They don't care about us little guys. They give those subsidies to the big-time farmers, and we sit out here and they don't give us a dime. Not a stinkin' dime.

"And our taxes. Do they ever go down? No, they do not. Damn government keeps raisin' the taxes, especially taxes on my land. I only got 120 acres, and they tax the hell out of me."

"Taxes are a problem for farmers," Josh offered.

"You damn bet they are, and you can write that in your story too," Burman said. "Then there's the DNR. That damnable Department of Natural Resources. I tell you, we'd be better off if every damn one of them DNR people got fired. They can be such a pain in the ass. Take them damn game wardens. We got the most snoopy game warden in the world right here in Ames County. Name is Natalie Karlsen. No business a woman being a game warden. But we got her. She's a piece of work. Everyday she's out snoopin' for people she thinks is breaking the law. I tell you—we could sure get along without her."

"How about crops, what kind of crops do you grow?" Josh asked, trying to move the discussion away from the conservation warden.

"Well let's see, I grow maybe ten acres of corn—enough for the hogs and the few steers we raise. Raise a few goats. Got a few acres of pasture. We got a big garden. Keeps the kids busy in the summer. Old lady cans a lot of the garden stuff. We grow an acre of potatoes. Sometimes have a few extra potatoes and squash to sell at the farmers market in Willow River." Burman paused for a minute. "Got about fifty acres of woods that runs up to the river. Grow me some deer and rabbits, some squirrels, and a few partridges there." He laughed as he told about his woods.

"Can't do much about the wild game. Damn game warden says I gotta have a license to shoot anything. Imagine that, having a hunting license to kill something you grow on your own land. Country's gone to hell. Gone completely to hell." He rubbed his hand with the knife in it across his whiskered chin.

"So you're making a living out here," Josh said.

"Survivin', that's about all we're doin'. Survivin' from one year to the next. Got five kids, you know. All in school right now. Ride the bus, they do. Doin' well in school, too. Proud of every one of 'em."

"Kids help out around here, do they?" Josh asked.

"You bet they do. Help out a lot. Have their chores to do every day before they go to school and when they get back home again. Chores is good for kids. Teaches 'em how to work. People don't know how to work anymore. They sit behind some desk with one of them computers on it and call it work. That ain't work. Gotta get your hands dirty before you can call workin' work."

"I hear what you're saying," offered Josh. He was busy scribbling notes in the pad on his clipboard. "Anything else you'd like to share?"

"Nope. Probably said more than I should already. What paper did you say you were from?"

"*Farm Country News.*"

"I heard of that. Good farm paper. Been around a long time, hasn't it?"

"Yes, it has. Started right after the Civil War. Well, I'll let you get back to your meat cutting."

"Enjoyed talkin' to ya. Say, you wouldn't want a hunk of this here goat meat, would you?"

"No thanks, but I appreciate the offer."

As he left the barn, Josh did not see the deer heads and hides stashed deep in the shadows of the old building. He crawled into his pickup, turned around, and steered down the narrow driveway toward the country road. As he left he noticed Mrs. Burman looking out the kitchen window. Her face was expressionless.

Farm Country News

Josh arrived back at the courthouse around four in the afternoon.

"How'd the interview go?" Ben asked when Josh entered his office.

"Burman's quite a character. Down on the government. Down on the DNR. He seems to be a tough old codger."

"Yup, that sounds like Burman. I don't know him very well. He's never set foot in my office, but he's hanging on. Making a living out there on that poor river-bottom farm."

Just then, Warden Natalie Karlsen knocked on Ben's office door a couple of times and stuck in her head.

"Sorry to interrupt, but are we on for lunch tomorrow?" asked Natalie.

"Yup, got it on my calendar. Meet you at the Lone Pine at noon." Ben regularly met with the county forester, the DNR warden, the fellow doing soil conservation work, the Farm and Home Administration person—people whose work overlapped with his.

"Got it," said Natalie. She was wearing her warden's uniform, complete with sidearm.

"I want you to meet someone," said Ben. "This is Josh Wittmore, a writer for *Farm Country News* who just moved back here and is working out of the head office. Josh grew up here in Ames County, on a farm just out of Link Lake."

"Good to meet you," said the warden. "I know your boss, Bert Schmid, well. Good newspaperman. Good guy. Good farm paper too." She shook Josh's hand. He noticed she had big brown eyes and a nice smile. Could this be the person Dan Burman was talking about? The dreaded, overly snoopy DNR game warden?

"Josh is writing about the Tamarack River Valley and all the changes going on out there," said Ben.

"Just getting started," said Josh. "I was talking with Daniel Burman this afternoon. He was butchering a couple of goats."

"Goats?" asked Natalie.

"Yup, that's what he said." The warden's expression changed to that of someone who looked like she'd figured something out—had put some pieces of a puzzle together.

"Got to be going," said Warden Karlsen rather abruptly.

"Nice meeting you," said Josh.

"Same here," she said, smiling. "See you around."

"Wonder how she takes all the guff," Josh said after Natalie left.

"Yeah, she gets a lot of it. Especially from the folks over in the Tamarack River Valley."

"So I noticed."

Josh and Ben talked for a few more minutes about poor farmers in Ames County, and about other people Josh might interview to flesh out his story. Then he drove to the Farm Country News office, south of Willow River on Highway 22. He arrived a few minutes after five. The clerical staff had left, but Josh noticed that the lights were still on in Bert's office.

Bert looked up when Josh walked by.

"Josh, you got a minute?"

"Been doing an interview out in the Tamarack River Valley. Thought I'd check my e-mail and see if I had any phone calls."

"Have a chair," said Bert, a rather rotund man in his mid-sixties with nearly white hair. He wore wire-rimmed glasses, which he removed when Josh entered the cluttered office. Papers and books were piled everywhere on the floor and overflowed from the old wooden desk where Bert sat, staring at sheets of numbers spread out before him. Several plaques hung on the wall: "Best Agricultural News Editor—1990," "Friend of 4-H Award—1992," "Service to Agriculture Award—Farm Bureau—1985."

"Drop those papers on the floor," he said, motioning to a chair by the desk. "Take a load off."

Josh expected him to ask about his story and what he'd been learning, how the interviews were going, and how he might help Josh as he put it all together. He didn't expect what he heard.

"Not a good year for *Farm Country News*, Josh. Not a good year at all," said Bert. He put on his glasses and pointed to some numbers on the page in front of him.

"I thought we'd run some pretty good stories. Maybe as good as we've ever done," said Josh. "That stuff we did on the Lazy Z got a lot of attention."

"Yes, it did, but I'm not talking about the stories, Josh. The stories have been great. We're just not making enough money. Can't run a paper without money." Bert stabbed his finger at a number on the page.

"How bad is it?" asked Josh.

"It's bad, Josh. Worse than I thought. This year, for the first time in our history, we're probably going to lose money. We've been in the black every year since *Farm Country News* came out, and that was 1868. Wasn't long ago we scarcely had room for all the advertising that came our way; now we're lucky to keep some of the oldest accounts."

"What's going on? People seem to be reading our paper."

"Not like they used to. First off, we've got only a fraction of the farmers in this country that we once had and we're losing more every year. Farmers are our best customers. Our subscriptions have been dropping every year since the 1960s—not a lot in any one year, but enough so that it adds up."

"Maybe we need to do more promotion, show up at more farm shows, make sure we get to the state and county fairs," said Josh.

"That's how it once worked, but now our pencil pushers tell me it's not profitable any more. It costs more to put up and staff an exhibit than it's worth," said Bert. "And, as you know, subscriptions don't pay the bills. Never have. It's advertising."

Josh had never paid much attention to the *Farm Country News* advertising department. His sense of journalistic ethics had always told him that what he wrote and how he wrote it should never be influenced by who does or does not advertise in the paper.

"Advertising revenue keeps us afloat," Bert continued. "And the Internet is killing us. Our want ads have essentially disappeared. Now people can go to the Internet and advertise for nothing. It doesn't cost them one damn nickel to advertise on Craigslist. I can't blame people for doing it."

Quietly, Josh sat listening to his boss and wondering about the future— his future as a journalist. He had worked at *Farm Country News* since he graduated from the University of Wisconsin and was now especially pleased to be working out of the paper's main office and living back in his home county.

"So, what are you gonna do?" asked Josh, a feeling of dread beginning to roll over him.

"What I thought we'd never do. We'll have to close down some bureaus. I'm trying to decide which ones we can keep. Hate to close any. Never laid off anybody before. Fired a few people, but that's different."

"That's terrible," said Josh.

"It's the worst thing I've ever known. It's not for public consumption yet, but the first to go will be our Springfield, Illinois, bureau. That's one of the reasons I moved you up here, so you wouldn't get the wrong idea when I closed the place down."

Bert had a sorrowful look on his face. Once more he removed his glasses and looked Josh in the eye.

"What do you think, Josh? Is there another alternative? I've given up on Illinois, and the Indiana bureau isn't doing very well either, nor is Ohio. Minnesota seems to be doing OK, same for the Iowa bureau."

Josh, not sure if he should share what he had on his mind, said quietly, "I have one suggestion."

"Let's have it; I need all the ideas I can come by."

"Have you thought about us putting out an online edition?"

Bert's reaction was like someone setting off a bomb in the office. His face turned beet-red, and he clinched his fists. "It's the goddamn Internet that's ruining us—ruining all the newspapers in the country. I would never do that. Never do that." Bert slumped back in his chair.

Josh, surprised at the outburst, sat quietly. Josh knew that Bert was the majority stockholder in *Farm Country News*, so he knew the man had a lot at stake in whatever decision he made.

"You know what happened to the *Milwaukee Sentinel*, you've heard about the *Capital Times* in Madison, and the *Rocky Mountain News* in Denver—it had published since 1859. And the *Tucson Citizen*, in the business for 138 years. And the *Ann Arbor News* in Michigan—around for 174 years. And lots more. Their print editions all gone under. Killed off by the goddamn Internet," said Bert. He was rubbing both of his hands through his thick gray hair.

"The last thing I want to do is be taken in by that thing that seems to grab everybody's attention these days. I thought we would be immune. We're one of those so-called niche papers. But it's happening to us, too. Damn Internet is out to get us, like a tiger on the prowl, without one ounce of ethics or concern about accurate news."

Josh could think of nothing else to say. He stood up to leave. "I'm sorry," he said. When he looked at his boss, he could see tears in his eyes, something he had never seen before.

Natalie quickly put two and two together when she heard Josh's comment about Dan Burman cutting up goat meat. Two plus two did not equal goat; two plus two equaled venison. Deer killed out of season, the result of poaching, something that she had high on her agenda to stop.

Natalie called Sheriff Clarence Bliss and asked if he'd like to ride along to the Burman place. She told him she had a hunch Burman might be poaching deer. Both she and Bliss knew that such a visit could be dangerous; a poacher cornered is an unpredictable person. Of course all poachers had weapons, usually powerful ones.

Bliss, in his mid-fifties, bald, and on the plump side, agreed to ride along—"Always agree to ride shotgun for a lady cop," he said. Bliss didn't differentiate among police officers, deputy sheriffs, state troopers, or conservation wardens; he called them all cops. He had accompanied Natalie on other arrests, especially when she thought things might become a little dicey. Of course, Natalie served as a backup for the sheriff on occasion as well.

It was about eight in the evening, a moonless night, when Natalie pulled by the sheriff's office. On the way out to the Burman farm, she described how she had heard rifle shots the other night, when she was out on patrol, looking for deer poachers. She hadn't seen anything and had no evidence that Burman might be involved. But she'd heard rumors about the Burman family and how dirt poor they were and how they regularly killed a deer or two to help them through the long Wisconsin winters.

"You ever think about giving old Burman a pass?" the sheriff asked. He knew about the Burmans' situation, probably better than the warden because he had been in Ames County for twenty years.

"I can't do that," Natalie said curtly. "You let one poacher off the hook, and before you know it, every Tom, Dick, and Harry will be shooting deer out of season."

They traveled along the narrow country road in silence for several miles, neither saying anything. Soon, they arrived at the Burman farm and turned in.

"I'll go up to the door," Natalie said. "You stay here in the truck until I find out what's what."

A skinny farm dog raced out to meet the warden's truck, barking loudly. The kitchen door opened and a tall, thin man appeared, framed by the light behind him.

"Who is it?" he yelled into the night.

"Conservation warden," Natalie said. "Natalie Karlsen. Are you Daniel Burman?"

"That's what folks call me. Whaddya want?"

"Wondering if I could look around a little."

"What in hell for?"

"Just want to look around a little."

"In the middle of the night? What in hell you expect to find in the middle of the night?"

"It's only eight-thirty."

"Who you got with you in your truck?"

"It's Sheriff Bliss."

"The sheriff. What you got him along for?"

"Can we look around a little? Check some things out?"

"Go right ahead. Look till you're blue in the face."

"You wanna come along with us?"

"Why the hell for?"

"Just thought you might like to see what's going on."

"Gotta put my shoes on. Good God almighty. What's the world comin' to?" Burman muttered as he disappeared into the house.

"Keep your eye on him, Sheriff, I don't want to see him coming through that door carrying a deer rifle," said Natalie. The sheriff had gotten out of Natalie's truck, quietly closing the door.

"I'm way ahead of you," the sheriff said as he stood off to the side, his hand ready to pull out his sidearm.

In a few minutes, Burman appeared wearing his barn coat and dirty cap; both reeked of cow manure. He carried a flashlight.

"Well, you just go look around to yer heart's content," Burman said. "What you lookin' for anyway?"

"I'll tell you if we find it," Natalie said. "What building is that?" she asked as she pointed to a little shack-like structure a short walk from the house.

"It's my woodshed. You wanna look in my woodshed?"

"Might as well," said Natalie. She and Burman walked to the small, dark outbuilding.

"Nothing here but wood," Natalie said after flashing her light around the inside of the little building. "What about the lean-to on the barn? Can we have a look in there?"

"Sure, look away."

The trio walked over to the lean-to. Burman pulled open the door. The hinges squeaked.

Natalie flashed her light around the lean-to and spotted two skinned animals hanging from a crosspiece.

"Well, well," Natalie said. "What have we here?"

"Couple of dead goats. Ain't no law against butchering your own goats, is there?" Burman said. He tugged on his dirty cap.

Natalie and the sheriff walked close to the carcasses. They saw a couple of fresh goat hides on the floor, along with the severed heads.

"Yeah, they're goats all right," said the sheriff.

44

"Sorry to have bothered you, Mr. Burman," Natalie said. "We're doing a little checking. Heard there had been some deer poaching going on in these parts."

"Figured that's what you were lookin' for. You satisfied now?"

"Thank you, Mr. Burman. You've been most cooperative. Good night, now."

Natalie and the Sheriff climbed back in her pickup, and she drove out the Burman driveway.

"Somebody must have tipped him off," Natalie said. She pounded her hand on the steering wheel. "Wonder who that could have been? Nobody knew I suspected Burman except maybe that reporter from the *Farm Country News*. He said he'd been out here earlier today and saw Burman cutting up some meat. That reporter, his name was Josh Wittmore, didn't say anything about seeing a couple of goats hanging." She pounded her hand on the steering wheel again.

"Damn," she said.

The sheriff, with the hint of a smile on his face, said nothing.

Tamarack River Ghost

Oscar Anderson and Fred Russo stood on the banks of Tamarack River at the former Ira Osborne Commemorative Park, now known simply as the Tamarack River Park. It was a warm, sunny October day. The maples were showing off their fall colors, deep reds mixed in with a few yellows. The oaks on the higher ground above the river were just beginning to show their fall colors—browns and quiet reds. The sky was a deep blue with no hint of cloud or haze.

Fall rains had increased the river level a little, but not much.

"Well, whaddya expect we'll catch today?" asked Oscar as he tossed his jointed fishing lure out into the river and began slowly cranking the handle of his spinning rod.

"What was that you said?" asked Fred.

"Fish, what kinda fish we gonna catch today?"

The river was a bit noisy in front of the park; a rocky rapids stirred up the current.

"Yup, think you're right about that," answered Fred.

"Right about what?"

"What you just said."

"All I said was 'What kinda fish you think we're gonna catch?'"

"Hell, I don't know what kinda fish we'll catch. We'll be lucky if we catch anything," said Fred. He was concentrating on his bobber, which had floated off into a little pool of still water where the river made a turn by the park. Fred liked to fish with worms and a bobber every chance he got. He let his friend fuss with fancy stuff, the bright-colored lures with hooks hanging everywhere, and the fancy Daiwa fishing rod and reel his kids gave him for Christmas last year. Fred used an old Shakespeare Rod and Johnson reel he bought thirty years ago. He saw no need to replace what he had as long as it worked, and it worked just fine.

As the sun climbed higher, the day warmed and the fall colors became even more intense.

The two old men sat staring into the water, dozing in the warm sun.

"Say Oscar, I've been thinking about the old ghost that lives on this river."

"Why?"

"'Cause that's what I'm thinking about."

"I probably know more about that ghost than you do," said Oscar. Each year Oscar Anderson, at the opening ceremonies for the Tamarack River Winter Festival, recited "An Ode to the Tamarack River Ghost," a somewhat embellished version of how Mortimer Dunn met his fate.

Fred laughed. "I know that. I suppose now you'll tell me you've seen the ghost and heard the song."

"I might have," said Oscar quietly. "I just might have. Happened last spring. It was a still night, right after the ice on the river went out. I was right here in this park, came here to see the ice break up. Something to see, you know. Big chunks of ice spilling over those rapids, smashing into little pieces."

"You didn't tell me you'd seen the ghost," said Fred.

"Well, I don't tell you ever'thin'."

"Guess not," Fred said, a bit miffed at his friend.

"Anyway," Oscar continued. "I was standing here, thinking about that log drive back in 1900. It was early in the morning, sun hadn't got up yet. And a bit chilly, too. Couldn't sleep, so I came down here to watch the river ice go out."

"So when you can't sleep, you come down here to the river?"

"Not always, but I did that day. Ice going out is always kind of interesting to see; I like the sound of the river when it's running full, too. Nice sound."

"What about the ghost? You gonna tell me about the ghost?"

"Well, hold your horses, I'm gettin' to it."

"About time."

"I was just standing and taking it all in—the coming of spring, the old river runnin' wild, the smell of the season's first new growth—when I heard it. Had to listen real careful, 'cause the sound was kind of dim, kind of dim it was."

"That's because your hearin' ain't so good anymore," said Fred.

"Speak for yourself, but I could hear it. Could hear the sound pretty good. It was the sound of a little bell, the kind of bell that hung from the collar of the ghost's dog. It was that kind of sound, clear as could be, after I focused in on it."

"Probably ice melting and chunks running over the rocks—sometimes that sounds like a little bell ringing."

"Ah, but there was more. Wasn't just the bell ringing. I could smell it."

"Smell what?"

"Tobacco smoke. Pipe tobacco smoke. And I remembered Mortimer Dunn smoked a pipe."

"Musta been somebody else in the park, smokin' a pipe that morning."

"Fred, there was nobody else here, I was all alone. And I know what I heard and what I smelled."

"That it? That's all to the story. You heard a bell ringing, and then you smelled tobacco smoke."

"There's more."

Oscar reeled in his line and tossed it out again.

"Well, you gonna tell me the rest?" asked Fred.

"You wanna hear it?"

"Well, sure. You don't tell a damn story and then stop in the middle of it without tellin' how it ended. What kind of story is that?"

"Thought maybe you wanted to go back to payin' attention to your fishing."

"I am payin' attention to my fishing. You gonna finish the story or not?"

"Ain't much more to it," said Oscar. He cleared his throat and continued. "And this part's a little more sketchy."

"Well?" said Fred.

"I felt like another person was standin' right next to me. I couldn't see nobody, but it sure felt like somebody was standin' there. And the weirdest part, when I sensed the other person nearby, the smell of pipe tobacco smoke was strongest."

"Couldn't see nobody else, huh?"

"That's what I said, but sometimes you can't see a ghost. The more I thought about it, the more sure I became that the Tamarack River Ghost was watching the river with me that morning. That old ghost is out there lookin' for his resting place, and when he ain't doin' that, he's takin' care of this valley. You bet he is."

"Gives me the shudders just to think about it," said Fred. "You oughta add what you just told me to the tale you tell at the festival. Put a little scare in the folks."

"I might just do that. Might do that." Oscar reeled in his fish line. "Damn fish ain't bitin'. Think I'm going home and have a beer. You wanna beer, Fred?"

Nathan West Industries

*J*osh flipped on his computer and waited for it to boot up. He looked out his office window and thought about the conversation he'd had with his boss. He knew about the demise of several major newspapers around the country, but somehow he never believed it would happen to *Farm Country News*. He thought that the paper's niche audience, people interested in farming and agriculture, would continue subscribing and advertising. He was obviously wrong about that.

Before the conversation with Bert, he hadn't thought much about his future as a journalist. He'd been far too busy researching and writing stories—like the series that he'd just done on the Lazy Z feedlot operation in Missouri—stories that he hoped made a difference for the future of farming and agriculture in general. Now he began to wonder if he even had a future in journalism.

The computer screen glowed, and Josh clicked on his e-mail program. Since he'd been working undercover at the Lazy Z, he'd not kept up; now he stared at a list of 150 messages waiting to be opened, most of them junk—online shoe stores, sporting goods specials, deals from three different computer companies. He worked down the list, starting with the oldest and moving to the most recent, systematically deleting the junk and sifting through it for anything that might be important. He double-clicked on a message with the subject line "Nathan West Industries Expanding Operations." The body of the message was a press release:

Nathan West Industries (NWI), with corporate offices in Dubuque, Iowa, announces today the purchase of substantial acreage in Ames County,

Wisconsin. NWI plans to build a major hog-raising, farrow-to-finish operation on this new property. Once the company obtains the necessary permits, NWI will construct state-of-the-art buildings and equipment to care for a herd of 3,000 sows that will farrow about 75,000 hogs a year.

Nathan West Industries has hog operations in Iowa and North Carolina; this will be its first in Wisconsin. The company has a long history in agriculture, beginning as a grain storage and shipping operation in 1868, when the company bought midwestern farmers' wheat and shipped it by steamboat down the Mississippi River.

In 1960, NWI opened its first broiler-chicken operation; it started its first feed-processing plant in 1965, which specialized in hog, beef, and poultry feed. Its first beef feedlot operation began in 1970. In 1985, NWI opened its first farrow-to-finish hog operation near Monona, Iowa.

Today, Nathan West Industries is the third largest agribusiness firm of its type in the United States. NWI is looking forward to a long and profitable future with its new operation in Ames County.

Josh hit the print button and a couple of minutes later was back in his boss's office. He dropped the e-mail on Bert's desk.

"Do you know about this, Bert?" Josh said.

His boss skimmed the piece of paper, then rubbed his hands through his shock of unruly gray hair.

"When'd you get this?"

"Just now."

Bert took his wire-rimmed glasses and rubbed his eyes.

"This is a big story," he said. "Could be as big as the Lazy Z feedlot series."

"Nathan West hasn't been accused of any wrongdoing, has it?" Josh asked.

"Nope, not that I know of. But the company keeps a lid on everything it does. It's privately owned; nobody knows how big it really is or how much money it makes. I do know that it's one of the biggest integrated meat-producing outfits in the country."

"I can see where this conversation is going," Josh said.

"Yup, get out there and find out as much as you can about them. Folks here in Wisconsin need to know before they give the final OK for NWI to build."

"There's one thing I'm not going to do," Josh said.

"What would that be?" Bert asked, smiling.

"I don't think I'll apply for a job there. I don't need another brick missing my head by a few inches."

Bert sat back in his chair and laughed his characteristic deep belly laugh. Josh had to laugh too, even though his experience working undercover at the Lazy Z feedlot was still a bit fresh.

"I'd suggest you start at the university in Madison. Talk to Bill Evans in the agribusiness studies department. Saw some research findings from that department about these big hog production operations."

"I took a course from him when I was in college," Josh said. "Wonder if he'll remember me. I sure remember him. Could hardly stay awake during his lectures."

"Try to stay awake this time, Josh." Bert laughed again.

Josh returned to his office and began searching the Internet for everything he could find about Nathan West Industries before traveling to Madison and meeting with Evans. His phone rang, breaking his concentration.

"This is Josh Wittmore," he said.

"Mr. Wittmore, this is Natalie Karlsen; we met in Ben Wesley's office."

"You're the conservation warden."

"Yes, I am. I was wondering if we could meet for coffee," she said. "Ben suggested it; he said we might be able to help each other."

"Sure," Josh answered. He remembered that underneath the gun belt and badge he'd seen quite an attractive young woman. Besides that, she might be a contact to have and the source for some news stories. "Where and when?"

"How about tomorrow at ten, the Lone Pine Restaurant. You know where that is?"

"I grew up in this county; I know the Lone Pine. See you there."

*F*ive minutes before ten, Josh pulled open the door of the Lone Pine Restaurant. He had not been inside the place since he'd returned to Willow River; it hadn't changed. A mounted deer head with glass eyes stared down on all who entered the place. A stuffed northern pike hung next to the deer head, and shotguns and deer rifles of various sizes and calibers graced another wall of the restaurant as they had when Josh last visited the place. An old-timers' table at one end of the big noisy room had its usual half-dozen to sometimes ten retired farmers and merchants from the area, discussing everything from who was sleeping with somebody else's wife to why the president of the United States wasn't paying more attention to farmers. For Josh, it was like the place hadn't changed at all since he left ten years ago. Mazy, Lone Pine waitress, greeted him as soon as he stepped inside.

"You look familiar," Mazy said.

"Josh Wittmore."

"Of course. You've grown up."

"Haven't been in here in a while. Quite a while." Mazy had put on a few pounds and her hair had streaks of gray, but otherwise, like the rest of the place, she hadn't changed.

"You back in town?"

"I am. Working for the *Farm Country News.*"

"You don't say. That's a good paper."

"I'm having coffee with Natalie Karlsen," Josh said.

"The game warden?" Mazy lifted an eyebrow.

"One and the same."

"Find yourself a booth or a table, your choice. I'll point her in your direction when she comes in."

Promptly at ten, Natalie came through the door. Josh watched as Mazy motioned toward where he was sitting. Eyes turned when the warden walked across the crowded restaurant floor, as they did whenever a law enforcement officer entered the place. Some of the old timers couldn't get used to the idea that the county's conservation warden was a woman.

"I tell you, what are we gonna see next?" one old timer muttered. "Who ever heard of a game warden being a woman?"

"Well, there she is," another fellow said. "Quite a looker, too."

Good to see you again," Natalie said when she arrived at the little table in the back where Josh had sat down.

Josh stood up and wondered if he should shake her hand or just stand there. Somewhere he'd heard that you never shake the hand of a lady unless she offers it first. Josh figured this would be especially so if the woman wore a badge and carried a firearm on her hip. Do you ever shake hands with a law-enforcement person? He didn't have the answer. For some reason, she unnerved him.

Natalie offered her hand. It was soft and warm, yet her grip was firm and authoritative. Josh had known lots of women, but never one wearing a badge. Natalie quickly picked up on Josh's discomfort. She smiled pleasantly, and once more Josh was drawn to the big brown eyes that defined her face, eyes that sparkled when she talked. Her blonde hair was tied back in a ponytail. She wore no makeup.

"How's it going?" she asked.

"OK," Josh said. "Trying to find my way around a new office." Josh wondered why she wanted to meet with him. He had become quite wary as the years passed. When people wanted something, some coverage in the paper, they contacted him. But often times when he called someone, they avoided him. He'd come to understand that some people just didn't like "the press." Josh had also become quite good at reading people, seeing through the veneer and uncovering who they really were and what they really wanted. But he was having trouble reading Natalie Karlsen. He had no idea what she had on her mind, but he doubted she merely wanted to get acquainted with him.

"Lots going on here in Ames County these days," Natalie said.

"It seems that way," Josh answered. He wondered how long it would take her to say what she really wanted. Josh had little patience for small talk—he saw it as a major waste of time. He wished when people had something to say, they would say it. But he also knew that farm and small-town people seldom got to what they had on their minds until they marched around the topic several times. Over the years, he had learned to listen patiently and wait for information he was seeking. And now this good-looking young conservation warden, who Josh noticed was not wearing a wedding ring, was doing the same thing. When he met her, he wouldn't have taken her for the beat-around-the-bush type. He soon discovered that she wasn't.

"Remember when we met the other day?"

"Of course," Josh said.

"You mentioned that you'd just interviewed Dan Burman and had seen him cutting up some goat meat."

"Yes." Josh wondered where Natalie was going with the conversation.

"Did you know Burman is suspected of poaching deer?"

"No, I didn't."

"Well he is. I got a solid tip that he had had been shooting deer out of season."

"Really," Josh said. "He told me he was cutting up goat meat."

"I know, that's what you said. I don't know how to say this politely, so I'll just ask." Natalie looked more than a little uncomfortable when she blurted, "Did you tip off Burman that I might be paying him a visit?"

"Did I what?" Josh asked, a little too loudly, wondering if he had heard correctly. People at nearby tables glanced over, and he lowered his voice.

"I haven't talked to him since the day I was out there."

"Well, I think somebody did. The sheriff and I drove out to his farm—and all we saw were two goats. No venison."

"Well, it wasn't me," Josh said, pushing back from the table and sounding more defensive than he intended. He had hoped for a much more pleasant meeting with Natalie, but she sure knew how not to impress a man. *Unbelievable*, he thought. *She has the gall—but maybe her attitude just goes with her work. And maybe she is like me—never trusting anybody.*

"Sorry," she said smiling. "I couldn't imagine that you had done it, but I had to ask."

Josh said nothing as he sipped the coffee Mazy had delivered to their table.

He couldn't think of how to reply. Inside, he was furious. No one had ever accused him of anything like this before. He took a last drink of coffee, stood up, and said, "Got to be going; got a big story brewing." He tossed some money on the table and stomped out the door. As he left, he thought, *There's a woman I'll avoid.*

Dr. William Willard Evans

Josh Wittmore turned his pickup onto Highway 22 and headed for Madison and the University of Wisconsin campus there. He'd made the trip many times when he attended the UW in the late 1990s, and he remembered it as a pleasant drive. It was but eighty-five miles from his home farm, and only seventy-five miles from Willow River. He was surprised how little traffic had increased since he'd left the county ten years ago—only a car now and then. As he drove south from Montello, he passed the occasional Amish buggy, with a single horse trotting alongside the road, the buggy's occupants deep in the vehicle's dark interior shadows.

As he drove, he scarcely noticed the fall colors that were appearing everywhere. The long hills lining the big marshes between Montello and Pardeeville were especially striking, as they were studded with bright red and yellow maples. October was a beautiful time in Wisconsin, but Josh drove on, noticing not much of anything out his window.

Josh planned to think through the questions he wanted to ask his former professor about these relatively new massive hog operations that had sprung up in several parts of the country. He'd done enough exploring on the Internet to learn what was going on in North Carolina, where some of the largest operators did business. He'd learned that one company alone had more than fifteen hundred operations, with seven hundred thousand sows total, in that state alone. That same company operated a slaughter-house there that butchered thirty thousand hogs a day.

All these facts and figures swirled around in his head as he drove, but he couldn't concentrate. He kept coming back to his meeting with Natalie. He was furious with this woman, conservation warden or not. Nobody had ever accused him of doing something dishonest, but she had. Why would she even think that he would tip off Dan Burman about a possible conservation warden visit? All he said was that he'd interviewed him and saw him slicing up some goat meat. No crime in cutting up your own goat meat. He felt sorry for the man, dirt poor with scarcely enough food to take his big family through the winter.

Josh had met people like the warden before: those who jumped to conclusions before they had all the facts. When people had done this to him previously, he'd crossed them off his list of contacts and tried to avoid them. He couldn't easily do this with Natalie. But he would try to stay out of her way. He would do his job, and she would do hers, and when they overlapped he'd be cautious, very cautious. But something else had happened at their meeting. Something about Natalie had gotten to him. True, she'd unnerved him with her accusation. She didn't know how close she'd come to having Josh Wittmore jump up and tell her off. He had a bit of a temper, which had gotten him in trouble before. Now, he was asking himself why he hadn't said more. Why hadn't he confronted this badge-wearing, gun-toting woman? He didn't know why. And that's what was troubling him as he drove on toward Pardeeville and then south to Arlington, Deforest, and on into Madison.

*E*vans had sent Josh a permit for the university parking ramp next to Steenbock Library on the College of Agricultural and Life Sciences campus. Josh parked his pickup, walked around the library, and headed up the hill toward Agriculture Hall, to the offices of the Department of Agribusiness Studies. It had been ten years since he'd been in Agriculture Hall, and memories of his college days came flooding back. The agribusiness offices were on the third floor of the old building; the stairs creaked as they did when he had climbed them to the auditorium where several of his classes met. It was in the Agriculture Hall auditorium that he suffered through Professor Evans's Introduction to Agricultural Economics in 1997. Thinking back to the course, in which he'd received a C, he wished he'd paid better attention. So much of what he wrote about these days required a solid grounding in the economics of agriculture.

He stuck his nose through the Ag Hall auditorium doors—students filled nearly every seat, and a professor stood on stage, pacing back and forth while the students stared at a PowerPoint presentation. The screen was filled with mathematical formulas. Josh remembered his college days, when his math professors wrote with chalk on a huge blackboard that stretched across the front of the big room. PowerPoint seemed an improvement. At least he could read the numbers.

He continued up the stairs to the third floor and found the offices of the Department of Agribusiness Studies, which had been called agricultural economics when he was in school. An administrative assistant directed him to the office of Dr. William Willard Evans, department chair. She gently knocked on the door.

"Come in." Josh recognized the deep voice.

"Josh Wittmore, good to see you," said the big man with bushy gray eyebrows and penetrating gray eyes.

"Thanks for taking time to talk with me," Josh said.

"I always take time for a former student," Evans responded. Josh wondered if he remembered him—part of him hoped that he didn't. He had not been a prize economics student. "How can I help?"

"You've surely heard that Nathan West Industries has bought land in Ames County for a major hog operation."

"I have," said Evans. "Should be an economic boon to the area. That part of Wisconsin could use a boost. Lots of low-income folks there."

"That's true," said Josh. "You may not know that I grew up in Ames County and recently moved back to Willow River, headquarters for our paper since 1868."

"So how can I help?" asked Evans.

"What can you tell me about Nathan West, beyond what I read on the Internet?"

"Oh, I guess you could say that it's one of those companies that represent the future of agriculture in this country. The people there seem to know what they're doing and are doing it well."

"Aren't they responsible for driving a bunch of the little family farmers out of business?" Josh asked, trying to dig deeper for his story.

Professor Evans bristled a bit. "Most of the little family farmers drove themselves out of business. Surely not the fault of Nathan West. The world of agribusiness has little room for small-time family farmers. These days, you either learn how to compete, which means getting bigger, or you get out. Simple as that."

Josh scribbled notes on his pad, making sure to write down Evans's comments as he heard them. He prided himself on accurate reporting.

"What can you tell me about the difference between contract farming and company-owned farming?" Josh asked.

"Company owned is just what the name implies—the company owns everything, from the land, hogs, and buildings to the feed supply, slaughter-house, and distribution system. Another word for it is vertical integration. I must say, from an economic perspective, it's the way to go. The company is in control of all segments of the operation. It's one way to maintain high quality."

"Not as many risks as dealing with individual farmers who contract with them?" Josh offered.

"For sure," said Evans. "Hard to control quality when you're dealing with a bunch of farmers scattered all over the place. Some of them are good managers, many of them not so good."

"I guess that makes sense. But when the company owns everything, where does it leave these farmers?"

"The good ones find jobs with the company—lots of employment opportunities on these big hog farms. The not-so-good ones, well, they find other work."

Evans said it in a matter-of-fact way, as if it were a foregone conclusion that the independent family farmer, even one with a contract with a big company, might not have much of a future.

"Nothing especially new about these big agribusiness firms; they are but one example of vertical integration," Evans continued. "Take the big oil companies; they're vertically integrated. They own the oil wells, the refineries, and the gas stations where you fill up your car. Nobody in between; they have full control. Nathan West is just like that, except it deals with hogs, not oil."

"So you think vertical integration in agriculture is a good thing?"

"I didn't say that. What I said is that's what's happening. The free market working at its best. Never want to argue with the free-market system. It's what made this country what it is today."

"Milton Friedman's ideas," Josh said. Deep in the recesses of his mind he'd remembered an economics lecture about Milton Friedman, a world-renowned economist. Friedman advocated a free market based on as little governmental involvement and control as possible.

"What about the disappearance of the small family farm?" Josh asked.

"Not for me to worry about. My job is to teach, conduct research, and try to understand what's happening, not make judgments about what should be happening. What should be happening? That's for the policy guys to debate, the politicians and the farm organizations. That's their business. My job, and the mission of the Department of Agribusiness Studies, is to provide scientifically based, unbiased research."

Josh was jotting notes as fast as he could, writing while looking at Evans, a technique he'd learned some years ago. When he looked at people, they kept talking. When he looked down to write, they tended to stop.

"Anything else you'd like to share?" asked Josh. He tried to keep his voice steady and not reveal in his questions or his demeanor how he really felt about the responses to his questions.

"If you want some cutting-edge research information, I suggest you schedule a meeting with Dr. Randy Oakfield and sit in on one of his lectures. He's one of our new hires, did his doctorate at Cornell."

Evans paged through some papers on his desk and picked one up. "The title of his dissertation was 'Vertical Integration in Agriculture: An Economic Analysis.' It's a good, solid piece of work. He and his graduate assistant, Emily Jordan, she's new too, have a grant proposal pending for a study of vertical integration in the pork industry."

"I'll do that; thanks for the suggestion," Josh said as he jotted down their names. "I won't take any more of your time. It was a pleasure talking with you. And thanks for the good information."

"Any time," Evans said. "Always here to help. I especially like to work with former students." Josh couldn't decide if he meant what he said or not.

Dr. Randy Oakfield

A few days after Josh returned to Willow River from his visit in Madison, he got a call from Dr. Evans.

"Hi, Josh," he began. "I enjoyed our conversation the other day, and I'm following up on my suggestion to have you sit in on one of Dr. Oakfield's lectures. I checked with Oakfield and he's presenting a lecture on vertical integration in agriculture next Thursday at 11:00. I asked if you could attend, and he said, 'Of course.' Can I tell him you'll be there?"

"I'll be there," said Josh. "Thanks for setting it up."

"No problem at all. Always ready to help out a former student."

*D*r. Randy Oakfield stood in front of a class of eighty-five undergraduate students, mostly sophomores, who signed up for his Agribusiness 205 course, Integrated Agricultural Systems. This was the first university course he had ever taught, having finished his graduate work last June. He'd been teaching the course every Tuesday and Thursday at 11:00 a.m. since September, but he was still nervous when he clipped on his microphone and looked out over a sea of young, mostly apathetic faces. Agribusiness 205 was a required course for all undergraduates enrolled in the College of Agricultural and Life Sciences, so a fair number of the students Randy faced wished they could be about any place other than listening to his lectures and attempts at humor, which seldom evoked more than an occasional chuckle.

Oakfield noticed that a stranger had slipped into one of the back seats and surmised it must be the newspaper reporter Dr. Evans had mentioned. He had decided he wouldn't make any adjustments to his lecture simply because a member of the press was in attendance, and besides, he had agreed to meet with him after the lecture.

Randy grew up on a livestock farm in Indiana. Until he landed this job at UW–Madison, he had been in school constantly, from the day he enrolled in kindergarten. He went to college at Purdue, where he majored in animal science and earned a graduate research assistantship in agricultural economics at Cornell. He liked numbers and was attracted to the study of economic theories. He'd found the field challenging. He'd become interested in food systems, especially the production end. This interest led him to the study of vertical integration in farming.

With his new PhD in hand, Randy was extremely pleased to land an assistant professor position at UW–Madison—such jobs had become scarce at the big agricultural universities, which all faced budget cuts and various kinds of entrenchment. He'd expected to do at least a year and maybe as many as three years of post-doctorate work before competing for a tenure-track faculty position.

Randy looked like the stereotypical scholar—he was tall and thin and wore thick glasses, rumpled khaki trousers, and a nondescript shirt with a necktie loose around his neck. And although it was October, he still wore sandals. Though just in his early thirties, he had already gained considerable respect in the field of agricultural economics. His published article in the *National Agribusiness Journal* had won first place in its competition for young scholars.

He snapped on the computer projector and pushed a button on his laptop. Words in big red letters appeared on the screen behind him.

Vertical Integration: When all production stages for a commodity are under one owner

"I assume you've all read the assignment, and that you had no trouble finding the material on the Internet." A few heads nodded in agreement, but most just sat staring at him and the screen, their notebooks and pencils at the ready. Several of them wanted only a passing grade, for which they had to pass the six- and twelve-week and final exams. And to pass these, they needed to pay attention to the professor's comments. Having taken the six-week test, they knew everything on the exam came from the lectures.

"In the last twenty to twenty-five years we have seen a tremendous increase in vertical integration in agriculture in this country," Randy continued. His voice was not especially easy to listen to, because he spoke with little inflection. But he didn't lack for enthusiasm for his topic, which soon became evident to the minority of students in the room who had turned their initial apathy to interest.

"Much of our meat—whether beef, pork, or chicken—is produced by but a handful of big firms that own everything: the feed that the animals consume, the animals and their facilities, and the slaughtering plants that prepare the meat for our tables. These firms own an entire food production system from top to bottom, which is why we call it vertical integration." Randy paused and poked a button on his laptop, causing a new visual to appear on the screen: a historic family farmstead with house, barn, and outbuildings with cattle grazing in a nearby field.

"This photo represents the family farm that was so important to the history of this country. These farmers owned their land and their animals. They decided what and how much they would produce. They both depended on and supported their local communities, including the local feed mills, hardware stores, and agricultural supply centers. When they shipped their animals to market, they were often sold at auction to several processing plants that bid against each other. It's a system the country knew for many years, and it worked reasonably well.

"Most of these family farms were diversified, that is, they may have raised beef cattle, hogs, and chickens, and here in Wisconsin, most had small dairy herds. They grew most of their feed on their own land. The farmers' families provided most of the labor. Then, a new kind of agriculture came along and slowly began replacing the small family farm."

Josh wrote furiously in his notepad as Randy continued his lecture. He'd also brought along his digital tape recorder, to make sure he captured everything the young professor had to offer.

Dr. Randy Oakfield

Once more, Randy pushed the button on his laptop, and another image, a set of low-slung metal buildings, stretched across the screen with the caption

CAFO: Confined Animal Feeding Operation

"All these buildings are owned by Nathan West Industries, the third-largest agribusiness firm in the United States, with stakes in beef, poultry, and pork production. This photo shows one of NWI's Iowa hog operations. These hogs never see the outdoors; the operation is known as a CAFO, a confined animal feeding operation. It is a prime example of vertically integrated agriculture. At this production site, NWI owns the land, the buildings, and all the hogs. Those who operate the farm are employees of NWI.

"NWI has similar facilities scattered across Iowa, North Carolina, and a handful of other states. The fattened animals are shipped to NWI slaughterhouses. They have a huge processing plant in Dubuque, Iowa."

Randy went on to explain in considerable detail all aspects of the NWI operation. He noticed that several students were busily taking notes and listening intently to his lecture. Several others seemed to be dozing off or staring into space. His fellow professors told him to expect that not all of his students would be interested—one of the problems associated with required courses.

A new image appeared on the screen. Big green letters spelled out

Comparing CAFOs with Family Farms

"The historic family farm surely had its problems," Randy continued. "Problems with unpredictable weather, low prices received for products, and meeting mortgage payments on land and property. But small family farms had advantages, too. Probably the most important and far-reaching advantage—the farmer was his own boss. He owned and managed the land, and if he was a good manager and had some luck with markets and weather, he made enough money to feed and clothe a family. The family farm, by definition, involved everyone, young and old, working together—sometimes three generations. At a deeper level, important values about work, responsibility, and caring for the land resulted from the close working relationship the farmer had with family members. These family farms became the mainstays of rural communities, where not only family members helped each other, but neighbors also worked together, worshipped together, played together, and sustained the small towns and villages that served the farms.

"The values and beliefs that sustained these rural communities became a part of the makeup of the young men and women who grew up in them. This dimension of the small family farm is often overlooked and seldom discussed."

A hand shot up from a student near the front of the room.

"Yes," Randy said, recognizing the student.

"You've been talking about family farms and how valuable they were to rural communities," the young man said.

"Yes, there is considerable evidence to prove my point."

"Perhaps. But haven't we passed the era of the small family farms—shouldn't we drop them in the dustbins of history along with steam engines, horse-drawn reapers, and threshing crews?"

Another hand from the left side of the room was quickly thrust into the air.

"I was born and raised on a family farm, and I beg to differ—the family farm will long continue to be the mainstay of American agriculture. It's our history, but it is also our future. When a family farm disappears, more disappears than merely the farm and the people who worked it. An entire way of life is gone."

The first student's hand was in the air again, but just then the bell rang, announcing the end of the class.

"We'll continue this discussion next time," said Randy, pleased that he'd gotten several students interested in the issue of large farms versus family farms.

As Randy was unplugging his laptop and putting his notes away, Josh stepped forward and extended his hand.

"Josh Wittmore, *Farm Country News*," he said.

"Pleased to meet you," said Randy. "You work for a great paper—well respected in the agriculture community. In fact, I've got on my desk right now a copy with an article about beef feedlots in Missouri."

Josh was pleased that not only farmers were reading *Farm Country News* but professors as well.

"Nice job with the lecture," he said. "Integrated agriculture can be a complicated, touchy, and often political thicket, to say nothing about the emotions involved when you talk about the demise of the family farm."

"Tell me about it," Randy said, smiling. "What can I do for you?"

"Heard you and your graduate assistant are working on a research project dealing with integrated agriculture systems."

"We are. We're waiting to see if we'll be funded."

As Josh and Randy walked toward the back of the lecture hall, they met Randy's graduate assistant, a pleasant young woman with red hair and a bright smile. She was nearly out of breath when she reached them.

"Mr. Wittmore, I'd like you to meet Emily Jordan, my research assistant. Emily is working on her PhD and will be working on this research—assuming we get funded."

"Pleased to meet you," said Josh.

"And so pleased to meet you as well. Dr. Oakfield said you might be attending his lecture today. He has a lot of information to share."

Randy blushed.

"I've got good news, Dr. Oakfield," she said. "Very good news."

Research Proposal

*W*hat's up?" asked Randy as he walked from the Agriculture Hall lecture room with Emily. Josh had said his goodbyes and was on his way back to Willow River.

"Dr. Evans called while you were in class," she said. She was still out of breath, obviously having run from Randy's third-floor office, where her desk was just outside his office door.

"What?" asked Randy. Emily, who had bachelor's and master's degrees from Ohio State University, had begun working with Randy at the beginning of the fall semester. Randy had been impressed with her academic record—more than one reference described her as brilliant. Dr. Evans had assigned Emily to Randy when she first arrived. "You've got some common interests," he had said.

They did have common interests. At Ohio State, Emily studied integrated farming systems, an area of inquiry she wished to continue at Wisconsin. When Randy reviewed her application to the department, he noted that she was the same age as he was, thirty-two. He was a little concerned about that; he expected to work with graduate students some years younger. But the two of them had gotten along very well. Randy had taken a little ribbing from some of his friends because not only was Emily brilliant, she was also beautiful. Randy, always the scholar, had scarcely taken time to look at any woman. For the past five years, his graduate studies and research had consumed nearly all his time. And now, as a new assistant professor, Randy knew that he had to work exceedingly hard if he was to earn tenure and a permanent teaching/research slot in his department.

"So, what's up?" he asked again.

"Our research proposal to National Affiliated Hog Producers has been approved. Can you believe it? We're getting the money," she gushed.

"Thanks to your hard work," Randy said, smiling broadly.

"They were your ideas, Dr. Oakfield. Ideas that for sure caught their attention."

The two climbed the stairs to Randy's office. Randy slid into the chair behind his desk, and Emily sat across from him. They both knew that lots of work lay ahead, for putting together a research project was no small task. They also knew that both of them would benefit greatly from the project—he on his way to gaining tenure, she getting research data for her dissertation.

Dr. Evans poked his head in. "Congratulations, Randy. I got the news this morning that your proposal was approved. Let me know how I can help further."

"Thanks, we appreciate your support. Looks like we've got our work cut out for us," Randy said. He looked at Emily when he said it.

Randy was a little skittish about National Affiliated Hog Producers as a funding source for the project; its members consisted of the major hog producers in the United States, including Nathan West Industries. But Evans as well as the staff at National Affiliated Hog Producers had assured him there would be no conflict of interest. "You have complete freedom to develop the project as you see fit—following the plan you submitted to us, of course," the NAHP research project coordinator said.

When Randy had mentioned the potential conflict of interest of the pork industry financing a research project about attitudes toward big pork producers, the department chair scoffed. "It's dang hard to find financing these days. The federal government is cutting back on research. The state hasn't got any money. I suppose we could have submitted the proposal to one of the big environmental groups, but they are so biased against big agriculture that you'd have a tough time running the project without them interfering."

Randy agreed Evans was probably right. He wanted to say that maybe the big producers might be a bit biased in what they wanted to see as research results as well, but he decided not to bring up the topic. He didn't want to do anything to prevent the research money from coming in—he needed the funding. In addition to this research project, he was also developing a new theoretical model for explaining the economics of integrated agricultural systems. Data from the new research project could feed into his new model.

That afternoon Randy and Emily worked on finalizing the survey instrument they planned to use. They'd earlier constructed the questionnaire form and had field tested it with a small group of land owners to detect any problems with the wording. They had been sitting on the project for several weeks as they awaited a decision on funding.

The project amounted to drawing a random sample of property owners in Iowa communities with large, confined hog operations. They wanted to assess people's attitudes toward these operations—whether they liked having large hog operations in their neighborhoods or not, what benefits they saw, and what negative features they were aware of. Now, since Randy knew about NWI's plans for the Tamarack River Valley, they would sample residents in Ames County, with a subsample from people living in the Tamarack River Valley. Questions would relate to what residents thought about the company locating in the valley.

Randy glanced up at the clock. "It's past five," he said. "You have time tomorrow to finish this up—another couple hours should do it."

"Sure," Emily said. "I've got time tomorrow. I have another idea. Come over to my apartment tonight for supper. We need to celebrate a little. It isn't every day that money for a major project comes through. I'll ask some others to come as well. We'll have a little celebration."

"Nah, I'd better not. You go ahead, though. Sounds like a good idea."

"But you've got to be there; you're the project leader."

"I've got hours of journal reading to catch up on."

"Dr. Oakfield, you need a night away from the books," Emily said firmly. But she was smiling.

"Thanks anyway. You go ahead and celebrate. I've got work to do."

Randy felt good. It isn't every day that an assistant professor landed a major research grant. He could already imagine several journal articles where he would discuss his new theoretical model for understanding the economics of integrated agricultural systems. He thought about the words "associate professor" behind his name, which would tell everyone that he had indeed earned tenure at the prestigious University of Wisconsin–Madison. He also was pleased that he had such an able assistant working with him. Emily was a joy to work with, and she was smart and filled with good ideas.

Randy, as was his custom, was at his desk in Agriculture Hall by 7:30 the following morning. He was ready to wrap up the final work on the research questionnaire. Emily breezed into the office shortly after eight. She greeted the office administrator and receptionist and walked to her desk. On the way, she poked her head through Randy's open office door. "Good morning, Dr. Oakfield," she said. She was her bubbly self—one of her strong features was a pleasant personality. She got along with everyone in the department, which was certainly a plus, for graduate students, whether it was always true or not, saw themselves on the bottom of the academic pecking order. Since she and her major professor had just won a big research grant, she knew she would have to be even more pleasant. Several of her fellow graduate students had little or no funding for their research projects and certainly had a right to envy her good fortune. She now had a half-time salaried appointment to do research, the same research that she could use for her dissertation.

"When do you want to work on the questionnaire?" she asked. She was obviously all business this morning, with no thoughts of partying and celebration.

"Give me five minutes to catch up on my e-mail," Randy said as he typed on the keyboard in front of his computer screen. The two of them worked most of the morning, fine-tuning the questionnaire that they would send to a random sample of landowners in an Iowa county with several large hog operations and to a sample of land owners in Ames County.

Their research strategy was to send the questionnaires through the mail and then follow up with phone calls to those who did not respond in ten days.

"We should get at least a 75 percent response," said Emily.

"That seems pretty high to me," Randy said. "If we get something over 50 percent, I'll be happy."

"We'll do better than that, a lot better than that," Emily said.

Big Hog Farm Coming

Large Hog Operation Planned

Farm Country News, October 20

Nathan West Industries (NWI) of Dubuque, Iowa, this week has announced its plans to build a major hog production center in Ames County. This third-largest agribusiness firm in the United States has purchased the former Tamarack River Golf Course for its operation. The land has stood vacant since the golf course and condominium development recently declared bankruptcy. NWI has worked out a favorable purchase agreement with the bank, which held the mortgage.

NWI plans to build a complex of buildings and operate a farrow-to-finish operation, which means pigs will be born and not leave the facility until they are shipped to NWI's slaughterhouse in Dubuque. NWI plans to house 3,000 sows at this state-of-the-art facility, and farrow some 75,000 hogs a year. The operation will be similar to other farrow-to-finish outfits the company owns and operates in Iowa and North Carolina.

*O*scar Anderson and Fred Russo sat at a table in the back corner of Christo's in Tamarack Corners, a small village about fifteen miles from Willow River, on the banks of the Tamarack River. The building housing Christo's, once known as the River View Supper Club, was built in the 1930s for the tourists pouring into the area from Madison, Milwaukee, Chicago, and other major cities. It had done well until the early 2000s. A fellow from Milwaukee, a chef by training, name of Alexis Christo, and his wife, Costandina, bought out the place in 2010, renamed it Christo's, and completely remodeled it. The tourist crowds began finding the place once more, and so did the locals who had driven by without stopping in recent years. Alexis left the old bar part of the supper club mostly the way it was. Here one could find pickled eggs floating in brine, pickled pork hocks, enormous dill pickles, and a tray of fresh cheese curds—fresh most of the time. Since Wisconsin passed its smoking ban, the smells inside the saloon had changed from secondhand smoke and stale beer to a subtle tangle of the stale beer and the various pickled things on the bar.

Fred and Oscar liked to meet at Christo's for their regular Wednesday-morning coffee. They had refused to join the old-timers' group, largely made up of retired valley farmers and other retired guys who'd moved back to the valley in recent years. The group met every morning at 8:30 and drank coffee and lied to each other until noon. Oscar said one time, "If that's all I got to do, drink coffee every morning, you might as well stuff me in a coffin. Besides, those guys are as old as dirt."

Truth be known, both Fred and Oscar were older than but one or two of the guys in the old-timers' group. These two old friends enjoyed coffee once a week; that was enough. Fishing took up much of their other free time.

Costandina took care of the coffee crowd each morning, and she had even made a little wooden "reserved" sign that she placed on Fred and Oscar's table every Wednesday morning. When she saw the two come through the door, she knew to pour two cups of coffee, black, and put a fresh morning bun on a little plate in front of each of them.

"How are you this morning, boys?" she asked.

"Fair to middlin'," Oscar would say. "Still walkin' around," said Fred.

She asked the same question every Wednesday morning, and she received the exact same replies each time she asked. No surprises, no break in a long-established routine. Fred and Oscar liked it that way. One of the advantages of country life was its predictability, from the seasons changing, to coffee and morning buns on Wednesday mornings. Change disrupted the quiet predictability no matter where you lived these days, though, and change was coming to Ames County, dramatic change.

"Fred, did you see the *Farm Country News* this week?"

"'Course I saw it; carried it from the mailbox to the house."

"I mean, did you read it?" asked Oscar.

"You didn't ask if I read it."

"Well, I'm asking now. Did you read it?"

"Read some of it—always read some of it. Sometimes I read all of it. Depends on how much time I got. I'm a pretty busy guy, you know."

"Fred, you're just about as busy as I am, and that ain't busy at all. We're just about the laziest old coots livin' in the Tamarack River Valley."

"I rescind that comment," said Fred.

"Resent, Fred, resent. Not rescind."

"What?" Fred had a perplexed look on his face. "I did read about this big hog company buying the defunct golf course with all those fancy log condoms."

"Condos, Fred. They're called condos." Oscar smiled. He'd made the same mistake himself.

"That's what I said, isn't it? Well, anyway, what do you think about that?"

"About what?"

"About all those pigs coming to our neighborhood?"

"Don't think I like it much," said Oscar. "Pigs stink. They stink to beat hell. I raised pigs when I farmed. Had forty or fifty of them around most of the time. Pig manure stinks. Stinks like hell in the summer. Stinks in the winter, too. Stinks all the time. There's an upside to raising pigs, though. Always made some money selling pork. Yes, I did. 'Specially during the war. Made lots of money on my pigs then. Paid off my mortgage. Yup, that's what I did. Paid off my mortgage with those fifty hogs I sent to market every year."

"Well, what should we do about it?" asked Fred.

"About what?"

"About all them pigs coming to our neighborhood. Paper made it sound like the deal was all signed, sealed, and delivered," said Fred.

"Paper did say that, but we can still raise a little hell, put up a little stink of our own. That is, if we want to. They gotta hold some meetings, tell us their plans. They gotta get permits from the DNR, gotta get the zoning changed. They can't just come in here willy-nilly and plunk down a bunch of stinkin' pigs without first jumpin' through a few hoops," said Oscar.

"Think it would help if we raised a little ruckus?" asked Fred.

"Won't hurt. Gotta do something to keep the Tamarack River Valley from going to hell. Been a good place to live. Good place to farm, too. Don't think we need any of these big operators comin' in and changing ever'thin'. Don't believe we do."

"I agree with you there," said Fred. Costandina came by with coffee refills as the two old friends munched on their big morning buns.

"Too damn bad we're still livin' to see all this stuff goin' on. Too damn bad," mused Fred.

"That sure ain't no way to be thinkin', Fred. No way at all. We gotta let folks know about this. Put in our two cents' worth."

"Don't think it will help one damn bit."

"Well, we can still give her a try. Let the big shots know that old codgers don't just roll over when some big-assed new idea comes floatin' along. We gotta stand up for what's right, which means letting them know that this place has a history. Ain't just some bankrupt golf course on the river," Oscar said.

"Yeah, lots of history in the valley, that's for sure. Wonder if these big shots know about the cemetery in the corner of the golf course, the one where the Dunn family is buried? Wonder if they know that?" asked Fred.

"Expect they don't. And I'll bet these guys wearing their fancy suits don't know about the Tamarack River Ghost either. They get their operation up and going, they'll find out right quick, I'll bet."

"That they will. That they will," said Fred. "I heard that's why that big fancy golf course with its fancy houses went under. Some of them folks said they heard the ghost dog's bell tinkling on quiet nights. One fellow, he'd just bought one of the biggest log condos, and was spending his first night there when he heard singing coming from the river. Somebody told him he'd heard the ghost. Scared the hell out of him. He never spent another night there."

"Wonder who's gonna tell these fancy hog company people that there's a ghost hanging around this river. Wonder who that's gonna be," pondered Oscar.

"Also kind of wonder what effect a big hog farm is gonna have on Tamarack Corners," mused Fred. "Just got this old supper club all fixed up and doin' good. Wonder what that pig smell is gonna do to Christo's business."

"Wonder that, too," said Oscar. "Tamarack Corners ain't changed a whole lot since we was kids, has it? Always had the Methodist church across the road. Always had the Tamarack Trading Post with the barbershop in back. Barber only works three days a week, but he's still there. Yup, be a shame to see these places disappear because of the smell of pig manure and hog trucks clogging up the road. Dirty damn shame. Hardly know what folks would do without the Trading Post—they'd have to traipse way off to Willow River to buy a quart of milk or a six-pack of Leinenkugel's. Same for the barbershop. Who wants to drive fifteen miles for a haircut? Nobody. Not one person."

Dinner Date

A conservation warden's job can be a lonely one, even more so for a young woman in a place where gender roles have been carefully defined and agreed on for generations. Ames County was one of those places. Men did their work; women did their work. When the lines began blurring, eyebrows lifted and people raised questions. For some jobs it didn't matter much. People generally accepted women as doctors, foresters, even attorneys and veterinarians, but female firefighters and police officers took some getting used to, especially for the old timers. And whoever heard of a lady conservation warden? After all, weren't conservation wardens supposed to enforce the game laws of the state, and weren't most of the hunters and fishermen men? How could a woman, especially one as petite as Natalie, put the collar on a 250-pound guy who'd just shot a deer out of season? One flick of the big guy's muscular arm, and she'd be on the ground with a bloody nose and he'd be on his way. Yet, slowly, Natalie had gained the respect of Ames County citizens, especially those who had a history of bending and occasionally breaking a game law or two.

As a result of her hard work, though, and also because so much of what she did amounted to late-night stakeouts, weekend patrols, and unexpected circumstances—such as a car slamming into a deer at midnight, killing three of its occupants—her free time was not predictable. Thus, she essentially had no social life. This was clearly the downside of her job. Living in the Willow River community didn't help matters, either. Not many single young people lived in this town of just over three thousand people. When they graduated from Willow River High School, most young people left the community either for college or to find work in the

Fox River Valley—Oshkosh, Neenah-Menasha, Appleton, Green Bay. Or in Milwaukee, Madison, or maybe La Crosse or Eau Claire, on the other side of the state.

A few stayed behind to farm with their parents, work in the forestry business, or become part of the small but steady tourist business that tripled the county's population during the summer months. And a handful, like Josh Wittmore, left for a few years and returned.

Josh's phone jingled twice before he picked it up.

"*Farm Country News*, Josh Wittmore."

"This is Natalie Karlsen. You got a minute?"

"Sure," answered Josh, warily. He remembered her accusing him of tipping off Dan Burman, and he'd decided to avoid her if possible.

"I'd like to take you out to dinner," she said.

"What?" Josh's voice must have surely sounded his surprise at the invitation. All he could think of to say was, "Why?"

"Because I owe you a better apology than I gave you."

Josh was silent, speechless. In his mind's eye, all he saw was a very attractive young woman in a uniform and all wrapped up in her job. He could think of no response.

"Well, what do you say?" she pressed. Her voice was pleasant and smooth.

"When?" he finally blurted. Why was he spending any time talking to this woman who had powers of arrest and sidearm training? He didn't know she was more than just competent with her ever-present .40 caliber Glock—she had recently won a pistol-shooting contest with it.

"How about Saturday night? I'll pick you up at 6:00."

"OK," Josh muttered. This woman surely knew how to take control of a situation. He wondered if this was her natural tendency or if she was trained this way.

"Where do you live?" she asked quietly.

"Oh, yes. Where do I live? Right." Josh was clearly flustered. He gave her the street name and the number of his apartment in the Willow River Manor complex.

"I know right where it is. See you at 6:00," Natalie said.

Josh sat holding the phone in his hand. *What is it with this woman?* he thought. His defenses once more came into focus—*What does she want with me? What motive does she have for taking a newspaper reporter out to dinner?* He didn't even ask her where they were going and how much he should dress up. This was surely not like Josh Wittmore; he usually had a good sense of what he was doing, where he was doing it, and why. His feelings about Saturday night ranged from dread to anticipation. It had been a long time since he'd had fun with a good-looking young woman.

He had difficulty concentrating on his work the rest of the week. He continued to dig into everything he could find out about Nathan West Industries. Wearing his every-company-has-something-to-hide hat, he began searching for anything he could find that would provide a more complete picture. Firmly imprinted in his mind was something he had learned when he studied journalism in college—newspapers have a responsibility for digging beneath the surface of stories, for finding out things some people would prefer remain hidden. It was one of the things he enjoyed about newspaper work, the research and digging that often uncovered very interesting information.

For the first hour of his Internet search, everything he found about Nathan West Industries was laudatory. News articles in the digital archives of newspapers had nothing but praise for the company. True, its operations were often criticized by animal rights organizations, but no more than other firms involved with producing meat.

Several articles criticized industrial agriculture and the establishment of large pork, beef, and poultry operations. This had been going on for a decade or so, but nothing pointed to any wrongdoing on the part of Nathan West Industries. Growing larger was certainly not against the law, especially not in a society that prided entrepreneurial spirit, risk-taking, competition, and free-market success. These attributes characterized NWI well. Though an old company with a rich history, the company has prospered and has become a national leader, with its interests in several enterprises, ranging from grain storage and marketing, where it first started, to now owning and operating huge poultry, beef, and hog operations.

Dinner Date

Josh remembered well a recent trip he'd made to Duluth, Minnesota, where he had seen huge grain elevators with the words "Nathan West Industries" written in large letters on their sides. Oceangoing ships were tied up to the docks by the elevators, loading corn and wheat for transport to who knows where in the world. And of course, he, and everyone else, couldn't avoid seeing packages of beef and pork emblazoned with Nathan West Food's logo—a farm scene with barn, outbuildings, and cattle grazing in a pasture—in local supermarkets' meat cases. Occasionally a meat display was devoted solely to Nathan West meats.

The company had a good reputation, excellent marketing, and strong market share. Even with the recent push for consumers to buy locally, many people preferred to purchase the Nathan West brand. Unlike some other companies, it had never had a recall of meat contaminated with E. coli or salmonella or for any other reason.

Josh pushed on, a slight pain developing just above his right eye, the kind of headache he often developed when he was intently searching for something. With a few more clicks on the keyboard, he discovered a complaint a Minnesota community had lodged when a local pork processing plant (a subsidiary of Nathan West Industries) had closed and moved to Colorado. The community leaders claimed to have offered tax incentives, and after just five years, the plant moved to a Colorado community that offered even greater incentives. Josh thought, *This is something that happens all the time. Nothing illegal about it—perhaps a bit unethical, and maybe even a little immoral, but certainly not illegal.*

Another subsidiary, Nathan West Grain, got into more serious difficulty when it failed to obtain necessary permits for constructing a storage site in southwestern Wisconsin. Josh read with interest the details of the case. The president of the subsidiary, in effect thumbing his nose at the government regulations, began building structures without permits, even when he knew such were required. The president of the subsidiary was quoted as saying, "If we're caught without permits and are fined, we'll just write it off as a cost of doing business."

The subsidiary was fined $200,000 plus investigatory costs and DNR attorney fees. Nathan West, when it learned what its subsidiary had been

80

doing, immediately began its own investigation, turning over its findings to the DNR. The president and vice president of the subsidiary were immediately replaced, and the corporation faced no charges, and in fact was commended for assisting with the investigation.

Josh called a reporter friend in Dubuque to get his impressions of the company. He himself traveled there too, visiting the newspaper office and digging into its archives for information about NWI. He could find little evidence of wrongdoing in its long history. In fact, the company received glowing reports from people in communities where it had located its big operations and from the employees who worked for them. While in Dubuque, he interviewed three of the company's former employees, who told him that the employees liked to think of Nathan West Industries as a big family. Some even seemed to think that long-dead Mr. Nathan West was still at the helm and always prepared to take care of them, come thick or thin.

But try as he did to concentrate on what could potentially be one of the biggest stories of his career, Josh's mind kept going back to Natalie. So far the woman seemed a total mystery but, he had to admit, an interesting mystery.

When Saturday evening finally arrived, Josh decided to wear tan slacks, a blue dress shirt, and his navy blazer. He thought of wearing a coat, but these October days had been warm, in the sixties, and no coat would be necessary. He combed back his brown hair—thinning faster than he thought it should be—checked himself in the mirror, and smiled. He was as thin and trim as he had been the day he graduated from college. But he was nervous. He remembered how he felt on prom night in high school—except on that night he'd driven to pick up his date.

As 6:00 neared, Josh found himself glancing out the window of his apartment for Natalie's car. But he didn't even know if she drove a car. One time he'd seen her driving down Willow River's Main Street in a big Ford pickup. Maybe that's what she'd be driving tonight. He chuckled at the thought of it. They could play a little "yours is bigger than mine." She'd win—her Ford F-150 was considerably larger than his little Ranger.

Josh didn't see the little Honda Civic pull up in front of his apartment, so he was surprised when he heard a knock on his door. He pulled it open. His chin dropped.

"Hi, Josh. You ready?

"I . . . I think so," he stammered.

"You look nice tonight," Natalie said pleasantly.

"So . . . so do you." Josh could not believe what he saw. No DNR uniform, no badge, no .40 caliber Glock. Just a beautiful young woman with big brown eyes, blonde hair to her shoulders, wearing a blue party dress. She wore a subtle perfume; Josh caught just a hint of it as he closed and locked his apartment door and followed Natalie to her car.

He faced a dilemma. He wanted to be a gentleman; he had held the apartment door so she could go through first, but what about her car door, should he rush around and hold her car door for her? He decided he should, but when he grabbed the handle, it wouldn't move.

"Let me unlock it first," Natalie said, smiling.

Josh's face reddened. He felt a bit the fool.

She put the key in the lock, turned it, and stepped back. Josh opened the door, and Natalie stepped in.

"Where we headed?" Josh asked.

"I thought we'd do McDonald's or Culver's tonight," Natalie said as she pointed her little Honda toward Link Lake. She hesitated for a moment. "I was really thinking about the Lake Edge Supper Club. You must know it, having grown up here."

"Nicest place on the lake," Josh said. "I never ate there when I was growing up. My folks couldn't afford it. Besides, my dad always said the Lake Edge was for the tourists and lake people. Not for farmers. Few local people ate there."

They pulled into the nearly full parking lot at the Lake Edge, about twelve miles north of Willow River, and walked to the door. "Reservation for Karlsen," Natalie said when she saw the hostess.

The hostess showed Josh and Natalie to a table that looked out over the quiet waters of Link Lake; a big yellow moon was sneaking up over the horizon.

"Would you like a glass of wine, or maybe something stronger?" Natalie asked. "Everything is my treat tonight."

"I . . . I'll have a glass of Leinenkugel's Red," he said when their waitress asked about drink orders.

"A glass of merlot for me," Natalie said. "Nice evening, isn't it?"

"Beautiful evening. I've forgotten how beautiful Wisconsin can be in autumn; it was always one of my favorite times of the year," Josh said.

"Mine too."

Menus soon appeared in front of them. Josh hesitated before making a selection—some of the items were quite pricey, and he was sure a conservation warden's salary couldn't accommodate this kind of dining. He knew a newspaper reporter's salary surely couldn't.

The waitress took Natalie's order first—she ordered broiled walleye. Josh quickly did the same—it was a mid-priced item.

Josh slowly got past his concern about having dinner with an "officer of the law." Natalie worked hard at leaving her job behind; she made no mention of what she had recently been doing, although Josh was well aware of her concern for deer poachers in the Tamarack River Valley.

They talked about Natalie growing up in Wisconsin Rapids, where her dad was chief of police and her mother a middle school teacher. Josh talked a little about his growing-up days on a farm but four miles from where they were enjoying a great dinner. She said how much she had enjoyed attending the University of Wisconsin–Stevens Point, and he said that he had attended the *real* University of Wisconsin, the campus located in Madison. Natalie rolled her eyes at the comparison, one she had heard many times before.

A three-piece band began playing some old danceable tunes, "Moonlight Serenade" and "Shine on, Harvest Moon," which were especially appropriate for the evening, then "The Tennessee Waltz" and even a couple of polkas, leading off with the "Beer Barrel Polka."

"Want to dance?" Josh asked. This was the first time the entire evening he had suggested something.

"Sure," she said.

Josh was immediately surprised at what a good dancer she was. Was it possible that lady conservation wardens could dance? Old stereotypes still hung around his brain, but he knew enough to keep his tongue in control and not say anything.

Dinner Date

Josh noticed that several diners glanced at them—a beautiful woman with blonde hair dancing with a tall, dark-haired guy. He was also sure that no one recognized her as the Ames County conservation warden, since she was wearing a blue dress that subtly showed off her figure. Josh had been back in the community only a few weeks, after ten years away, so he was quite sure that no one recognized him either.

After dancing a polka, Josh and Natalie sat down, catching their breath. Josh hadn't danced the polka since he left Ames County after college.

"Halloween will soon be here," Natalie said, "which reminds me of ghosts. Josh, have you heard of the Tamarack River Ghost?"

"Ever since I was a little kid, when my dad told me about him."

"Do you believe in ghosts?" Her eyes caught his. Her question was a serious one.

"No, generally not. But I don't know about the Tamarack River Ghost. Over the years, lots of folks claim to have heard him, claim to have heard the log driver's song and the tinkling of a little bell. I don't know what to make of the stories; people that tell them surely believe what they've experienced.

"I've heard about the ghost several times since I've been here," Natalie said. "Even heard it was the main reason that the Tamarack River Golf Course development went under."

"I heard that same story," Josh said.

"Just this spring I heard another one," said Natalie. "A young couple was paddling down the Tamarack River. They'd been camping, and they wanted an early start, so they were in their canoe before the sun had come up. It was foggy and dead quiet. After a half hour of paddling, they heard the tinkling of a bell. When they glanced toward shore, through the fog and mist, they saw a man wearing a felt hat and a checkered shirt. He was standing there, staring at the river and smoking a pipe. They could smell the burning tobacco, a sweet, not unpleasant aroma. Alongside the man stood a big dog. When they got closer, they waved, and just like that the man and dog disappeared into the fog. A bit later, they pulled their canoe on shore and walked the short distance to Christo's for breakfast. While eating breakfast they asked the waitress about the man and the dog. 'Oh,

84

you saw the Tamarack River Ghost and his dog,' an old timer overhearing their story told them."

"Quite a story," Josh said. "Almost makes you a believer."

"It does," said Natalie. "This young couple swore by what they saw."

Shortly after midnight and considerable dancing, Natalie caught Josh yawning.

"Any time you want to go home, just say the word," she said, smiling. She had her hand on Josh's arm. She had the nicest, warmest smile; her hand was warm and friendly.

"I'm sorry," Josh apologized. "I guess I'm out of practice. Been a long time since I've had this much fun."

"I'm glad."

Natalie drove them back to Willow River, parked in front of Josh's apartment, and turned off the Honda.

"Thank you for a great evening," Josh said as he reached for the door handle.

She pulled his arm away from it.

"I'm so sorry," she said.

"About what?"

"About accusing you of tipping off Dan Burman."

"Apology accepted," Josh said. "Thank you again for dinner and a great evening."

"You're welcome."

Josh reached for the door handle again, opened the door, and stepped out into the night. He walked toward his apartment door, turned, and waved. Natalie waved back before starting her car and driving off.

14

Ice Fishing

*J*osh's mother had taught him well. When someone gives you a present, or does something nice for you, you send them a thank-you note. An e-mail message doesn't count. It must be a handwritten note, placed in an envelope and sent through the regular mail. The day following dinner and dancing with Natalie, Josh penned the following note:

> *Dear Natalie,*
>
> *How unexpected it was for you to buy me dinner last night. I want you to know how much I appreciate it—you certainly didn't need to do it. The food was excellent, the conversation interesting, and, although my dance steps need some work, I don't recall when I had so much fun.*
>
> *Thank you again. Next time it's my turn.*
>
> > *Sincerely,*
> > *Josh*

He folded the message, placed it in an envelope, and then realized that he didn't know Natalie's home address. He wrote her DNR office address on the envelope and then wrote personal across the bottom. He hoped some office worker wouldn't slit open the envelope and cause Natalie some embarrassment. But at this point, he really didn't care. He had a great time and he wanted her to know it.

*T*hose who've lived in Wisconsin know that November is usually the transition month from fall to winter, no matter that the calendar says winter doesn't begin until December 21. By Thanksgiving week, when the annual deer hunting season rolled around, the first snow had usually arrived and daytime high temperatures struggled to reach the high twenties.

This November, several nights in a row area thermometers showed zero degrees, which meant the smaller lakes had frozen over, as had the backwaters of the Tamarack River.

Josh wanted to ask Natalie out for dinner, but he knew that deer hunting season was one of the busiest times of the year, so he did not contact her. He was pleased that her work had made the lead story of the *Milwaukee Journal Sentinel*:

Conservation Warden Nabs Hunter with Fake Deer

Natalie Karlsen, Ames County DNR warden, arrested Joe Zims of rural Link Lake for firing a deer rifle while standing on a county road. State law requires hunters to be a minimum of 50 feet from the center of a public road before firing their weapons.

Warden Karlsen had placed a battery-operated, ten-point-buck replica that she calls "Freddy" alongside a well-traveled road.

"People just don't learn," she said. "Freddy has so many bullet holes in him the patches covering bullet holes have patches on them. Every year I arrest several hunters for shooting poor Freddy."

The week after deer season, when the hullabaloo about how many deer were shot in the state and why the DNR wasn't doing a better job of managing the deer herd had subsided a bit, Josh's phone rang.

"*Farm Country News*, Wittmore," Josh answered.

"This is Natalie."

"Natalie, how are you?"

"Surviving."

"Say, I saw your Freddy story in the paper. Good one."

Josh heard Natalie chuckling.

"The reason I called is, I was wondering if you'd like to do a ride-along—come with me tomorrow afternoon while I check some fishing licenses. I'm going over to the Tamarack River. It might be a chance for you get another Tamarack River story."

Josh glanced at his calendar. "Sure, what time?"

"How about I pick you up at your office at 1:30? I'll have my truck."

How different Natalie looked when she was in uniform! And she was different. Josh looked for a hint of the attractive young woman who'd bought him dinner and who had snuggled up to him when they danced. This Natalie, this woman with a pistol on her belt, was all business.

"What's this?" Josh asked when he climbed into the pickup. He saw a leather-bound book lying on the seat. He picked it up.

"Oh, sorry," Natalie said as she took the journal from Josh and stuffed it in the glove compartment. "It's just my journal."

"You keep a journal?"

"I try to. I don't have a whole lot of time to write what I want to write."

"I've got the same problem," said Josh. "What I write is for the paper—seldom do I have time to write anything for myself."

They continued driving, neither speaking.

"Nice day," Josh said, breaking the silence. A bright sun on the fresh snow made everything sparkle.

"Beautiful day. Should bring out the ice fishermen. Ice fishing is usually best soon after the lakes freeze—the fish are still pretty active then," Natalie said.

She parked the big pickup in the parking lot at Tamarack River Park.

"Looks like I was right," Natalie said as she counted the cars and pickups in the lot.

The backwaters of the Tamarack had been a favorite ice-fishing place for as long as anyone cared to remember. A recently frozen area just around the corner from the park already had a half-dozen fishing shanties on it.

"You ready?" Natalie asked. She pulled on her parka. "Can get a little chilly out there with the north wind coming down the river."

"I'm ready," said Josh. He had a camera and a clipboard.

The first shanty they came to looked new. It was constructed of plywood with two-by-six runners underneath. A puff of wood smoke came from the stove pipe stuck through the shanty's roof.

As they approached they read the little sign above the door, "Oscar Anderson & Fred Russo, R.R. 1, Tamarack Corners, WI."

"In case you didn't know," Natalie told Josh, "there are several laws that refer specifically to ice fishing. One is that shanty owners must have their name and address on the outside."

Natalie knocked on the door of the shanty. "Conservation warden," she said in a firm voice.

"Come on in."

Upon entering, Natalie and Josh spotted two older gentlemen hunched over holes drilled in the ice. They each held a jigging pole, a short fishing pole with thin monofilament line attached.

"How you guys doing today?" she asked, by way of greeting.

"Fair to middlin'," answered Oscar as he pulled up his line.

"How many lines you got in the water today?" Natalie asked. She talked quietly.

"Well, let's see. I got one, and Fred's got one," Oscar said. "When you get our age, about all we can handle is one line apiece. Takes a younger guy to keep up with three lines."

From the answer to her question, Natalie quickly determined that these old fishermen knew that three lines was the limit.

"Could I see your fishing licenses?" she said politely.

"Yup, you sure can," Fred said as he began digging for his billfold buried deep within his heavy woolen trousers. Oscar began looking for his license as well.

Natalie glanced at computer generated, not-very-fancy-looking licenses and said, "Aren't you the guys who caught that big northern that burned down your shack a few years ago?"

"We are," said Fred. "Biggest dang fish we ever caught. Mean bugger, too. Came right up out of the fish hole, one just like this 'un. Fish took after us. Started floppin' around the shanty liked it owned the place. Well that damn fish tipped over our stove. Fish burned down our shanty, right down to the ice."

"I read the story in the paper," Natalie said, smiling.

"Yup, people didn't believe us. Didn't believe that big old fish had done what it did," said Oscar. "But we know the truth, don't we Fred? We know what happened."

"What'd you do with the fish?" asked Josh, quite taken by the story.

"Well that's the problem. When that old fish tipped over our stove and the shanty began burning, we got the hell out as fast as we could. You suppose we could find that fish—cooked or not? Nope, couldn't find 'im. Musta flopped back down the hole. That's what musta happened," said Fred.

"So what've you caught today?" asked Natalie, changing the subject.

"Nothin'. We ain't caught a single fish. Not one. Too nice a day, I guess. Fish takin' a vacation," said Oscar.

"Good day for fishin' though. Good day to be out on the ice. You wanna stop back a little later, we'll be fryin' up some of my venison sausage. Pretty good stuff."

"No thanks," said Natalie. "But thank you for the offer—and good luck."

"Thanks. Kinda looks we'll be needin' a little luck if we're havin' any fish for supper," said Oscar.

"What a pair of characters," Josh said when they walked toward the next shanty. He remembered that his father had talked about Oscar and Fred.

"That they are," said Natalie. "But they're good guys. Salt-of-the-earth types who wouldn't do anything wrong if their lives depended on it. Wish we had more of them around."

Josh noticed that several people were moving around from shack to shack. Obviously, the warden's presence on the ice had not gone unnoticed.

The next shanty, a few yards beyond Oscar and Fred's, had seen better days. At one time it had been covered with black tarpaper, which now was coming lose in several places. A piece of cardboard covered what had once been a window. The door hung crooked on its hinges. The words "Dan Burman, R.R. 1, Tamarack Corn——" had been painted in white on the shanty's wall. The words were badly faded, and part of the address had ripped away. Both Natalie and Josh recognized the name as that of the person Natalie had accused of game poaching.

"Conservation warden," Natalie said as she knocked on the sagging door.

She knocked again. "Conservation warden—anybody home?" Both she and Josh heard scrambling inside the dilapidated shack.

Natalie pushed open the rickety door to find Dan Burman and his son Joey frantically stuffing panfish down the ice hole in the middle of their shanty. Josh stayed outside.

"Conservation warden," Natalie repeated. Josh was astonished at how much authority she could put into her voice. "What are you doing?" she asked.

"Catch and release," Burman muttered. Both of his arms were wet to his elbows. Joey had just handed him a good-sized bluebill that he was prepared to push down into the fish hole. "Catch and release."

"I don't think so," Natalie said. "Just stop what you're doing and show me your fishing license, Mr. Burman." Joey dropped the bluegill back in the pail that stood next to him. Burman pulled out his billfold, found his license, and handed it to the warden, who looked at it and handed it back without comment.

"How old are you, son?" Natalie asked, looking at the nervous young man sitting on a wooden bench nailed to one side of the shanty.

"I'm . . . I'm fifteen," the young man stammered.

"Yeah, he's fifteen," the senior Burman said. "Big kid for his age. Good fisherman, too."

"Mr. Burman, is this your fishing shanty?"

"It is. Seen better days, but it's every bit mine," Burman said, a hint of a smile on his face.

"How many fish you got in that pail?"

"What pail?"

"That one standing next to your son."

"Got a few keepers. Most we throw back. Got us a few keepers in the pail. Make a few good meals for the family."

"What do you say we take the pail outside and count your keepers."

"OK by me," said Burman. "Joey, grab up that pail and take it outside."

"Would you dump the fish out of the pail, please," Natalie said to the young man once they had all exited the shanty.

Joey dumped the flopping fish and water onto the ice. Burman, his eyes adjusting to the bright light outside the shanty, focused on Josh.

"Say, don't I know you?" Burman asked. He had several days' growth of whiskers covering his craggy, weathered face.

"Yup," Josh said, extending his hand. "We met out at your place a little while back, when I interviewed you. Josh Wittmore."

"That's right—what you doin' traipsing around with the game warden?"

"Still doing stories on the Tamarack River Valley. Need to have something about ice fishing. Seems pretty popular."

While Burman and Josh chatted, Natalie counted fish. Burman's son looked on.

"I count forty-five," Natalie said. "What's your count?" she asked, looking to the young man.

"I get forty-five too," he said. Both the warden and the young man knew that twenty-five was the limit for each fisherman, and they were just five shy.

"Nice bunch of bluegills you got there," Natalie said. "Just make sure that when you get to fifty you pull up your lines." She didn't mention that she'd caught them pushing fish back down the hole—she had no idea how many they'd already caught past fifty, but without evidence, she could issue no citations.

"You guys have a good day, now," Natalie said as she and Josh walked on to the next shanty to repeat the routine.

On the way back to Willow River, Natalie and Josh chatted about the afternoon.

"I was a little surprised to see Dan Burman and his son out there," Josh said.

"I wasn't. Guy's a good fisherman, good hunter, too. Too bad he's always pushing the legal limits."

"He's got a big family to feed," Josh said. "He's barely making it."

"Still got to obey the law," Natalie said.

They drove on, neither saying anything for several miles. Josh, usually a good judge of character, simply was confused about the difference between Natalie Karlsen conservation warden and Natalie Karlsen dinner date. Today he had seen Natalie the conservation warden, and he had been impressed. She knew her job, and she knew it well. She was firm with people, yet pleasant. He still harbored the deeper question—what did she want from him?

Valley History

*J*osh sat at his computer at *Farm Country News*, working on the second in a series of stories he'd planned about the Tamarack River Valley. His brief history of the valley had appeared in *Farm Country News* this week, with a couple of photos he had taken of the river and an overview shot of the valley itself.

The Tamarack River Valley: A Brief History

The Tamarack River defines the western boundary of Ames County in central Wisconsin. The river and the valley surrounding it were formed by the glacier that ground its way through this part of what eventually became Wisconsin. The glacier began retreating about 10,000 years ago, followed by the return of plants and animals, and eventually Native Americans who lived on these lands for many years.

Although Wisconsin had become a state in 1848, this part of central Wisconsin remained Indian country until the U.S. government signed a treaty with the Menominee Indian Tribe that had lived on these lands for centuries. In 1851, government surveyors laid out the townships and created the section and quarter-section lines, before offering the land for sale. Since the area was settled, the Tamarack River Valley has seen many changes, although the river itself, flowing southeast toward Lake Winnebago, has remained a constant in the lives of the people who live and work in the valley. As one old timer said, "The Tamarack River is always the same but ever changing."

During the logging era in northern Wisconsin, from the mid-1850s to the early 1900s, the Tamarack River served as a "logger's highway." Each spring, when the ice went out, the logging crews that had piled huge logs on the river's banks during the winter dumped them into the river for their trip south to the sawmills in Oshkosh and Fond du Lac. Log drivers, daredevil loggers who rode the river south with the logs, accompanied the logs, keeping them in the current and breaking up logjams when they occurred. Injuries and even deaths were not uncommon during the spring log drives.

In the spring of 1900, a logjam on the Tamarack took the life of Mortimer Dunn, a farmer in the valley during the summer months and a logger during the winter. A family gravesite contains a marker for Dunn, but his body was never found. Some local residents claim that Mortimer Dunn's ghost still haunts the valley as it searches for his grave. Others say that the Tamarack River Ghost looks out for the valley and the mighty Tamarack River.

Farmers, many of them immigrants from northern Europe, but some from upstate New York, first settled the valley. From the 1850s until the 1880s, the majority of these farmers grew wheat. But then, over a period of a few years, wheat yields declined because of disease and an insect called the chinch bug, which sucked the juices from the wheat plant. Most valley farmers then took up dairy farming. Many also raised hogs, sometimes a few sheep, occasionally some beef cattle, and small flocks of chickens that provided eggs and meat for the table, and a little extra money for groceries. They became diversified farmers, not depending solely on one enterprise for their income.

The Depression years of the 1930s challenged the Tamarack Valley farmers. A few lost their farms because they couldn't make mortgage payments. But most hunkered down and carried on. Cucumbers and green beans became popular cash crops for most of the valley farmers, especially those with large families. From planting to harvesting, both crops required considerable hand labor. From late July through August, valley farm kids could be seen in their cucumber and bean patches, earning enough money for school clothes and supplies, Christmas presents, and sometimes even enough for a new bike or a .22 rifle.

The valley land was not rich, especially not as fertile as farmland in the southern counties of Wisconsin. But for several generations the

Tamarack River Valley supported the family farmers who lived there, raised families, and sent them to school.

Electricity did not come to the Tamarack River Valley until after World War II. In the late 1940s and early 1950s, valley farmers also bought tractors and put their draft horses out to pasture, although they would not sell them. "Never can tell when a good team might come in handy" was a comment often made by farmers who had grown up driving horses and had come to love and respect them.

In the southern part of the Tamarack River Valley, several cranberry growers established cranberry marshes in the years following the Civil War. Most of these cranberry growers still operate, and in recent years they have done well with an expanded cranberry market in the United States and around the world.

Today, the Tamarack River Valley faces two major outside forces— developers who see the river property as prime land for golf courses and condo development, and industrial agriculture that sees relatively cheap land that can be used for large, confined animal operations. Future stories will discuss these new challenges for the people of the Tamarack River Valley.

Fred and Oscar

*F*red and Oscar enjoyed another day of ice fishing in their little shack on the backwater of the Tamarack River.

"Say Fred, you gettin' any bites on that fancy new rod you got for Christmas?"

"Does it look I'm gettin' any bites? You going blind as well as senile?" answered Oscar, who fished from a second hole within their little shack.

"Well don't get huffy about it. Ain't my fault your new rod don't work."

"New rod works just fine. It's the fish that are the problem," said Fred.

"Now it's the fish you're blaming."

"Gotta blame something. Probably that lady game warden's really the problem. She put a jinx on our fishing. That's what happened. You get a lady game warden prancing around on the ice checking on fishing licenses, and you just don't know what's gonna happen," said Fred.

"Kinda of a looker, she is," said Oscar, smiling.

"'Looker,' what in hell do you know about who's a looker and who's not?"

"I may be old, but I ain't blind. Underneath all that uniform and badge and stuff is a helluva good-lookin' woman," said Oscar.

"So now you're like an X-ray machine, huh?" said Fred.

"Gotta use a little of your imagination, Fred." Oscar touched his finger to the side of his head. "Keeps life interesting. Yup, it does. Keeps life interesting."

"I don't know about you, Oscar. You're not only getting senile, you're acting like you're eighteen again."

"Nothing wrong with thinkin' that you're eighteen. Helluva lot better than thinking that you're eighty. Helluva lot better."

The two old men sat quietly for a time. A stick of pine wood they had stuffed into their little box stove crackled and snapped. A stiff breeze from the northwest blew down the Tamarack River and whistled around the corner of their comfortable fishing shanty.

"What'd you think about the history piece in the *Farm Country* newspaper, Fred?"

"What history piece?"

"You read the paper, don't you?"

"Every time it comes."

"Well what'd you think?"

"About what?"

"The story about the history of the Tamarack River Valley," said Oscar as he put down his fishing pole and reached for his thermos of coffee.

"Oh, that piece."

"Well what'd you think?"

"It was okay," said Fred. "You got any more coffee in that thermos?"

Oscar reached for Fred's nearly empty coffee cup and refilled it.

"Just okay? I thought it was pretty damn good," said Oscar.

"I wouldn't go that far. That guy ridin' around with the lady game warden is the one that wrote it. You knew that, didn't you?" said Fred.

"Is that right? Nope, I didn't put that together. Seemed like a decent sort. Name is Josh Wittmore, I recall. His old man is Jacob Wittmore—has a farm over by Link Lake."

"Yeah, I remember Jacob."

"Didn't you read the fine print, Oscar? This guy Wittmore is writin' a whole series on the Tamarack River Valley. Probably we'll be in his next story, two sorry-assed ice fisherman that don't catch nothin'."

Both men laughed as they went back to fishing, intent on at least catching enough bluegills for an evening meal.

"Liked what Wittmore wrote about the Tamarack River Ghost," said Oscar.

"Yup, he got that part right. Got that right for sure. That old ghost is still around and doin' all kinds of mischief—mostly scaring the bejeebers out of folks who don't know about him," said Fred.

Fred stuffed a couple of sticks of oak wood into the little stove and glanced out the window of the ice fishing shanty. It had turned out to be a nice January day. A good day for ice fishing, even if the fish didn't bite.

"Say, Fred. You thinkin' on showing up at the big meeting over at the Tamarack Town Hall next week?" asked Oscar.

"What meeting is that?"

"Big meeting."

"You said it was a big meeting before. Big meeting about what?"

"You didn't hear about the meeting?"

"I may have; I hear about lots of meetings. Which one you talking about?"

"Geez , Fred. Some days you are dense as hell. Meeting about the big hog factory comin' to the valley."

"Oh, that meeting. Yeah, thought I might show up."

"Thought I might come too," said Oscar. "Before that I thought I might gather me up a few facts on how they grow hogs these days."

Skiing in the Park

This time Josh took the initiative. It was a bright, sunny Sunday in January, a fine day to be outside. He decided to call Natalie to see if she'd like to go cross-country skiing. It was a wild idea. He didn't even know if she knew how to ski. And besides, this might be one of the weekends she worked.

She answered on the first ring. "Sure, I'd love to go," she said when Josh posed the question. "I'll rustle up my skis and be ready when you get here."

Josh now remembered he didn't even know where she lived. "Where is 'here'?" he said.

"Oh, you don't know where I live, do you?" She gave him the address, a cabin on Copperhead Lake, a couple of miles east of Willow River.

The temperature hung around twenty degrees, but without a wind and with bright sunshine it was about as nice a winter day as anyone could ever want. The snow piled along the road was still fresh and clean, since the latest snowfall had only been a couple of days earlier. Josh decided on the Tamarack River Park; it had new trails that spread out along the Tamarack River and snaked through the nearby pine woods and marshes.

They traveled along the snow-packed road for several miles in silence, enjoying the winter views. How different Ames County looked in winter: all of nature's sharp edges were rounded. The vivid colors of summer were now blacks, grays, and whites, with an occasional pine tree providing a splash of green.

Their skis crunched over the cold snow. Otherwise the park was quiet, not a sound as they moved along the trail. Snow hung from the pine trees, the white contrasting with the green. And a bright blue sky with a warm sun added the final note to perfect the scene.

When they stopped to rest, Josh dug his camera out of his pocket.

"Can I snap a picture?" he asked.

"Sure, snap away," said Natalie, a big smile spreading across her face.

"Want to see it?" asked Josh. "It's a good one."

"Nah, let's move on."

They skied along quietly for nearly a half hour, one following the other, enjoying the winter day and each other's company. Josh turned a corner in the woods and stopped abruptly. A person holding a gun stood next to the ski trail. He was smiling.

"Mr. Burman," Josh blurted out. "I didn't expect to see you here." By this time, Natalie had caught up with Josh and turned the corner as well, and saw Burman with a gun.

"Mr. Burman," she said. Burman was wearing snowshoes, the old-fashioned kind made of bent wood and leather.

"Madam game warden," said Burman, bowing a bit. He held the gun in the crook of his hand, the barrel pointed downward.

"What . . . what are you doing out here?" asked Natalie. She wished she were wearing her sidearm and badge.

"Huntin' rabbits," said Burman. "Tryin' to find me a few rabbits. Kids like fresh fried rabbit meat."

"With a deer rifle. You're hunting rabbits with a .30–30 Winchester?"

"Yup, I am." Burman smiled, knowing that rabbit season was still open and that deer season had closed back in late November.

"Seems the rabbits here in the valley get just a little harder to kill every year. Started huntin' them with a BB gun when I was kid, then turned to a .22 single shot, then a .22 semi-automatic. Then got me a .410, which worked pretty good for a few years. But now, well now, it takes a .30–30 to knock over one of these Tamarack River bunnies." He said all of this with a straight face, knowing full well that he was blowing smoke at the conservation warden.

Natalie did not smile at his little firearms litany.

"Well, I'll be on my way, then," said Burman. "You folks have a good day now." Burman pushed off into the woods on his snowshoes, the snow packing under them. He did not look back.

"Burman has the gall. He's hunting deer out of season and in broad daylight, too."

"Said he was hunting rabbits," Josh said, a big smile spreading across his face.

"Right, rabbits. We both know what he was doing, and he knew we knew it, too. One of these days I'm gonna catch him. You just wait. One of these days. Meeting him sure spoiled a decent round of cross-country skiing. Ruined it." Natalie's face was red.

"It's not quite that bad. Still a nice day. Sun is shining, snow is sparkling," said Josh. "Hey, let's ski back to the truck, and I'll buy you a cup of coffee over at Christo's; it's only a skip and a jump from here."

Natalie quickly perked up with the thought of coffee.

At Christo's, several other people were drinking coffee and hot chocolate and enjoying the view out the big window that faced the snow-covered, solidly frozen Tamarack River a hundred yards away.

"Nice view," said Natalie.

"It is that," answered Josh after ordering two cups of coffee from Costandina. He hung his parka over the back of his chair and helped Natalie remove her parka and hang it over her chair. She wore a wine-colored sweater that went well with her blonde hair and brown eyes. With her parka removed, she let her hair settle over her shoulders.

"What do you think about the big hog farm proposed for this valley?" asked Josh.

"The DNR is watching the whole thing closely—they've got to pass muster with our people before they can get their permits."

"Think they'll get the permits?"

"If they meet the requirements. How are things going at *Farm Country News*?" Natalie asked, changing the subject.

"Not so good. Electronic media are killing us. Our advertising is drying up. Our subscription list is down."

Natalie quickly realized that she shouldn't have asked the question.

"The paper is closing down some of its bureaus—one of the reasons I'm here is we had to close down the Illinois bureau," said Josh.

"That's too bad. I've read other papers were having problems. I didn't know the farm papers were in trouble too."

"I've told my boss we should do more things electronically—maybe even have an electronic edition. But he'll have none of it. He's an old-school editor—darn good one, too. But he's not about to change much. He knows what good journalism is all about, and he doesn't waiver from it. Not one bit."

"I expect it's good to have principles," said Natalie.

"It is. No question about it. But I keep hoping that those of us in the newspaper business can keep our principles and keep our jobs, too."

"It's a challenge," said Natalie. "State keeps cutting back our budget too. We're all expected to do more with less. That's been the state's mantra for the last few years. I try to keep my principles though. Try not to cut corners."

After a few minutes, their coffee arrived, and Josh and Natalie sipped the fresh, strong brew Christo's had become known for. They looked out the window at the winter scene—sunlight bouncing off the snow-covered landscape and a snowmobile hurrying down the frozen, snow-covered river. In the distance they could see where the river turned as it hurried on toward Lake Winnebago.

"Paper did come up with a new idea though," said Josh, still thinking about their conversation. "We've decided to accept what we are calling community contributions—it's what we used to call freelance writing. We'll see if that'll generate some interest, maybe even increase our subscriptions a little. We're running the announcement in this week's paper."

"Sounds like a plan," Natalie said.

"According to Bert, we gotta do something, or we may very well go under. I can't believe that will happen—we've been around since the 1860s."

Josh took another long drink of coffee, looked out the window at the winter landscape, turned, and smiled at Natalie, who sat across from him. She smiled back. They both sat quietly for several moments, neither saying anything.

"Place will sure be different if there's a big hog farm just down the road," said Josh.

"Change is inevitable. Everything is always changing. That's just the way it is."

"But does it have to be that way?" asked Josh.

Natalie didn't answer. She stood up, and Josh helped her into her parka. He caught a hint of her perfume.

Informational Meeting

Josh needed a break. He'd been hunched over his computer keyboard most of the morning. On his way for his third cup of coffee, he walked by his boss's open door.

"Josh, you got a minute?" Bert asked.

"Sure, how are things with you?"

"I'm afraid I've got more bad news. Have a seat."

"So what's happening?" asked Josh.

Bert took off his wire-rimmed glasses and put them on the pile of budget sheets in front of him.

"I had to close the Indiana and Ohio bureaus this week. Laid off twelve people. I hated to do it, but had no choice. Only three bureaus left: Iowa, Minnesota, and Wisconsin. And things don't look good in Minnesota."

"Advertising revenue still down?"

"Way down. We just lost another big account. National Beef Feedlot folks—pulled their ads and said they'd never run another ad in our 'decrepit paper,' to use their exact words."

"They didn't like my stories?"

"That's about it. Damn fools couldn't see that the stories you wrote would help them in the long run. Help them police some of their bad actors so the public would get off their case about animal treatment and air and water pollution."

"That's how it goes some days. I wrote what I saw, and it wasn't pretty."

"That's what a newspaper is supposed to do. Dig out the facts and let them fall where they may. No holds barred. That's what a good newspaper does, and that's what this paper has done for nearly 150 years." Bert pounded his fist on his desk to make his point.

"Of course, it's the damn Internet that's killing us. Just killing us. People are not reading print newspapers any more, especially the young people. And advertisers, well when subscriptions go down, advertisers began disappearing too. I just don't know where it's headed, Josh."

Josh was one of the first to arrive at the Tamarack Town Hall on this cold January evening. A foot of snow had fallen the previous day, and although the snowplows had been through to clear the roads, a stiff northwest wind continued to blow, making for questionable visibility and difficult driving. He wondered if many people would turn out for the meeting, which had been announced in the *Ames County Argus* and over the local radio station as "an opportunity to learn about Nathan West Industries' new hog operation planned for the Tamarack River Valley." When Josh opened the door, he spotted the county agricultural agent, Ben Wesley, setting up folding chairs.

"How you doing, Josh?" asked Ben.

"Doing okay, kind of miserable night to be out."

"That it is. You forget how winter can be up here in central Wisconsin?"

"Nope, I didn't," said Josh. He stamped his boots to remove the snow from them, took off his coat, and began helping Ben with the chairs.

By 7:30, a steady stream of people had trudged through the snow, howdied each other, and crowded into the little building. The Tamarack Valley School had closed in 1955, and at that time the township purchased the building for its meeting and voting place. Most of the time, the building, which could hold up to seventy-five people, was sufficiently large for town board and community meetings, but by 8:00 p.m. it was bursting at the seams. Every chair was taken, people stood in the back, and still others were trying to push through the door.

"Looks like we got ourselves a hot topic," Curt Nale, town chairman and vegetable grower, said to Ben.

"Appears so," said Ben. "These big factory farms stir up people, both pro and con."

Ben motioned toward Josh. "Curt, I want you to meet Josh Wittmore; he works for the *Farm Country News* these days, but he grew up on a farm over near Link Lake."

"Heard you'd moved back to Ames County." Curt shook Josh's hand.

"Glad to be back. One of my assignments is writing a series on the Tamarack River Valley. Didn't expect a hot issue would be a part of the story," said Josh.

"Valley's been pretty quiet. Folks got a little upset a few years ago when the golf course came in with its fancy log condominiums; just like they were upset when it came, they were upset when it went bankrupt. Some of the people around here get pretty agitated about land taxes, their own mostly. When the golf course left, the tax base went down a little," said Curt.

A red-faced man, overweight and out of breath, walked up to Ben and shook his hand. "How you doing, Billy," said Ben. "Meet Josh Wittmore with *Farm Country News*, he just moved back here from the Illinois bureau."

Josh shook hands. "Josh, this is Billy Baxter, editor of the *Ames County Argus*."

"Great to meet you," said Josh. "You don't know me, but I know you. My folks still live near Link Lake, where I grew up. And we forever subscribed to the *Argus*."

"Glad to hear it," said Baxter. "Glad to hear it. Keeping subscribers these days can be a challenge."

"Tell me about it," said Josh. "It's a challenge for *Farm Country News* as well."

The two newspapermen continued chatting as a man clutching an armful of equipment came through the door and hurried to the front of the room. Ed Clark, the regional representative for Nathan West Industries, was in his mid-forties and balding. He wore khaki pants, a blue blazer, and a sport shirt open at the collar. When Clark spotted Curt Nale, he put down his equipment and shook the town chairman's hand. He also said hello to Ben and shook his hand as well. It was obvious that Clark had made sure that he knew the community leaders well ahead of scheduling this meeting.

"Ed, meet Josh Wittmore from the *Farm Country News*," said Curt. "Josh, this is Ed Clark, with Nathan West Industries."

"Pleased to meet you," said Clark. Josh noticed his firm handshake and his way of looking you straight in the eye when he shook your hand. Josh was impressed with the man's confidence; he had surely faced many crowds of doubters and naysayers about large-scale farming over the years. Big hog farms, multi-thousand-cow dairy operations, huge poultry-raising enterprises, and cattle feedlots had split the rural communities where they located. People were either for or against them, with feelings strong on each side. The situation reminded Josh of what he'd heard from his folks about the closing of so many one-room country schools just like this one. In the 1950s, the issue had torn up rural communities to the point where some neighbors still didn't speak to each other because of how they came down on the issue. He hoped this planned hog facility wouldn't do the same thing.

Clark, who worked out of NWI's Dubuque headquarters, had been in the community for a couple of days, driving around, talking to people in both Willow River and Tamarack Corners and walking over the land his company had purchased. With the former Tamarack River Golf Course covered with snow, it was a bit difficult for him to envisage just where they would place their buildings, and he had no idea yet what the company would do with the vacant log-faced condo buildings. When the company purchased the property, it had considered the condos as possible housing for employees—that still seemed a reasonable idea, except there were far more condo units than potential employees.

A few minutes after eight, Curt Nale called the meeting to order.

"I'm pleased to see so many of you on this cold, blustery, wintry night. We'll get to the business at hand in just a few minutes. But before we get to talking about pigs, Ben Wesley, our county agricultural agent, has a word."

Ben walked to the front of the room to applause; nearly everyone in the room had worked with him at one time or another, and he was well liked.

"Thank you," he said. "Ames County is changing, as most of you know. And agriculture is changing, sometimes faster than some of us want it to. Tonight we're going to learn about a new farming operation that is planned for Ames County. I know many of you have questions—that's a good thing—we all should be well informed when we face change. I want you all to know that I am always open to your questions about agriculture and land use, as I have always been. Give me a call or stop by the office. Now I'll turn the meeting back to Tamarack town chairman Curt Nale. Curt."

"Thank you, Ben. As you all know, Nathan West Industries of Dubuque has purchased the old Tamarack River Golf Course and plans to establish a hog farm there. It is seeking a zoning change from the county to return the golf course to agricultural land, and it has submitted its plans to the Department of Natural Resources to obtain the necessary permits. But I'll let Ed Clark from Nathan West tell you all about what the company has in mind. Oh, before I turn the podium over to Mr. Clark, let me say that this is not a decision-making meeting—that is, we'll not do any voting about anything. We are here to learn what Nathan West is planning. A lot of rumors have been floating around, so let's find out what these folks really have in mind. Mr. Clark."

The audience applauded politely, waiting to learn more about its potential new neighbor in the valley and what this internationally known company planned to do with land that had once been three family farms. A tall, thin young woman standing in the back of the room raised her hand and then began waving it back and forth so Clark might allow her to speak. He ignored her.

"Thank you for the opportunity to share some of Nathan West's plans for something I'm sure you'll all find exciting," Clark began. "We plan to become your new neighbor in the valley, and we want to get off on the right foot. First, let me tell you something about Nathan West Industries."

Clark snapped on his computer projector and ran through a series of slides showing grain elevators, barges on the Mississippi River carrying grain, the company's big meat-processing plant in Dubuque, and, finally, some shots of a couple of Nathan West hog farms in Iowa.

"Let me tell you a bit more about our hog operations, because the one we are planning for the Tamarack Valley will be similar, but even more modern and technologically up to date than any of these."

The audience watched and listened intently; as the session went on, some foot-shuffling could be heard, and some whispering. It was becoming obvious that people had heard enough lecturing and wanted to ask questions. A hand flew up from in back of the room.

"Say, we gonna have a chance to ask you some questions?" Oscar Anderson asked, his friend Fred Russo seated next to him. Oscar was generally rather quiet, but he obviously had something on his mind and wanted to get his idea out there while people were still fresh and not too enthralled by what they were hearing from the well-spoken Nathan West representative.

"You bet you will," said Ed Clark, who shut off the projector. "Let's get to your questions right now." A buzz could be heard as people turned to each other and then to Oscar, who stood up from his chair. Wearing a bright plaid flannel shirt, he leaned on his ever-present cane and began speaking. His voice was deep, his speaking style slow and deliberate.

"I was born in this valley eighty-six years ago," he began. He wiped a wrinkled hand across his mouth. "I've got a few things to say about this big pig production outfit you got planned for our neighborhood."

"Go right ahead," said Clark. Josh had his notepad at the ready. He had done his own research about the history and current operations of Nathan West; now he was curious what people in the valley thought of the idea.

"First question I got for you, Mr. Clark, is this. Are you aware that pig manure stinks?" Oscar asked with a straight face. A tittering of laughter flowed across the audience; most of its members were either now or had once been farming, and they knew full well the intensity of smells coming from a hog yard.

"Yes, I am," answered Clark, without a hint of a smile. "Anyone who knows anything about farming knows there are some smells associated with it."

"Do you know how much smell can come from a pig pen with twenty pigs?"

"Yes, I believe I do," answered Clark.

"Can you imagine what the smell from several thousand hogs might be, the number you are suggesting that will be raised on your farm?"

"We do everything we can to keep the smells in control and want you all to know that we meet every law and regulation that's required of us; we always have, and we always will." Clark's response sounded like he had it memorized and had repeated these words many times and in many communities. Josh wrote it down on his notepad word for word. Oscar frowned when he heard the response but said nothing further.

A tall, thin, older woman with short gray hair stood up. "My name is Phoebe Henderson," she said, a bit haltingly. "I've spent my life working in Chicago and recently retired here in the Tamarack River Valley. I grew up here in the valley and for many years looked forward to retiring to this beautiful place that I remember so well. My home and my five acres are but a half mile from here, overlooking the river. My question to you, Mr. Clark, is how bad are these hog smells going to be?"

"Thank you for your question, Ms. Henderson. Nathan West Industries prides itself in being a good neighbor. I believe you will find us a good neighbor when we become established here in what you so correctly describe as a beautiful place." Again Josh noted the question and the response—and wrote, "Didn't touch the smell problem."

"Might I have a word?" asked a thin fellow near the front of the room.

"You certainly may," said Clark.

"Well, my name is Dan Burman. I own a little farm just down the road a piece from here. As a kid, I spent lots of time in this building when it was a country school. My old man grew up in this valley. My kids are growing up in this valley. I'm tryin' to make a livin' on the farm where I was born and raised. I'm glad you're comin' to the valley. Property taxes are so damn high, none of us can hardly pay 'em." He paused for a moment and rubbed a hand across his three-day stubble. "This worthless golf course has been sittin' here moldering," Burman continued. "Need a tax-paying company like yours to come in here. So hogs stink a little? There's lots in life that stinks, including high taxes and the damn government sticking its nose in our lives."

There was brief applause following Burman's words.

"Thank you for those comments," said Clark.

"Other questions?" asked Clark, as he continued to ignore a young woman who continued standing with her hand up, red faced and frustrated.

A young man standing off to the side back raised his hand. "Yes," Clark said, recognizing the speaker.

"My name is Clyde Mueller, and I'm a vegetable farmer here in the valley. I'm concerned about the Tamarack River. We recently had some pollution problems with the river, and now that it's cleaned up we don't want any more. The river gives our community its name; it's a place where we fish and swim. Its history is our history. Can you assure us that an operation of your size won't pollute our river?"

"I can guarantee it," said Clark. "We follow to the letter every DNR regulation. We have the most up-to-date approach for storing and spreading our manure. I can assure you that this beautiful river, and it is beautiful, will remain so."

Several people turned to each and either smiled or frowned, depending on their take on large-scale farming and confined-animal operations such as the one Nathan West was planning.

Clark finally recognized the young woman who had been waving her arm from the back of the room. He had ignored her for several minutes because he knew what was coming. She wore a loose-fitting T-shirt with the logo of a prominent animal-rights group printed in bright orange across the front.

"Yes," Clark said.

"Ladies and gentlemen," she began. She obviously had something to say to the entire crowd, not just to Ed Clark. She had a strong voice.

"I am appalled that you are even considering allowing this company to establish itself in your community. No animal should have to endure what pigs endure in these big factory farms. How we treat our animals is a disgrace to the human race, to say nothing about the fact that we kill and eat them. Pigs have feelings too, just like we do, yet look what we do to them. We must all join in an effort to block this company and all companies like it that promote the raising, killing, and eating of animals." Her loud voice could be heard in every corner of the building. When she finished her speech, she sat down. The room was quiet for a moment or two. And then, from somewhere near the front, a loud "boo," and then another even louder "boo."

Clark held up his hand and waved it downward, to signal to the persons booing that they'd made their point. A number of other questions followed:

"How much will the traffic in the area be affected by trucks coming and going?"

"Should not be a problem."

"How many people will Nathan West employ?"

"At first about fifteen or so."

"When do you plan to start building?"

"As soon as we have all our permits and the county zoning committee rezones our property as agricultural."

"Will Nathan West purchase its hog feed locally?"

"We will purchase as much as we can, but several thousand pigs eat a lot." A few old farmers chuckled, as they knew about the eating habits of hogs.

"What about water?"

"We'll pump our water from deep wells."

"What will you do with the cemetery that is on your property?"

"Nothing. We have great respect for cemeteries."

"Do you know about the Tamarack River Ghost?" Now a considerable chuckle could be heard in the audience.

"Yes, we know about the Tamarack River Ghost."

"What will you do about it?"

"What would you suggest?" asked Clark.

No response.

When it looked like the meeting was about to close, an older gentleman who had been sitting in the back stood up. He was slightly stooped and had white hair and a white beard.

"My name is Amos Slogum. Most people around here call me Shotgun," he said with a clear voice. "I was born in this valley and have lived my entire life here. The Tamarack River and I have been friends for a long time."

Most people in the audience knew Shotgun, knew he was a vegetable grower and had a small cranberry bog. Most also remembered that Shogun had a mind of his own and he was not the least bit shy about letting others know what he was thinking.

"I've been sitting here listening to all this palaver about pigs, pollution, and the smell of hog manure for the last hour or so. I hate to say it, but the entire discussion is old fashioned and out of date. Let me digress a moment to make my point. You all know how much we depend on oil to run our cars, keep our tractors moving, keep our economy buzzing along. We also know that we're running out of the stuff. What do we do—we just keep looking for more, in places where it's hard to look, like a mile beneath the sea."

Some people were beginning to fidget; they were tired after an already long, drawn-out meeting. They knew Shotgun had a point somewhere in his words, and they wished he'd get around to making it so they could go home.

"We need a new major energy source to replace oil and begin using a lot less of it," Shotgun said. He paused briefly and then said, "We also need to quit eating so much meat."

"So, what's your point?" someone sitting toward the front asked. It was not a belligerent question, merely an inquiry.

"My point is, we here in the Tamarack River Valley should stand up and say we don't need another hog farm, not here, not anywhere. And the sooner all these pork farms begin closing down, the better it will be for all of us—for our health, and for the health of the environment. For the sake of the planet, we must quit eating meat."

The room was silent. No one questioned or challenged Shotgun— some thought he was just probably getting a little senile, others believed it was another of his wild ideas that generally made no sense. But Josh heard him well and was both recording his comments and taking notes as rapidly as he could. He knew he had a story that was different from what he'd been hearing of late—big-time hog farming versus small-time hog farming. This Slogum guy was suggesting no hog farming at all, and no meat eating.

Ed Clark stood, ready with a response for Shotgun. But Curt Nale motioned for him to stay seated.

"The hour is late. I suggest we close this meeting and give a round of applause to Ed Clark, who has, I think, been straightforward in answering your questions."

The applause was considerably greater than it had been at the beginning of the meeting. Glancing at the old schoolhouse regulator clock that hung on the town hall wall, Josh saw that it was 11:30. He moved through the crowd so that he could talk more with Shotgun Slogum, to see what else he had to say about his no-more-meat perspective.

Opposing Positions

Don't Eat Meat

Farm Country News, January 25

Amos "Shotgun" Slogum, longtime resident of Ames County's Tamarack River Valley, says it's time that we quit eating meat. He was one of several who spoke at an informational meeting, held in the Tamarack Town Hall last Tuesday evening, about a new hog operation planned for the valley. At the meeting, citizens of the valley heard Ed Clark, a representative from Nathan West Industries, explain his company's plans for a large hog operation at the recently purchased former Tamarack River Golf Course.

Attending citizens seemed evenly split between those who welcomed a new use for the golf course and an increase in the tax base and those concerned about harm to the environment and negative effects on the community and its people because of odors and increased traffic. A representative from an animal rights organization argued that confined hog operations were inherently cruel to animals, but those in attendance largely ignored her comments.

Amos "Shotgun" Slogum stood up at the end of the meeting and spoke in opposition to the proposal. He said, "We don't need another hog farm, not here, not anywhere. And the sooner all these pork farms begin closing down, the better it will be for all of us—for our health, and for the health of the environment."

Stunned silence followed his comments, but because it was already late in the evening, no debate ensued. Interviewed after the meeting, Slogum softened his comments somewhat by saying, "I didn't mean we should stop eating meat, I meant we should eat a lot less of it." He cited research indicating that people in the United States yearly eat about 220 pounds of meat per person.

"If we ate less meat, say half as much, we'd be healthier, the environment would be less stressed with water and air pollution, and we'd have more grains available for human consumption."

When asked if he had a proposal for encouraging people to eat less meat, he said, "We can start by not approving any more big factory farms like the one Nathan West is proposing on the old golf course."

The Ames County Zoning Committee will meet at the library in Willow River on April 17, its regularly scheduled meeting. Prior to the meeting, the committee will hear citizen comments about rezoning the former golf course, changing it from recreational to agricultural. If the committee votes in favor, the new hog facility in the Tamarack River Valley will be on the fast track for development.

20

Fred and Oscar

On a late January morning, Fred and Oscar sat at their regular Wednesday table at Christo's, each with a fresh cup of coffee in front of him.

"Well, whaddya you think, Fred?" asked Oscar, breaking the silence.

"About what?" Fred put down his coffee and looked at is old friend.

"About the meeting the other night?"

"What am I supposed to think about it?"

"Hell, I don't know what you're supposed to think about it, I wanna know what you do think about it," said Oscar.

"Well, to tell you the truth, I was a little surprised that you stood up and shot off your mouth."

Oscar smiled. "Sometimes you gotta do that, Fred. Sometimes you gotta stand up and say what you think. Let folks know where you stand."

"Oscar, you can't hardly stand without a cane. Ain't you a little too old to be saying what you think?"

"Old? No, I'm not too old to say what I think. More old people ought to do that: let the younger folks know that we old timers got experience, that we've been around the tree a couple times and have learned a few things because of it."

Fred took another drink of his coffee, contemplating what Oscar had just said.

Oscar continued, "It's one of the things wrong in our society these days—everybody thinks the young people have got all the ideas, have figured out where things are headed, and wanna let you believe they know how to move into the future. I'm not sayin' we shouldn't listen to these young folks; we should. But they ought to listen to us, too. There ought to be a mix of ideas comin' from all directions."

"So whaddya think of what old Shotgun had to say about not eatin' meat?"

"I think he's got a point. Yes, I do. And by golly, he's got a right to express it too. You notice that reporter guy, that Josh somebody, picked up on what Shotgun said and wrote about it in the newspaper today?"

"Yup, I did see that," said Fred. "Can't see it happenin' though. People been eating meat since they lived in caves."

"How do you know that?"

"Know what?"

"That people ate meat when they lived in caves."

"I just do. Read it in a book when I was in second grade."

"You could read when you were in second grade?"

"You damn betcha I could, and I remembered stuff too." Fred touched the side of his head as he spoke.

"So where do you come down on the idea of a big hog farmer comin' into our valley?"

"Ain't thought about it much."

"Why not?" asked Oscar.

"Why not what?"

"Why haven't you thought about it?"

"Other things to think about. Lots of other things to consider," said Fred.

"Like what?"

"Well, my arthritis has been kicking up lately. Been thinkin' about that. Been thinkin' about getting old—been thinkin' about that a lot."

"Good God, Fred, you gotta get your mind away from arthritis and worrying about gettin' old. You should think about something else. Something important."

"Arthritis and gettin' old are pretty damn important to me."

Oscar sipped his coffee and didn't say anything for a half minute or so.

Fred broke the silence. "So you agree with me that I got other things more important to think about than a bunch of smelly hogs comin' into the valley."

"I didn't say that," said Oscar, picking up his coffee cup.

"So what are sayin', then? Just what are you sayin'?" Fred raised his voice a little.

"You don't have to yell. I ain't deaf," Oscar said quietly.

"I ain't yellin', I'm just wondering what you're drivin' at."

Oscar put down his coffee cup and looked Fred straight in the eye. "Are you for or against this big hog operation comin' into our valley?"

"I figure it ain't none of my business," said Fred.

"None of your business?" Now Oscar raised his voice.

"That's what I said. Now if I was to stand up and say what I think, people are gonna call me and write to me and put my name in the paper. I don't need that kind of attention, I just wanna live what I got left of my life by myself, without anybody botherin' me. I don't want anybody messin' in my business, and I figure I shouldn't be messin' in anybody else's."

"So you don't care that when you wake up in the morning all you can smell is pig manure? You don't care about that, huh?"

"I don't wanna smell pig manure when I wake up in the morning."

"So, you do have an opinion on the matter."

"I didn't say that."

"Sounded like you said that."

"Well I didn't."

"Know what, Fred?" Oscar hesitated for a moment before he continued. He didn't want to criticize his friend, but then he thought, *Why not*, and he continued.

"Do you know that you are a middle-of-the-roader?" said Oscar.

"What does that mean?"

"It means you sit right in the middle of road, trying not to take on a position on either side."

"Expect that's right."

"Know what happens to middle-of-the-roaders?"

"What?" asked Fred. He took another sip of coffee.

"They get run over by traffic goin' in both directions."

Fred laughed. "I ain't been run over yet."

"Know what else?"

"What else?"

"People who don't stand up and say their piece when decisions are being made have no right to shoot off their mouths when they don't like what happens."

"Why not?"

"'Cause they didn't have guts enough to stand up and say what they thought when the idea was bein' discussed."

Fred drained the last drop from his coffee cup, stood up, and put on his John Deere cap.

"I gotta be goin'," he said. "See you around." He walked toward the door of Christo's, leaving Oscar alone with a half cup of cold coffee.

Yes or No to Factory Farms

Josh Wittmore was working at his office computer when Bert Schmid stuck his head through the open door. He carried a copy of the latest issue of their paper, which had the Nathan West informational meeting story on the front page.

"Looks like we got ourselves an issue," said Bert.

"You bet we do—and we should make the most of it," said Josh as he turned from his computer to face his boss.

"This story will give our paper a chance to tell folks what's going on in agriculture and at the same time let them know a little more about this quiet river valley here in Ames County," said Bert.

"Sure wasn't quiet the other night," said Josh, smiling.

"What's next?" Bert asked.

"Well, I'd like to visit one of Nathan West's farms over in Iowa, see firsthand how they operate. Check on the smell. Talk with some of the locals to see what they think about having a big hog farm in their midst."

"That's a good idea. You want me to set up something? I'll call their head office in Dubuque."

"Appreciate it," Josh said. A half hour later Bert was back in Josh's office.

"What a bunch of cautious people. They're scared to death of animal rights activists. I had to convince them that you weren't gonna do a hatchet job on them."

"Well, did you convince them enough so I can visit?"

"After three phone calls, I talked with one of their vice presidents, who finally agreed you could visit."

"So, when do I go?"

"Not until March. The veep's gonna set up a visit with what they call their 435 unit—they give each location a number. It's near Decker, Iowa. By the way, Josh, here's what we've gotten so far in our request for community contributions. I haven't opened anything yet."

Josh returned to his office, sat down, and slit open the envelopes Bert had just handed him. The first contained several handwritten pages, a story titled "Horses I Have Known" by Clyde Emersol, with a Waupaca return address. Josh began reading:

> I grew up driving horses on the home farm back in the years of the Great Depression. The first team my pa had, he named Joe and George, Percheron horses they were. They were big horses, nearly a ton apiece. Pa often said they was the best team we'd ever had on the farm. Of course they was Pa's horses. They didn't like me much. Old Joe would try to bite me every chance he got. Mean horse, he was. And George was just plain lazy. Nothing worse than a lazy horse, to my way of thinking. But when I'd say that to Pa, he wouldn't listen. He kept bragging up that pair of horses to everyone who'd listen.

Josh chuckled occasionally as he continued reading, enjoying Emersol's down-home way of writing. When he finished the piece, he decided to recommend they publish it—just the way it was, no editing, no correcting of grammatical errors.

The next envelope he opened had no return address; the postmark was Link Lake. He found two neatly typed sheets of paper with a poem written on each of them. At the bottom of each were the initials "M.D." He'd tried to think of someone around Link Lake with those initials and came up blank. But he'd been away for a decade, and he knew several new families had moved into the community, maybe one of them had the initials M.D. He'd have to check the phone book.

He read the first poem:

Farms and Factories

Factories make things.
Ships and stoves and automobiles.
Tables and chairs
And fancy gadgets.
Farms grow things.
Vegetables and grains.
Milk and pork.
Lumber and beef steaks.
Farms are not factories.
They never were.
They never will be.
They never can be.
Farms are of the land.
The land that feeds us all.
Factories produce the extras,
Beyond what's necessary for life.

M.D.

Josh read the poem a second time, then put the paper down and sat back.

I'm not much of a poet, he thought, *but there's something here that might cause people to think a little more about the big hog farm that's headed for the Tamarack River Valley. M.D. surely has a point of view. I wonder if M.D. lives in the Tamarack River Valley and not near Link Lake? Who in the valley might write like this?* He couldn't come up with a name. He tried to recall some of the people who had spoken up at the meeting back in January; he wondered if it could be one of them. This writer surely was on the side of small farms and the river.

Josh took the story and poem into Bert's office. "Well, anything worth running in the paper?" Bert asked when he looked up from the ledger in front of him.

"I think so," said Josh. "Got a nice nostalgic piece about horses that I think many of our readers will like. Also got a poem, maybe not a poem, but just ideas strung together to look like a poem."

"Here, let me have a look."

He read through the poem, then read it a second time.

"Who is this M.D.?" he asked when he looked up, still holding the poem in his hand.

"I have no idea. No return address, but a Link Lake postmark."

"Person has a point of view," said Bert. "Definite point of view. I think we'll run it. Might tick some people off, might get some others thinking. Poem fits right in with the discussion about the big new hog farm in the Tamarack River Valley. Wish we had some more material from M.D. Need a little controversy; might gain us a few more subscribers. Might lose us a few too," he said with a chuckle.

22

Winter Festival

*T*he Tamarack River Winter Festival began in 1910 when several farmers in the area who worked in the logging camps during the winter months gathered to show off their lumbering skills and tell tall tales of life in the winter woods. Those early festivals mostly consisted of competitions between teams of woodcutters and individual contests, such as what team of two could saw a log fastest, who could shinny up a pine tree quickest, who could toss an axe and hit the center of a target, that sort of thing. Considerable drinking and partying went on into the dark winter nights of the first weekend in February. The festival was always held on that same weekend, no matter what—even if it was a fierce blizzard or thirty below zero. The competitions took place on the banks of the Tamarack River—in the old days, all out in the open. Today, the local organizers erected a big tent, fully enclosed and even partially heated, in Tamarack River Park. The old timers scoffed at the tent, especially the heaters. "Don't know about this present generation. Gotten pretty soft," one old timer was heard to say.

Everyone looked forward to the event with more than a passing interest; the festival had long ago become a tradition. The locals seemed to understand, although few people put it in words, that traditions are what make a community, tie people together, give them a common purpose. The festival attracted people from throughout Ames County and the neighboring counties, but people also came from Madison, Milwaukee, and the Fox River Valley, and even a few snowmobilers from Chicago came to participate in the races held on the frozen river on Sunday afternoon.

Josh planned to attend both days of the event and had asked Natalie to accompany him.

"I can't go on Saturday, but I can on Sunday," Natalie had said.

Wanting to get a broader picture of the Tamarack River Valley and its various activities, Josh drove alone to the festival on Saturday, but he was thinking about Sunday, when Natalie would be with him, which would be more fun.

Saturday dawned partly cloudy and not especially cold. Thermometers in the valley read twenty-five degrees above zero, mild for early February, which was the heart of a northern winter, when the temperatures usually reached their lowest levels. One longtime resident recalled a year—he was a little fuzzy on whether it was 1939 or 1942—that the temperature dropped to thirty below on the opening day of the festival.

"Went right ahead with it," he said. "People in those days didn't let a little cold weather get in the way of a good time."

Earlier in the week, it had snowed nearly a foot, but county crews had done a good job clearing the parking lot at the park and removing the snow from the place where the tent went each year. Volunteers had put up the tent, which held about a hundred people, on Wednesday, pounding the metal tent pegs into frozen ground, laying out the canvas and ropes, and then pulling the structure into place.

The Saturday-morning sun struggled to break through the smoky gray clouds as people, Josh included, found chairs in the heated tent. They came prepared. Almost all wore down-filled parkas of some kind, and most wore heavy felt-lined boots. The opener for the festival, scheduled to start at ten, featured "An Ode to the Tamarack River Ghost," recited by Oscar Anderson. Oscar had recited the piece every year for more than twenty. With a new haircut and wearing freshly washed overalls and a red-and-black-checked shirt, he stood when this year's festival chair, Alexis Christo, introduced him. Oscar, using his cane, walked slowly to the podium as people clapped—a rather strange, subdued "whomp, whomp" sound, as everyone wore either thick gloves or down mittens.

"An Ode to the Tamarack River Ghost," Oscar said quietly.

"Louder," came a voice from the back of the tent.

Oscar began once more, this time louder: "An Ode to the Tamarack River Ghost." He paused briefly, then continued.

When the wind is down and the moon is up, we sometimes hear him. We hear his song, and we hear the clear sound of his dog's little bell. We are reminded of the story of the Tamarack River Ghost, the ghost that haunts this valley, the ghost of Mortimer Dunn. We are reminded of that day in April during the year nineteen aught aught, the day that Mortimer Dunn met his fate. The day that Mortimer Dunn drowned in the river. Drowned in the Tamarack River, the river we all know so well.

Mortimer Dunn was a log driver, but more than that, Mortimer Dunn knew logjams, understood them, studied them, pondered their creation, and learned how to spot the key log and pull it loose. Learned how to take apart a jam so the logs would once more flow free on their journey down the Tamarack River on their way to the sawmills in Oshkosh and Fond du Lac.

Mortimer Dunn was also a family man with a wife and children, a storyteller, and a woodcarver. He carved many things, but his specialty was whistles. Little wooden whistles that he made from green willow branches. He carried one of these in his pocket and used it to call his big dog, Prince.

It was a beautiful day in April. The logs floated free, and the log drivers were singing:

> Ho Ho, Ho Hay, keep the logs a-going.
> Keep 'em rolling and twisting.
> Keep 'em moving, keep 'em straight.
> On the way to the lake called Poygan.
> Ho Ho, Ho Hay,
> What a day, what a day.

But then what often happens when things are going well, when progress is being made, when celebration is in order—a turn of fate. An unexpected logjam develops, the river is plugged, the logs are stopped. A day that started with beauty and hope becomes one filled with agony and sorrow. So today, and every year on this weekend, we celebrate the life of Mortimer Dunn, who died in this river. All that was found of him was his little wooden whistle, with the initials M.D. carved on it. The whistle washed up right here at Tamarack River Park. You can see it on display at the Trading Post in Tamarack Corners.

On this day we celebrate the Tamarack River Ghost, for Mortimer Dunn's grave on the banks of this river stands empty. When the wind is down and the moon is up, his ghost is searching, searching, constantly searching for his empty grave. In the still of a moonlit night, we sometimes hear him; we hear his song. And we remember. We remember the Tamarack River Ghost.

Oscar made a slight bow, smiled, and returned to his seat. Everyone stood and clapped. Although he was eighty-six years old, Oscar Anderson's voice was powerful and his presentation exemplary.

M.D., thought Josh. He immediately thought of the poem the paper had received. *M.D. stands for Mortimer Dunn. Is someone pretending to be the ghost of Mortimer Dunn? Why would anyone do that? But maybe there really is a ghost contacting the paper from the great beyond; wouldn't that be something?* Josh shuddered a bit at the thought.

The members of the Willow River High School Band found their places on the little makeshift stage at the end of the tent. As they were doing so, people in the audience turned to each other, visited, commented on Oscar's presentation, and waited for the band to get itself in order. There was no impatience, no sense of urgency. Winter was a time for slowing down, for doing things deliberately. People living in the valley knew this and appreciated it, for they, like rural and small-town people everywhere, were tuned to the cycle of the seasons. The band could take as long as it needed. It finally led off with a rousing rendition of "Old Man River" and followed with a series of river songs, another festival tradition: "Rolling Down the River," "Cry Me a River," "Down by the Riverside" (everyone in the audience joined in the clapping), a fun rendition of "Row, Row, Row Your Boat," with various instruments taking turns playing the lead, and ending with "Michael Row the Boat Ashore."

After the final piece, the audience clapped loudly, for the Willow River High School Band was in good form, giving its best performance people could remember. Just outside the big festival tent, bratwurst and chicken cooked on a long, charcoal-fired grill, and just beyond that, in a small three-sided tent, two men, bundled in long gray parkas with fur-edged hoods, served beer on a portable bar that stretched across the front of the tent. They also offered soft drinks, coffee, and hot chocolate.

When the concert finished, people filed out of the tent. Some walked around, looking at the various ice sculptures in progress. A half dozen artists chipped away at what were once fifty-pound hunks of clear ice, fashioning bears, penguins, eagles, pine trees, and other wintry creations. A small crowd gathered around Brittani Martin, including Ben Wesley, who had not seen any of his office manager's creations before now. Brittani had been taking sculpting lessons at the university in Stevens Point and discovered she had a talent for making something out of something else—of making art, as her instructor had told her. For the past several weeks, after work and on weekends, she had practiced ice sculpting in preparation for the festival. Now, somewhat nervous with people watching, she slowly chipped away at the big block of ice in front of her. When they asked, she did not tell people what she was making.

"Figure it out," she said proudly.

"It's a rabbit," a youngster wearing a big red parka said. "It's not either a bunny," his sister said. "I think it's an igloo."

As people continued watching, they slowly saw a wild rose emerging from the ice, its five petals and stem clearly visible.

"Remarkable work," an older person said. "Remarkable work."

Brittani smiled.

The afternoon events featured an axe-throwing contest, an event held every year since the first festival. Chair of this year's throw was Don Happsit, barber at the Tamarack Corners Barber Shop. Promptly at 2:00 p.m., he took the microphone. "Those interested in watching the axe-throwing contest should gather at the west side of the park shelter, near the river's edge."

This longtime festival favorite attracted contestants from as far away as Winnipeg, Manitoba, Canada. This year, an even dozen contestants competed for the Golden Axe, an old logger's axe painted gold, now faded after many years of being passed from winner to winner. The winners' names and years were inscribed on the handle. Last year, Dan Burman won the contest, with Shotgun Slogum a close second. Most residents in the valley had little to do with Burman, and he liked it that way. He did things his way, including breaking a few game rules from time to time. Slogum, long-time vegetable grower in the valley and a bit of an eccentric, had little to do with Burman, although they had both been born and lived their entire lives in the valley.

Happsit continued his announcement after the contestants and a substantial audience had gathered. "The rules for the contest are these. Each contestant gets one practice throw and three throws at the target, which is exactly twenty feet away. Hitting the bull's-eye is five points, the next ring four, and so on to the outer ring, which is one point. You must use a double-bitted axe with a blade edge no larger than six inches. Each axe handle must be at least two feet long but no longer than forty inches. An axe must weigh at least two and a half pounds. Are there any questions?"

The audience gathered a bit closer to watch as the contestants stretched, hefted their axes, and made throwing motions with their arms.

"Are we ready to begin?" asked Happsit as he motioned to the first contestant, selected by drawing the contestant's name from a hat.

"Our first contestant is Freddy Jones, from Milwaukee. This is his first year competing for the Golden Axe Award. We're ready when you are."

Freddy, in his early twenties, tall and muscular, wore a jaunty French voyageur-style cap and a plaid wool shirt. He stepped up to the line, hefted his axe, pulled his arm back, and tossed it hard.

"Whack." The axe stuck into a pine tree alongside the target. He had completely missed.

"Remember folks, each contestant gets one practice throw, so Freddy's miss doesn't count."

Freddy retrieved his axe, hefted it once more, spit on the handle, pulled his arm back, and tossed it. "Whack." The axe stuck the target firmly in the blue ring, for four points. With a big smile on his face, he walked up to the thirty-six-inch target, firmly attached to pine boards, and retrieved his axe. After two more tries, he'd earned twelve points, a respectable score, especially for a newcomer.

Each contestant in turn threw his axe, once for practice, and three that counted. Burman achieved a perfect score—all three tosses stuck firmly in the bull's-eye. Two contestants later, Shotgun Slogum did the same thing. The crowd swelled to watch these two competitors, both experienced and both previous winners, do another round to break the tie. A tossed coin determined that Slogum should go first. All four of his tosses, including the practice toss, landed in the bull's eye. Burman, a serious look on his face, and his reputation as the best valley axe thrower at stake, faced the target, carefully hefted his axe, and threw it hard. He drove nearly the entire blade of his axe into the bull's-eye. Same for tosses two and three. But something happened with the fourth toss. Something broke his concentration. No one really knew what it was—a baby crying in the audience, a snowmobiler making a practice run down the river in preparation for Sunday's snowmobile race, loud laughter coming from the beer tent. Anyway, the fourth toss landed in the four-point ring, and Shotgun Slogum was declared winner of the Golden Axe.

Slogum came forward to retrieve the award, smiling, but not broadly. He was not one to show much emotion, especially when he was being recognized for something.

"Thank you," he said quietly when he received the trophy axe. He turned to walk away, and there stood Dan Burman, directly in front of him.

"Congratulations," said Burman as he extended his hand to Slogum.

"Thank you," Slogum said.

The two men parted, neither saying another word to each other.

Sunday, Josh stopped by Natalie's cabin a little after 12:30, and they drove on toward the Tamarack River Valley. A few flakes of snow gently struck the windshield of the Ford Ranger as they drove on.

"Looks like a few flurries," Josh said. "A little snow shouldn't stop anything at the festival."

"Surely not the snowmobile races," said Natalie. "They'd race in a blizzard. They're a tough bunch of guys."

The falling snow increased in intensity soon after they arrived at the park. They walked by the now snow-covered ice sculptures and the equally snow-covered artists, who were standing by their creations to answer questions and talk. Josh and Natalie chatted for a bit with Brittani.

"This is really nice work," said Natalie as she looked carefully at the wild rose, its edges now covered with freshly fallen snow.

"Thank you," Brittani said, smiling.

The snow continued falling as they walked among the other sculptures, waiting for the snowmobile races, scheduled to begin at 2:00 p.m. on the river. The wind had come up a little, blowing swirls of snow across the parking lot and making it difficult to see any distance. By the time of the snowmobile races, it had become impossible to see across the frozen river. The announcer's voice, sometimes lost in the wind and swirl of snow, began giving instructions for the race, a straight-away half-mile course. Over the wind, Josh and Natalie heard the first group of racers revving their engines and then tearing down the river, the sound of the machines soon lost in the storm. No one could see them. The race watchers soon drifted off toward their cars, now covered with three inches of snow, with more on the way, from the looks of the sky and the feel of the wind. Josh and Natalie found shelter in the big festival tent, its canvas roof beginning to sag a bit from the accumulating snow. A few others were there as well, waiting for the snow to let up so they could watch the rest of the races, which continued without pause. Josh bought paper cups of hot chocolate from the beer tent, where coffee and hot chocolate had become far more popular than Wisconsin's famous craft beers.

The snow did not ease but continued falling, even harder. The wind, now from the northwest, swirled the snow about the park, festival tent, beer tent, and park shelter. The ice sculptures were nearly buried when Josh and Natalie headed for Josh's red pickup, which, fortunately, had four-wheel drive.

"Still game for dinner?" asked Josh as they both brushed snow from the truck's windshield.

"I'm starved," answered Natalie.

"Might be a little tricky driving back to Willow River, even if it is only fifteen miles."

"So, what kind of a truck is this, anyway?" she said, smiling. Both knew that she was comparing his little red pickup to her much larger one.

Soon they were seated at a table in Christo's, near a window facing the Tamarack River, which gave them an opportunity to watch what had become a blizzard, with snow blowing down the river in walls of white, the river sometimes disappearing into the storm.

"I love blizzards," said Natalie as she gazed out the window. She wore a cherry-red knitted sweater, and her blonde hair hung loose on her shoulders. "It's like we are sitting inside the storm and looking out." Her brown eyes sparkled as she talked.

"A good old-fashioned blizzard makes the world slow down. Reminds us that we aren't in control of things as much as we think we are," said Josh.

Costandina came by with menus. "Prime rib is the special," she said. "With all the trimmings." They agreed on the special and, while they waited for their food, shared a bottle of merlot. They looked out the window and watched melting snow make little rivers down the glass. They could hear the wind tearing around the corner of the restaurant, swirling the snow, piling it up in drifts. For a long time, neither said anything.

"Any thoughts on the new hog farm coming here to the valley?" Josh asked, breaking the silence.

"As a DNR employee or as Natalie Karlsen?"

"So, you really are two people?" Josh said, remembering an earlier conversation. Natalie laughed, and her eyes brightened. Josh liked that.

"As long as Nathan West meets all the requirements, jumps through all the hoops, it's the company's right. No law says a hog farm should be a certain size."

"What about this old river we can't see this afternoon? How will the Tamarack River and a Nathan West hog factory farm get along? What about the people who live here in the valley, people who like it quiet, hold annual winter festivals, fish on the river, walk in the park, live out their retirement years in little cabins? What about a factory farm and these people?" asked Josh.

"I worry about these things, Josh. This is me talking now. Not an employee of the DNR. I think about these questions a lot."

Natalie was looking out the window, staring at the swirling snow and the rivulets of water that trickled down the window.

After a few moments of silence, Natalie said, "How about some dessert at my place? I baked a cake."

"You baked a cake?" Josh asked. Natalie wrinkled her nose at the comment.

Back in Josh's pickup, he immediately punched the 4x4 button. They carefully made their way out of the restaurant's parking lot and onto the county road that led to Willow River. As Josh drove, trying to keep his eyes on the tracks of the few cars that had traveled ahead of him, the truck's wipers slapped against the windshield, scarcely able to keep up with the falling snow. He could not see more than ten or fifteen feet in front of his truck; he felt like he was driving into a wall of snow that constantly retreated as he entered it—at a top speed of twenty miles an hour. They finally arrived in Willow River; Main Street was deserted, and snow swirled around the street lights, casting eerie shadows. They drove through town, toward Natalie's place. Josh pulled into the drive that led to Natalie's cabin; he could feel all four wheels digging into what had become more than a foot of snow. He shut off the engine and turned off the truck lights.

"Quite a ride," he said, letting out his breath.

"Come on in. We'll start a fire in the fireplace and watch the storm over the lake. And have some of my chocolate cake."

"You didn't say it was chocolate. I like chocolate."

"Most people do. You know how to start a fire in the fireplace?"

"I do," Josh said. He crumpled an old newspaper, checked the damper, and balanced a few sticks of kindling wood on the paper, then struck a match to the little pyramid he had made. Soon a brisk fire was crackling.

Outside the big picture window, snow swirled and the wind howled, but it was cozy and warm in Natalie's cabin.

"Like some more wine before dessert?"

"Sure; whatever you've got would be fine." Soon, Natalie was back with the wine. She sat down beside him in front of the fire.

"Nice place you've got," said Josh.

"I like it. I rented it shortly after I got here. Couldn't see living in an apartment. Too many nosy neighbors around. Here, I'm all by myself."

"Isn't that a little dangerous, I mean being out here all by yourself?"

"You forget; I do know how to use a gun. . . . Would you like me to rub your neck? I'll bet it's killing you after driving through a blizzard." She began rubbing his neck and his shoulders, relieving the tension. It had been a long time since Josh had felt this good; it had also been a long time since he sat like this with a good-looking woman.

Soon, they were eating chocolate cake and drinking more wine. The blizzard had not let up; in fact, it had grown in intensity. One time, Josh looked out the window at his truck in the driveway, and it appeared nearly buried; a drift of snow had crawled up one side, and the hood was covered with what looked like at least six inches of the white stuff.

At eleven o'clock, Josh stood up and said he should probably make his way home.

"You should stay here tonight," Natalie said quietly, putting her hand on his knee. It was warm and friendly. "You shouldn't be out in a storm like this." She smiled when she said it. She leaned toward him.

Fred and Oscar

Damn, it's cold this morning. Colder'n a witch's tit," said Fred when he joined Oscar at Christo's for coffee the Wednesday after the Winter Festival. Fred rubbed his hands together as he spoke. "Quite a snowstorm on Sunday. Ain't had one like that for a while."

"Sit down, and quit complaining," said Oscar, who already had a cup of steaming coffee in front of him.

"I ain't complaining. Cold enough to freeze the balls off a brass monkey, though. Twenty below zero this morning," said Fred.

"I didn't think it was that cold. You sure your thermometer ain't broke?"

"My thermometer ain't broke. It's just plain colder than hell." Fred hung his red-and-black-checked wool Mackinaw over the back of his chair. "How'd you get your coffee already?"

"If you'd get goin' a little sooner in the morning, you'd get early coffee too."

Costandina, unbeknownst to both of the old men, was standing off to the side, taking in the conversation and smiling from ear to ear.

"You like some coffee, Fred?" she asked. She had an empty cup in one hand and a steaming pot of coffee in the other.

"You betcha I would. Need to warm up. Cold out there today." He rubbed his hands together again.

"Looks to me like you got yourself a new haircut," said Oscar.

"Yup, I did, had my ears lowered. Cap fits better now."

"That's one of the reasons you're so damn cold."

"What's one of the reasons?"

"You got your hair cut, dummy. Nobody gets his hair cut in the winter. Hair keeps you warm. Olden days, nobody got a haircut in the winter. They let 'er grow."

"Well, this ain't the olden days, Oscar. If you haven't noticed."

"So, what'd you make of the winter festival?" asked Oscar.

"Saturday was pretty darn good. About the best Saturday we've had in years. That high school band over at Willow River, boy those kids are good. No question about it. Those kids know how to toot on them horns. Expect you'd like to hear what I've picked up about your ghost performance," Fred said.

"What'd you hear?"

Fred smiled, hesitated, and took another sip of coffee.

"Well, what'd you hear?"

"Hate to have to tell you this," said Fred, trying to be serious.

"What?"

"Folks said it was the best performance you ever gave. Best goll-darn ghost recitation you ever did." Fred was smiling broadly. He took another sip of coffee.

"Pleased to hear it. Pleased to hear it," Oscar said. "Sunday kind of fizzled, didn't it? They did the snowmobile races—at least I think they did. You could hear 'em roaring down the river, but you couldn't see 'em. Wonder how them snowmobile drivers could see where they was goin'? I wondered about that."

"I didn't stay. Drove on home when it started snowin' hard. Tires on my pickup ain't the best any more. Traction's not so good," Fred said.

"Say, you been reading the *Farm Country News*?" asked Oscar.

"Yeah, I read most of it the day it comes out. Sometimes I read all of it. Depends on how busy I am. Sometimes I'm pretty busy."

"Well, did you read that stuff that somebody using the initials 'M.D.' wrote?"

"Yeah, I read it. Supposed to be poetry, I expect. Do you think it's poetry, Oscar?"

"Doesn't matter what it is, matters what it says and who says it."

"I'm just not sure it's poetry. Set up like poetry, short lines stacked up on top of each other, but isn't poetry supposed to rhyme?"

"Damn it, doesn't matter if it's poetry or not. What'd you make of it, Fred?"

"First off, whoever M.D. is, he doesn't think much of the new pig farm comin' into the valley, does he?" answered Fred.

"He sure doesn't, and I pretty much agree with him," said Oscar. "I don't think havin' that many pigs on one piece of ground is a good idea."

"But them pigs ain't gonna be outside. They're gonna be in buildings, big, new buildings," said Fred, taking another sip of coffee.

"There's still pig manure, Fred, inside a building or not. Pig manure's gotta get outside sometime or another. And pig manure stinks."

"But don't we need something to lower our taxes? Property taxes are just about killin' us. Keep goin' up every year. Need a new business to increase our tax base."

"That we do, Fred; that we do. I agree with you there. Say, who do you think is writing these poems? Who do you think M.D. is? Could it be one of our doctors in Willow River? They're all MDs, aren't they?"

"Nah, don't think it's no doctor. Those folks are so darn busy, they don't have time to do anything but help sick people."

"I think I know who M.D. is. I think I know," said Oscar.

"Well, you gonna tell me, or just keep it to yourself?"

"You're testy this morning; you get up on the wrong side of the bed?"

"Maybe. Maybe I did. None of your damn business what side of the bed I got up on. So who is M.D., in your well-informed, intelligent way of thinking about things?"

"I think M.D. stands for Mortimer Dunn, the Tamarack River Ghost."

Fred laughed out loud. "You serious? Old Mort Dunn's been gone since 1900, hardly think he's up to writing poetry or whatever that stuff in the paper is."

"The ghost could be workin' with a livin' person, givin' him the ideas to put down on paper and send in," said Oscar.

"Oscar, I saw it comin' your way, and I think it's now here. Yup, I think it's now here," said Fred.

"What the hell you thinkin' about now?"

"I'm thinkin' about you."

"I thought we was talking about who M.D. was."

"We were."

"So, what about me? What's coming my way?"

"Senility, the old-timer's disease," said Fred.

"Hell, Fred, I ain't no more senile than you are."

"So why'd you think 'M.D.' might stand for Mortimer Dunn?"

"'Cause it just might. Say as you will, that old Tamarack River Ghost is still around. Still around. You can bet your bottom dollar on it," said Oscar.

Paper Problems

*J*osh Wittmore, ad manager Bixby Billings, photographer Steve Atkins, and Bert Schmid sat around an old oak table in *Farm Country News*'s conference room on the Wednesday afternoon following the Tamarack River Winter Festival. The conference room also served as the lunchroom, archives collection room, photocopy room, and a place where extra stuff was stored—such as newspapers from around the country, farm magazines, and the like.

Bert had written rows of numbers on the blackboard that hung on one end of the room. Above each row, he wrote a year, starting with 1965, and a year for every ten years since. The numbers represented profits, and from 1965 to 1995 they showed a steady increase—1995 was a peak. Since then, the numbers had been dropping. The newspaper was losing money, more each quarter.

When everyone was seated, Bert stood up and walked to the board. "You all know that we've got financial troubles, but I wanted to take a few minutes to show you how bad it really is. There's a clear danger we might go bankrupt."

The room was quiet. "The numbers speak for themselves—so, do you have any questions?"

"Have we had any increase in subscriptions since we started running some of the community contributions?" asked Josh.

"A little. A few more subscribers. We need all the subscribers we can find, but our big problem is advertisers. We need more advertising money. That's how we've survived in the past; that's the only way we can survive in the future. Bixby, what's your take on increasing advertising revenue?"

Bixby Billings, a round-faced, bald, moderately overweight man, was prone to wearing loud neckties and bright shirts. He generally had a positive, I-can-get-it-done attitude. But not today. "I'm trying everything," he said. "I tried various kinds of special offers. I make the rounds of the farm shows, talking to the big machinery and feed guys. I'm working ten-hour days, and when all is said and done—I just don't know what to do. The Internet is killing us. No question about it. The big companies, the farm machinery companies, the feed companies, the chemical companies—they have as much advertising money as before or more than ever—but they're advertising through their own websites and on dozens of other farm-related websites. I don't know how to compete with that."

"Josh, what's your take on all this?"

"I think Bixby's got it right. The Internet is the future for lots of people, farm people included."

"Damn Internet," Bert said, pounding his big hand on the table. It's gonna destroy all of us. How in hell do you fight something you can't see? Tell me that?"

The room was silent, as everyone knew Bert's attitude toward computers and the Internet. Bert insisted on writing his stories with a manual typewriter—the paper's secretary retyped his work onto the paper's server so it could be sent to their printer, which refused to accept anything that wasn't digital.

"One last hope we've got," said Bert, rubbing his hand through his thick, unruly gray hair. "That's the Nathan West story. That'll probably be the biggest story we've ever done, after the feedlot stories, that is; we sure got people talking about how beef cattle are fed for market. Folks are split every which way about the coming of this big factory farm to the Tamarack River Valley. Soon as you do your visit to the farm in Iowa, we'll step up our coverage. Get people reading about Nathan West—and arguing. Can't beat an issue like this for stirring up interest."

"I hope you're right," Josh said quietly. "I hope you're right."

Josh returned to his office. He was worried about his future with *Farm Country News*, but at the same time more than pleased with how his relationship with Natalie was developing. At his desk, he opened a plain envelope postmarked Waupaca. It contained two more submissions signed

"M.D." Josh had given up trying to identify the writer. What he did know was that people were talking about M.D.'s writing, and that's what was important. It didn't matter if they were for or against the writer's positions; what mattered is that they talked about it—and bought more newspapers.

He read this week's submission—a short essay and a poem.

The Mystery of the Tamarack River

To those who know, and those who don't, the mighty Tamarack River is a mystery and a history. From the seeping springs that give birth to it in the far north in the land of the Ojibwe, the Tamarack twists and turns its way south through the pinelands and the lowlands, through the cranberry marshes and the tamarack forests.

Twisting and turning, it's moving, always moving, and ever growing larger as it welcomes the many little streams that feed it and give it strength and vitality as it hurries along through wide quiet stretches, over rapids and around tight turns on its way to the lake called Poygan and then to the mighty Winnebago, the largest lake in Wisconsin.

For ten thousand years this river has run, since the last great glacier gave up its icy grip on the land and retreated to the north, leaving behind a scattering of lakes and rivers, like the Tamarack and the Wisconsin, the Fox and the Chippewa, the Wolf and the Peshtigo.

The Tamarack River is always the same but constantly changing. The water we see today is not the water we see tomorrow. It is predictable and unpredictable. It is a source of solace and a place to fear, a friend one day, a foe the next. But it is always the river, the mighty Tamarack River. Those who know the Tamarack respect it and love it. For there is nothing like it. Nothing like the Tamarack River.

M.D.

Factories and Rivers

Factories and rivers don't mix.
History is filled with examples.
Polluted water and dead fish.

A factory farm and a river never mix.
They never will;
It's impossible to think they should.
So save our river!
The mighty Tamarack River.
Stop the factory hog farm.
Send it packing.
Keep our river clear and running pure.
Save the fish and other river creatures.
Keep the factories off the farm.

                                                              M.D.

Josh read both submissions a second time and decided to run them both in the next issue of the paper. He was sure the second one would generate some interest. Reading the material took his mind off the paper's problems and his own, should the paper go under. He thought about how much money he had in the bank—not much—and how long he could live without a job. For the first time since he'd begun working at *Farm Country News*, he pulled up his résumé on his computer and scanned it. It would take him a while to bring it up to date. He'd prepared his last résumé when he graduated from college. Lots had happened in his life since then, lots of water under the bridge, even though until now he had kept the same job.

He thought again about Natalie and her cabin, how warm it had been while a fierce blizzard raged outside and they drank wine and ate chocolate cake in front of a blazing fire. He thought of the smell of her hair and her subtle perfume, and the touch of her gentle hands on his neck—and more.

Smear Tournament

After living in central Illinois for ten years, Josh had forgotten how miserable the month of March could be in Wisconsin. One day a promise of spring, with temperatures creeping into the high thirties, the snow turning mushy and eaves from the snow-covered rooftops dripping, and the next, another snowstorm and temperatures hanging around zero. On the one hand, a depressing month, with seemingly constant reminders of winter, and on the other, a month of giddy anticipation at subtle hints of spring—the first green grass on the south side of a building, Canada geese winging north in long *V*s, the first sandhill cranes arriving.

Josh sat at his computer; he had difficulty focusing this Friday morning, even though the sun was up and, for the first day in several, it felt like spring when he stepped out of his apartment and walked to his pickup. He remembered how when he was growing up on a farm on a morning like this his father would say, "You can smell it; you can smell spring in the air."

He was thinking about Natalie; he hadn't seen her for several days and found it was hard to think of anything but her. He wondered what her true feelings were for him. He also couldn't take his mind off his newspaper, which clearly faced major financial problems, perhaps even more serious than his boss had shared. He forced himself to think of the emerging story about Nathan West. With the county zoning committee's approval, they would build a hog facility in the Tamarack River Valley and change that community forever. He thought about the questions he would ask when he visited the Nathan West farm in Iowa in a few days. "What do you feed the hogs at different ages? How many days from birth to market weight? How do the hogs react to close confinement?" He wondered how he would be received; many of the big factory farm operators were not that keen on letting reporters in on their operations. They had gotten too many black eyes from the anti–big farm movement that seemed to be growing in prominence in recent years.

He jumped when the phone on his desk rang.

"This is Natalie."

"Good to hear your voice. I was thinking about you this morning."

"That's good." Her voice was soft, so different from the voice she used when she was asking a fisherman for his license. "Would you like to go with me to the annual Smear Tournament at Christo's this weekend? It runs Saturday and Sunday afternoons. You and I could be partners."

"A what?"

"Smear Tournament—where we play cards and win prizes."

"I haven't played Smear since I was a kid; I don't think I remember how."

"Oh, you'll catch on quickly. Once you learn, you never forget."

"I've never been very good at card games, no matter what they are."

"I'll help you. I'll add an incentive, too."

"And what would that be?" Josh smiled when he asked.

"I'll cook dinner for us, at my cabin—complete with chocolate cake."

Shortly after noon on Saturday, Natalie pulled up in front of Josh's apartment in her little Honda Civic. She wore black slacks and a pale blue sweater and had tied her hair in a ponytail. "You ready to kick some butt?" she asked when Josh pulled open the Civic's door and stepped inside.

"If you mean, am I ready to play Smear, you've got to be kidding. I tried to remember how to do it, and I'm lost. Somehow I got the rules tangled up with seven-card stud."

"Forget about poker. Anybody can play poker; it takes a skilled card player to play Smear." She smiled broadly when she said it.

"That's what I'm afraid of—any card-playing skill I left behind when I was in high school."

"Oh, quit being such a worrywart; I'll show you how. The game is easy."

When they arrived at Christo's, they saw eight tables with four chairs at each.

"Sixteen teams of two start in the tournament," Natalie said. "I registered us two weeks ago so we'd have a place."

"Two weeks ago, before you even called me?"

"Sure, wanted to make sure we got in. People try to get in this tournament from all over the place. Several come from Wisconsin Rapids and sometimes as far as Oshkosh and Appleton. This is a big deal."

"Right," said Josh, smiling.

"Well it is. People around here take Smear seriously—you should remember that."

Josh and Natalie checked in with the tournament leader, Don Happsit the barber, himself a noted Smear player. He and his wife, Marcella, had won the tournament just two years ago. Once you win, your name goes on a plaque and you can't compete anymore.

At each table was a small laminated card, with the rules for the game. Josh began reading:

Smear (Four Players)

A deck for six-point Smear consists of thirty-four cards. The remaining cards are not used. The lowest card is a 7. Two players on the same team sit across from each other. Each player is dealt eight cards, with two tossed in the middle. The player to the left of the dealer bids first. This player may pass (no bid) or bid from two to six points, based on the cards the player holds. The bidding goes around the table; anyone can overbid the previous player. With the first card played, the bidder decides what is trump.

The count includes one point for each of following:

High (an Ace in the trump suit)

Jack (in the trump suit)

High Joker (always is trump)

Low Joker (always is trump)

Low (a 7 in the trump suit)

Game (the count of the cards taken by each team)—team members count cards together.

For purposes of game count, the value of the cards is:

Ace=4

King=3

Queen=2

Jack=1

10=10

all other cards=0.

Josh finished reading and looked across at Natalie, who sat patiently waiting. The second team at their table arrived, and they introduced each other. They learned their names—John and Florence Grabowski from Wisconsin Rapids—and found out that they had been participants in the tournament every year for the past ten. When Natalie explained that Josh had not played the game since he was a kid, they agreed to do a practice round. They had time, as the tournament wasn't scheduled to start for a half hour.

Natalie dealt the cards, two at a time, until each person had eight. She put the last two in the middle.

Josh looked at his hand and placed the cards in the same suit together. He had the 8, 9, 10, and king of diamonds, a 7 of clubs, an 8 of hearts, a jack of spades, and a queen of clubs. He stared at them, not having the first idea whether he should bid or not. Florence looked at her hand and bid three.

Natalie walked around and glanced at Josh's card hand, only because it was a practice hand. "Looks like the best you can do is pass—not a great hand."

"I told you I never have any luck," Josh grumped.

"Be patient, there's always the next round; remember it takes twenty-one points to win the game, and at best a team can earn six points in a round."

Now it was John Grabowski's turn. His hand included the ace, king, jack, and 7 of hearts plus the ace and king of spades. He bid five on his hand, with a sure count of the high (the ace) and the low (the 7) and, with the king, strong prospects of taking one or both jokers—without even needing help from his partner, or a lucky draw from the center two cards.

Natalie glanced at her cards, and quickly said, "Pass," knowing that she couldn't bid six, which would be a near perfect hand. John reached for the two cards in the center; they were a 7 of diamonds and a queen of spades, no help to his hand, so he discarded both of them.

They began playing, with John taking all the tricks; not only did he have all the counting cards—high, jack, two jokers, low, but he also had game, the sum of all the cards taken in the tricks.

By now, teams had filled in at all the tables, and Don Happsit began his little welcome spiel, which included reminding people to look at the instruction cards on the tables for any questions about which cards counted for what. "Also," he said, "if there are any questions about anything, I'm the guy with the final answer." He said it with a big smile on his face, as he remembered how a couple of years previously a big argument developed over whether you had to always play a trump card if a trump card is played and you have one in your hand. You do.

Josh glanced around the room. He recognized Fred Russo and Oscar Anderson playing as a team on the far side of the room. Fred wore a red-and-black-checked wool shirt, Oscar a green-and-black-checked wool shirt. He saw Brittani Martin and a fellow he assumed to be her husband. The rest of the people were strangers to him.

With the tournament started, John Grabowski began dealing the cards, while Josh tried to remember what he had just learned in the practice round, attempted to recall some of the rules from when he played as a child, and glanced occasionally at the instruction card Natalie had placed in front of him. He passed the first round, and Florence Grabowski won the bid and earned four points for Team Grabowski. The next round, Natalie bid four, won the bid, and Team Karlsen-Wittmore took in six points. The very next hand, Josh, with an ace, king, and queen of hearts, bid four, and Team Karlsen-Wittmore took in another five points. He and Natalie were now ahead ten to four. Their luck holding, Natalie bid four the next hand, and, with Josh holding both jokers and the low, they won six more points, bringing them to a total of sixteen to four.

"Beginner's luck," John Grabowski muttered when Josh's next hand contained an ace, king, jack, and 10 of clubs, plus the 7, which was low. Team Karlsen-Wittmore picked up six more points and handily won the game, twenty-two to four.

They would play two more games with the same partners. The team winning at least two games would move up; the losers would be out. Josh's beginner's luck failed for the next two games—indeed he had become a little overconfident and had overbid his hand a couple of times, resulting in becoming "set," which meant his team had to subtract the amount he bid (and lost) from what it had already won. By 3:00 p.m., Josh and Natalie were back in Natalie's Honda, on their way to her cabin. Both had had a good time, even though they had not moved up in the tournament.

It was a pleasant drive back to Willow River. The temperature had climbed into the low fifties, the snow in the fall-plowed fields had mostly melted, and sprigs of green grass appeared along the roadside.

"Are you still planning to visit the big hog farm in Iowa?" Natalie asked. He had told her about the planned visit as a way to add another dimension to the story he was writing about the hog farm planned for the Tamarack River Valley.

"I am. In fact I'm leaving for Iowa tomorrow morning."

"So, what's your take on factory farms, Josh?"

"What do you mean, 'What's my take'?"

"Are you for or against them?"

"It's not that easy. The story is complicated. Besides, I'm a journalist, and we need to keep our own opinions in check when we're working on a story."

"So, you don't have an opinion?"

"I do. But I've got to keep an open mind. There's a lot of misinformation and a lot of emotion out there—on both sides of the question. My job is to sort through it all and come up with the truth."

"The truth, huh."

"Yup, I'm always searching for the truth. And to do that, I've got to be open to new ideas and new facts and allow the material to tell a story.

People understand stories, and I'm trying to dig this one out and shed some light on it."

"And then what?"

"I write the story, including facts, perspectives, arguments, pro and con."

"So you're not going tell me if you're for or against big factory farms."

"That's right."

"And I thought I was beginning to know you."

They drove quietly for several miles, neither saying anything.

"What's for supper?" Josh finally asked, breaking the silence.

"Just like a man."

"Just like a man what?"

"Thinking about your stomach."

"That's not all I'm thinking about," Josh said, a smile spreading across his face.

"Oh, really. And what else might the male half of Team Karlsen-Wittmore be thinking about?"

"Dessert."

"Chocolate cake?"

"It wasn't chocolate cake I was thinking about."

"Neither was I," said Natalie.

26

Nathan West 435

Josh was up early on Monday morning, his mind filled with thoughts of Natalie and the wonderful time they had at the Smear tournament, and the even better time they had at Natalie's cabin in front of a crackling fireplace. He looked forward to visiting the big factory farm in Iowa. As a reporter, he knew he must gather some firsthand information about a large-scale hog operation. Too many rumors floated around as to what occurred on one of these farms. Josh needed to see an operation up close, see the hogs, smell the smells, listen to the sounds.

Josh crawled into his pickup, traveled down Interstate 39 to Madison, and got on Highway 151 toward Dubuque. As he drove along, he wondered if Nathan West's operation, when he got to see it up close and smelled it, would be similar to the beef feedlot operation he visited in Missouri. Although he tried to be objective about these large-scale farming operations, his thoughts were far from positive. Having grown up on a small dairy farm near Link Lake, Josh remembered the hogs they raised, up to twenty-five or thirty a year that his dad shipped to the stockyards in Milwaukee. He didn't much care for hogs; they ate a lot, fought like the dickens with each other at the trough, and dropped a lot of smelly manure. His dad had told him more than once, "If you're gonna raise hogs, make sure the hog house is downwind from the farmhouse. Nothin' worse than the smell of pig manure."

In spring, when the hogs had access to pasture, the smells declined considerably, and the pigs seemed happier roaming around their three-acre lot that was fenced with woven wire to keep them confined. Unlike cattle, hogs used their noses for rooting in the dirt—and digging their way out and escaping from their enclosures.

Josh knew to keep his opinions to himself, but he wondered if he'd be able to do this when he confronted Nathan West's enormous hog facility. He also still had Shotgun Slogum's ideas from the town hall meeting floating around in his head—that we should eat less meat. He wondered if anybody in Ames County agreed with him. He doubted it, but you never knew these days.

Less than an hour out of Dubuque, Josh arrived in Decker, not more than a grain elevator, a church, a few houses, and a coffee shop. The town looked tired and worn, not unlike many midwestern farm towns that had seen tremendous changes in farming during the past couple of decades. Josh stopped at the Home Cooking Coffee Shop for lunch and picked a booth where he could spread out his materials and think through what questions he wanted to ask the Nathan West people. The counter was lined with what appeared to be retired farmers, several of whom had likely sold their land to Nathan West, and a few sales people of one stripe or another. He ordered the special, homemade meatloaf with mashed potatoes—$5.95.

The waitress was an older, gray-haired woman who walked with a bit of a limp. When she brought his food he asked, "Do you know about Nathan West?"

"Yup, I do. Everybody does. It's what we've got here in Decker. It's about all we've got anymore."

"What do you mean?"

"Well," she said as she lowered her voice a little, "Nathan West bought out most of the farmers around here; paid 'em good money, I heard. But before you could say 'Farmin' ain't what it used to be,' we got but one big farmer, if you can call Nathan West a farmer, and a few smaller ones that are hanging on."

"So what's your take on Nathan West?" Josh asked.

"Oh, I really ain't got anything against 'em, except they're all that's left. We used to have farmers all over the place; many of 'em were dairy farmers, some had a few hogs, maybe a few beef cattle. Most are retired or gone. Now we got nearly all our eggs in one basket, and it's called Nathan West."

Finishing his meal, Josh gathered up his bill, left a two-dollar tip, headed back to his pickup, and made the short drive to the Nathan West 435 facility. He topped a rise in the county road and saw a set of brilliant white, single-story buildings sprawled out on the right. He parked his truck in front of a sign that said "Office." Above the small sign was a bigger one: "The Home of Happy Hogs. Nathan West Industries, Facility 435." He opened the office door and stepped inside to meet a receptionist at the desk, working at a computer.

"What can I do for you?" the woman asked, looking up from her work. She had a pleasant way about her.

"I have an appointment with Kyle Jorgensen."

The woman appeared to be in her late thirties and had blue eyes and brown hair. She reached for a button on her desk. "What'd you say your name was?"

"I didn't. I'm Josh Wittmore with *Farm Country News*."

"There's a Mr. Wittmore here to see you," she said into the intercom.

After a moment or two, a man opened the door behind the receptionist and walked a few steps to where Josh waited. He extended his hand. "I'm Kyle Jorgensen," he said. He smiled as he spoke.

"Josh Wittmore, *Farm Country News*."

"Pleased to meet you. Always glad to work with the press—need to get the word out about how our food is produced these days. Not enough information available about that." Jorgensen wore a green dress shirt, open at the neck, with khaki pants. He had a shock of blond hair that appeared to defy combing. Josh figured him to be in his late forties.

"Thanks for taking time to talk with me and give me a tour. I appreciate it."

"No problem. No problem at all. As I said, we're always available for a visit from the press." Josh remembered the difficulty his boss had setting up the interview and tour, and how reluctant Nathan West was to have him visit, but he kept that information to himself.

"So, where do you want me to begin?" Jorgensen asked. He sat behind his desk with his hands folded in front of him. Cartoon pictures of smiling pigs hung on two walls of the office.

"You don't mind if I record our conversation, do you? I want to make sure I get all this right. And how about photos?" asked Josh.

"No problem, record away. Take whatever pictures you want." Josh thought about how different this was from the Lazy Z feedlot operation, where taking a picture resulted in a brick through his motel window.

Josh slipped his tiny digital recorder from his pocket and put it in front of Jorgensen. He then took out his pocket-sized digital camera and snapped a photo of Jorgensen sitting behind his desk.

"Let's start with the size of your operation. How many acres do you have at this site?"

"Well, we keep adding as farms come up for sale. Right now, I think we must have about three thousand acres."

"So you grow crops as well?"

"We sure do. We grow about twenty-five hundred acres of corn, about enough for all our finishing units."

"How many hogs have you got at this site?"

"This is one of four farrow-gestation units we have on this farm. We have three thousand sows here, all together about twelve thousand on our four farrow-gestation sites, at different places on our land."

"And how big are these farrow-gestation buildings?"

"Oh, let's see. Each one is 82 feet wide and 740 feet long."

Josh had a note pad in front of him where he scribbled, *Sow building almost two and a half football fields long.*

"How many little pigs do you farrow each year from this unit?"

"Let's figure it out. The gestation period for a sow is about 114 days, so we expect on average about two and a half litters per sow per year. Our average litter size is ten per sow. So, three thousand sows times two and a half litters and you come up with seventy-five hundred litters. Ten little pigs per litter times seventy-five hundred litters amounts to seventy-five thousand pigs coming out of this building each year—if everything goes right, and most of the time it does. You ready for a tour?"

"Sure," said Josh as he gathered up his notepad, camera, and recorder.

They entered a little hallway just beyond the office, where Josh saw a sign: "Bio-security."

"We work hard to keep all diseases away from our hogs. So, everyone coming into any of our buildings is required to shower and wear the company's clothing and boots while in the building."

Jorgensen pointed to a pair of shower stalls and a dressing area behind them. "You can leave your clothing here," he said, pointing to some hooks and a shelf.

"Even I shower every time I walk into the production unit," Jorgensen explained as he began unbuttoning his shirt.

Josh undressed, showered, dried himself with towels with the NWI logo printed on them, then stepped into the little dressing room, where he pulled on underwear, socks, and blue coveralls, with "Nathan West Industries" printed in gold letters on the back. He found a pair of knee-high rubber boots that fit. Leaving the dressing room, he spotted Jorgensen, dressed in similar fashion, emerging from his dressing room.

"You mind if I bring along my camera, notebook, and recorder?"

"No problem," Jorgensen said.

Josh snapped a photo of Jorgensen dressed in the blue disease-free garb.

"You ready?" Jorgensen asked as he reached for the handle on a heavy metal door.

Once inside Josh glanced around. As far as he could see were pens, each containing about fifteen big, white sows. What he expected was the terrible, nauseating smell of hog manure. But although there was a smell, it was mostly of ammonia—not altogether off-putting. He snapped several photos.

What immediately struck him was how clean the building was. Everything was painted white—the walls, ceilings, even the panels that made up the pens. The hogs, also clean and white, stood on slatted wooden floors. The building, with rows of bright lights, had no windows, and thus no sunlight entered. He remembered the hog pen and hog yard on the home farm. On hot summer days, the pigs wallowed in the mud and manure;

they were dirty from their snouts to the ends of their tails. And the smell was overpowering. So different from what he was seeing in this modern hog house.

The second thing that surprised Josh was how quiet the building was—none of the squealing that he remembered from hogs inside and feeding. On the home farm, the pigs fought with each other over a place at the trough—there was always a certain amount of pandemonium and considerable noise among a group of feeding hogs. Not here.

Josh commented on the quiet.

"Like the sign says, these are happy hogs. No reason for them to make any noise. We control the temperature to within two or three degrees; we control the humidity; we have huge fans to keep the air clean and fresh; and we have automatic, computer-controlled feeding stations in each pen."

"How do these feeding stations work?" Josh asked, pointing to what looked like a metal box with a little door on his end. He snapped a photo.

"Each sow has a tag in her ear. When she's hungry, she walks into the feeding station. A sensor reads the tag. It sends a message to a computer, which in turn drops the appropriate amount of feed in front of the sow, based on what she has or has not eaten so far that day."

As they talked, a sow approached the feeding station and entered. In a few seconds, Josh heard a whirring sound as the overhead auger-feeding system came alive and delivered just the right amount of feed.

"Pretty slick," Josh said. "What breed are these?" On his home farm they raised Chester Whites and Berkshires.

"They're mostly a Landrace-Yorkshire cross. They have large litters, are good mothers, and do well in confined situations."

"And they're big," said Josh, not remembering ever seeing sows so large.

"That they are; they'll weigh around 280, some a little more."

"This is a bit of a difficult question, but I'll ask anyway. Hog operations like this have been accused of inhumane treatment of hogs. How do you respond?"

"Maybe some operators treat their hogs poorly, but not many. You can't stay in business if you don't take good care of your animals," said

Jorgensen. "Our on-call veterinarian conducts classes on humane treatment of animals that all of our employees must take. All of our workers are certified for handling animals humanely."

"I didn't know that," said Josh.

"Lots of misinformation floating around out there. I'm glad you asked the question."

"What about your breeding practices?"

"It's all done with artificial insemination. Several of our employees are trained to do it. We get our semen from one of our subsidiary companies, which supplies all of our hog operations."

"What about those boars I saw when we came in?" Josh had seen four big male pigs in pens on one end of the building.

Jorgensen smiled. "Having the boars around helps bring the sows into heat so they can be inseminated."

Josh saw the stalls where the sows were bred, located on one end of the long hog house. He and Jorgensen walked through a hall on their way to the farrowing house, where the little pigs were born and kept until weaning age—about eighteen to twenty days. In the farrowing house were long rows of farrowing crates, one for each sow and her litter. Josh watched a sow nursing twelve little pigs, and he took several photos.

"Crates seem a little tight; sow can't even turn around," said Josh.

"That's true, but she also doesn't lay on her little ones and kill them, either. That can be a problem, especially with big sows."

Jorgensen and Josh walked the length of the farrowing house, where Josh saw hundreds of little pigs, happily nursing under climate-controlled conditions. Jorgensen explained, "Once the little pigs are weaned, they are moved to a nursery building, where they are raised to forty-five pounds or so. The male and female pigs are separated, each given their own special diets, and the male pigs are castrated. From the nursery, the pigs go to the finishing house, up to fifteen hundred in a building, where they are fed a ration preparing them for market. By the time they are five to six months old, they weigh from 260 to 280 pounds. When the hogs reach market weight, we ship them by truck to our packing plant in Dubuque, where they are slaughtered and cut up into hams, pork chops, bacon, and all the other cuts of meats consumers want."

"I've got another difficult question for you, Mr. Jorgensen."

"Fire away. If I can answer it, I will."

"What happens to all this manure? What do you do with it?"

"First off, we are monitored by the Iowa Department of Natural Resources. Of course, we need permits for everything that we do. We have a manure storage facility at each building, which we empty each fall. We put the manure on our land once a year. We don't really spread it: the manure is injected into the ground, so the smell is minimal. We hire a contractor to empty our manure storage units—our people don't do it."

Josh rapidly took notes, as manure handling and the associated smells were the most common issues asked about when a big hog facility sought a new location. He remembered well the questions from the informational meeting at the Tamarack Town Hall.

Jorgensen continued, "Before the contractor arrives to empty the manure storage facilities, we pull samples of the manure and send them to a lab for testing, to measure the nutrient levels. The amount of manure we can put on the fields is based on the crop yields for these fields and the amount of nutrients a crop needs. This way, we avoid excess buildup of certain nutrients that could eventually pollute the groundwater."

Josh continued making notes. He also checked to make sure his tape recorder was working.

"For instance, by measuring corn yields—on average we produce 192 bushels of corn per acre—we know how many nutrients such a corn crop requires, and that's what we put on the fields. Our fields are sampled every four years for yield information. Our numbers are based on crop uptake. We have a 10 percent cushion on nitrogen—we can exceed the amount we put on by that much. If we put on more than that, we are in violation."

"Sounds complicated," said Josh.

"It's really not. It's how we prevent overloading the soil with nitrogen, phosphorus, and potash, the natural nutrients in manure, and the nutrients needed by a crop to grow."

"So, what if you have too much manure?"

"We contract with our neighbors, who cash crop corn and soybeans. We pay them to put manure on their fields. They, in effect, are getting fertilizer for their crops and being paid to get it."

"Very interesting," said Josh as he continued writing. "Have you considered putting in methane digesters, turning all this manure into electricity?"

"We have, but the numbers just don't work. Too much water in the manure. Besides, the technology for methane converters needs some work. Methane gas is very corrosive, requires lots of equipment maintenance."

Josh finished writing and looked up. "I think I've got about what I need."

"You have any more questions, just give me a call. As I said, if I can answer your questions, I will. Always want to cooperate with the press."

Josh entered the little dressing room, removed his borrowed clothing, showered, and put on his own clothing. He shook hands with Kyle Jorgensen again, thanked him, and was soon back in his pickup and on his way to Willow River.

How could he best write a story about what he had just seen? Clearly, he had been impressed with about every aspect of this big operation. Perhaps these big hog operations, with controlled temperatures, computer-operated feeding, and constant monitoring, were the future. After all, with an ever-increasing global population, people still need to eat. Jorgensen had reminded him of that several times. What more efficient way of producing pork than what he had just seen? He doubted there was one.

As he drove back to Willow River, he couldn't help thinking of the conditions at the Lazy Z feedlot, where feeder cattle stood in manure and mud up to their bellies when it rained and were moved from pen to pen with electric prods. Here, the pigs were clean, content, and certainly appeared to be treated humanely. Josh was confused. Large-scale farms were surely not all the same. He'd just seen proof of that. He knew what he must write, but he didn't know what he thought about it. Was he like Natalie, who confessed that she was two people—a DNR employee and her own person? He was a reporter and also someone with opinions—how could he avoid tangling the two?

Decision Time

After his visit to Nathan West's large production farm, Josh wrote a long piece that he titled "The Future of the U.S. Pork Industry?" The piece featured details of his visit to Nathan West Industries' big hog operation in Iowa and interviews with University of Wisconsin officials, plus the words of local citizens both for and against large-scale farming. In that same edition, he penned the following editorial, titled "Nathan West Industries as a Neighbor?"

The Ames County Zoning Committee meets on Tuesday evening, April 17, 7:00 p.m. in the community room of the Willow River Library. At this meeting, the committee will vote on whether to change the zoning of the former Tamarack River Golf Course from recreational to agricultural use. The Ames County Zoning Committee is facing one of its most important decisions. If it votes in favor, Nathan West Industries will build a large hog production unit on this site.

The committee has invited the public to a listening session, which will begin at 7:00 p.m. and continue until everyone has had his say, or 10:00 p.m. At that time the committee will dismiss the audience and make its decision.

Farm Country News attended the informational meeting held in January of this year about the potential for Nathan West's factory farm. The discussion was spirited, the views expressed diverse. *Farm Country News* sees the following as advantages and disadvantages of large, confined animal operations:

Decision Time

Advantages

- Factory farms ensure that food will be available at the lowest possible cost to the consumer, as these large farms are able to operate following a business model that emphasizes efficiency with all the advantages of large-scale production.
- A community with a factory farm becomes a symbol of the future and how food will be produced using the most modern genetics and the most advanced technological equipment for the feeding and care of animals.
- A factory farm employs a substantial number of workers in the community, contributing directly to the community's economy.
- On relatively few acres, a factory farm is able to produce an enormous amount of food.
- Consumers of food produced on large factory farms can be assured of a consistent supply throughout the year, whether eggs, pork, beef, milk, or poultry. There will be no times doing the year when the product is not available.
- Foods from factory farms, especially meat products, are conveniently packaged so the consumer can use them with little effort.
- Factory farms produce a uniform product. Pork chops purchased from a factory-farm supplier are essentially the same month after month, as are poultry, beef, and dairy products.
- In a world where population continues to increase, the only way food supplies will be able to keep up with demands is through means of large-scale production such as factory farms.

Disadvantages

- Factory farms, especially those producing animal products such as milk, eggs, and meat, produce an enormous amount of potential pollutants—especially manure. When not properly stored and managed, manure can pollute not only the air for miles around but also nearby streams and rivers and sometimes the groundwater.

- When a food product is produced in a centralized location, substantial transportation costs result from moving the product from producer to consumer. Food is often transported hundreds of miles before it reaches the consumer.
- Many factory farms are vertically integrated, which means one company, such as a pork producer, owns everything, from the farms growing the feed to everything along the production line, including the hogs—from the time the little pigs are born until the meat products are in the grocer's case. This can be an advantage for the pork producer, but it crowds out others, such as family farmers who want to raise hogs for market.
- Food safety can be a problem on factory farms. Because large numbers of animals are confined in one location, once a disease organism is established, it can raise havoc. A 2010 case of salmonella in eggs from factory farms in Iowa led to illness among hundreds of people who consumed the contaminated product. In another case, E. coli–related illness from contaminated hamburger resulted in the recall of thousands of pounds of that product.
- Many of today's meat and dairy products are in the hands of but a few large producers and distributors. The small family farm has been shoved aside, unable to produce a product as inexpensively as the factory farms.
- Animal protection groups consider factory-farm treatment of animals confined in close quarters—with no access to sunlight and fresh air—inhumane.

The day after the article and editorial appeared, Bert came into Josh's office carrying a copy of the newspaper. "Good writing," he said. "This ought to get people talking; at least now they've got some information, a better idea of how these big hog operations work."

"I did the best I could," Josh said. "I worked hard on these pieces."

"It shows. It's the kind of thing a newspaper can do well—get behind the scenes, dig out the facts. Keep the emotions and opinions at bay. I liked your summary of the situation, the advantages and disadvantages of factory farming."

"After doing a bunch of research, talking to the folks at the university, and visiting the big farm in Iowa, that's about the way I see it. I suspect some folks won't agree with what I wrote—but at least it should get them thinking," said Josh.

"Well, that's what a good newspaper is supposed to do. Give people the facts and then encourage them to make up their own minds," said Bert.

Tamarack Museum

A bright sun, a clear blue sky, and temperatures predicted to climb into the low fifties greeted Fred and Oscar when they climbed into Oscar's rusty old Ford pickup on a mid-April afternoon.

"Why'd you say we should go to Tamarack Corners today? Be a good day just to stand on the riverbank and watch the Tamarack hurry by," said Fred.

"Because we're gonna visit the museum, that's why. I told you that yesterday."

"You did? You sure? You sure you told me yesterday?"

"Fred, I think you're startin' to lose it. I for damn sure told you yesterday about what we had planned for today."

"How come we're visiting this museum, anyway?" asked Fred.

"'Cause there's something I want you to see."

"I don't care much for museums. They remind me too much of when I was a kid."

"What's wrong with that? You were a kid once, weren't you?"

"Yup, I was, but my old man had me workin' like a man by the time I got to be twelve years old."

"So did my old man, but that doesn't mean we weren't once kids. Besides it'll do you good to see this new museum, Fred. Do you good. Take your mind off your troubles."

"So, goin' to this museum is gonna cure my arthritis and fix my bad back."

"I didn't say that. I said it would take your mind off your troubles. Make you think about something different."

"So, now you're complainin' about how I'm thinkin'."

"Nah, just come on along and see the place, and maybe you'll learn something. Besides, I gave them one of my old hog troughs, a wooden one my dad made that we used for years to feed our pigs."

"So, that's the reason you're draggin' me along to the museum: to see that old trough you used to feed pigs. Hell, we had one just like it. Probably still sittin' out in the shed. Probably in better shape than yours, Oscar. Ours was about four to five feet long, made out of two pieces of wood, held together in a *V* shape, with square pieces nailed on each end to make it sturdy."

"Ours was just like that, and it's in the museum and yours ain't," Oscar said, smiling.

"Geez, going to a museum to see a hog trough. Your old one, besides."

"There's more at the museum than the hog trough, Fred. Lots more."

"Well, there'd better be. Hog troughs remind me of work, remind me of carrying two five-gallon pails of water, with a couple scoops of ground corn and oats dumped in each. Water'd spill on my pants when I walked from the pump house to the hog pen."

"Yup, I remember doin' the same thing. Especially remember how heavy them two pails was. My pa said carryin' two was easier than one. When you carried two, you were balanced—one hanging on the end of each arm. That's what he said. I expect he really just wanted me gettin' the work done faster."

"Something else I remember about our old trough," said Fred, the cobwebs in his mind receding into the shadows.

"What was that?"

"Them pigs of ours was always hungry, and when I came carrying them pails of slop they'd come a-runnin' from the far end of the pen—we had about twenty of 'em. Ran like bats outta hell they did. When I started pourin' the slop into the trough, they'd fight and bite and squeal. You had to stay out of the way, or you'd git yourself bit."

Oscar smiled when he heard the story. "Yup, same thing on our farm. Our pigs did the same thing. They'd bite each other's ears, push and shove, do the best they could so they'd be first at the trough. Every damn one of them wanted to be first."

"Something else I remember," said Fred. "The smell. God, do I remember the smell. Nothing stinks worse than pig manure. Mix a little mud in with it, and some spilled pig slop, and you got yourself a smell that lingers, stays with you down through the years. Never forget the smell of a pig pen. You just never do."

"I agree with you there, Fred. Which reminds me. Did you read the piece in the *Farm Country News* about that big hog farm in Iowa?"

"I did. That's the same outfit that's planning to put up a hog farm here in the valley. Pretty interesting story. That reporter guy, Wittmore, got himself inside one of their big operations. Sounds like Nathan West knows what they're doin' though. Remember what he wrote about how the pigs don't fight over what's in the trough, because there ain't no pig troughs, just a fancy feeding place where they git to eat, one at a time."

"I'm still not too sure we want one of them big operations here in the valley. Remember, we just had twenty or so pigs on our farms. They're planning to raise thousands of them," said Oscar. "And none of them ever gets to set foot outside. They never get to see the sun and the blue sky like we're seeing today."

"Oscar, you sound like you're stickin' up for the pigs. The only reason them pigs is on this earth is so we can eat 'em. That's all there's to it."

"Maybe so. But there's still something kinda nice when you see a bunch of pigs, maybe ten or a dozen or so, out in a green pasture with their little ones runnin' along behind 'em. Sight to see. Yup, a sight to see."

"Oscar, sometimes I wonder about you. You want our taxes to not keep goin' up, or not? You want people to have work so they can pay your bills? This is a new day. A new day. People are doin' things different from when we were kids. Them Nathan West folks appear to take good care of their pigs."

"Maybe so. But I'm still worried about all this. Worried where the country is headed with these big operations, these big factory farms jumpin' up all over the place," said Oscar.

The two old men drove on toward the museum in Tamarack Corners, neither saying anything. There was one other car in the small parking lot.

"Well, you ready to see my old hog trough?" Oscar asked, a big smile spreading across his face.

"Damn old hog trough. Seein' it will bring back a bunch of bad memories."

Zoning Committee Meeting

*E*mily, let's go over the material we're presenting at the Ames County Zoning Committee tonight," suggested Assistant Professor Randy Oakfield. "I need to be brought up to speed."

"There's no need," answered Emily Jordan. "I've checked the figures a couple of times. We're ready for this evening."

"Still, I'd like to look over the data."

"The surveys are in my apartment, and I just put my laptop with the PowerPoint presentation in the car. Trust me, everything is in good order."

*B*y 6:30 p.m., the community room of the Willow River Library was filled to capacity. The room had 150 chairs, with people standing in the back of the room. Josh sat in the front row with tape recorder and camera at the ready. Billy Baxter from the *Ames County Argus*, with a camera hanging around his neck, stood off to the side. Josh noticed Ben Wesley sitting toward the back, with a clipboard for note-taking. He also spotted Oscar Anderson, who had spoken up at the winter meeting. Several people coming into the room greeted Ben and shook his hand.

Cindy Jennings, member of the Ames County Board and chair of the Ames County Zoning Committee, called the meeting to order and made a few brief comments.

"We all know this is an important meeting, and we want to hear what you have to say. But please, let's be civil; don't interrupt when someone else is talking, and try not to repeat what someone else has said. And to make sure everyone has a chance to speak, we are holding you to three minutes. We have a timer: when it beeps, finish your sentence and please be seated. I'd add one more thing—please turn off your cell phones." She reached into her pocket, removed her Blackberry, and turned it off. "Almost forgot to turn mine off," she said, smiling.

Marcella Happsit, president of the Tamarack Historical Society, held up her hand and was the first to speak. "I would like to read a letter I recently received from Nathan West Industries," she began slowly:

Dear Ms. Happsit,

Thank you for the opportunity to visit your wonderful museum and your tour around your fine village. We at NWI wish to be good community neighbors.

As a small gesture of our good-neighbor policy, we are prepared to fund the building of a new library for Tamarack Corners, including the purchase of books and computers. We will also establish a fund to pay for library staff. Tamarack Corners has a rich history, going back to the logging days of the late 1800s. I've learned that the Tamarack River Trading Post supplied the logging crews that floated logs down the Tamarack River on their spring logging drives. The Trading Post replenished food supplies and sold the log drivers new clothing and equipment, such as axes and pike poles. We are prepared to fund the creation of a special exhibit about this rich history for your museum.

Also, as we have become acquainted with the village's history we have learned about Mortimer Dunn and the Tamarack River Ghost. We will fund the creation of a life-sized statue of Mortimer Dunn and his dog, to be placed in front of your museum.

Sincerely,
Ed Clark
Regional Representative
Nathan West Industries

"And," Marcella concluded, "we have already commissioned an artist to create the statue. This is a rare opportunity for the Tamarack Corners community. I can't see how we could possibly not favor Nathan West Industries becoming one of our neighbors."

A brief round of applause followed Marcella's comments.

The discussion began with questions and comments from every perspective. For Josh, it seemed a repeat of January's meeting, but this crowd was larger and the questions seemed better informed. It was clear that people had been doing their homework; some even quoted from *Farm Country News* about advantages or disadvantages of factory farming.

For nearly an hour, people stood, most voicing their opposition to Nathan West coming to their community. Some, impressed with the corporation's promise to contribute money to Tamarack Corners, seemed on the fence.

Shotgun Slogum raised his hand and slowly rose to his feet. "Most of you folks know me, and you also know that I am 100 percent opposed to this factory pig farm coming to our community. Those of you impressed with Nathan West's promises to the community should not be taken in. Do you know for sure NWI will keep its promises?" He turned to Marcella Happsit, who had a perplexed look on her face. "Of course you don't. Don't you see that this is merely a ploy to gain your approval, your good will? We need to send Nathan West packing. We don't need it stinking up our valley."

Another round of applause came from those who were adamantly opposed to Nathan West and its plans.

At 9:00, Cindy Jennings said, "I want to introduce Dr. Randy Oakfield, who is with the Department of Agribusiness Studies at the University of Wisconsin–Madison. Dr. Oakfield has been researching large hog operations for several months. His research has included surveying citizens here in Ames County. Dr. Oakfield."

Randy, with little experience talking to citizen groups, stood and walked to the microphone. He wore tan trousers and a dark brown corduroy jacket. His white button-down shirt was open at the top.

"Ladies and gentlemen," he said quietly, looking down at the notes he had put on the podium.

"Louder," someone in the back of the room said.

"Ladies and gentlemen," he said again with a bit more force. "My research assistant, Emily Jordan, and I have been studying citizens' reactions to large factory farms. We have not completed our final report—indeed there will likely be several of them—but we do have some preliminary results that I think you will find useful. I've asked Emily to share with you some of these early findings." He nodded toward her, and she stood and walked to the computer projector she had earlier set up and snapped it on. On the screen appeared the words "Preliminary Findings: Citizens' Reactions to Large-Scale Hog Farms."

"Hello, everyone," she said when she got to the podium. She had tied her red hair in a ponytail. And she wore a dark tan skirt with a matching blazer and a light tan blouse.

"How's everyone doing? Interesting meeting. Very interesting," she said. Where her professor seemed shy and tentative, she was bubbly and forthcoming.

"We've still got lots of work to do with these data, but we have some preliminary findings I think you'll find interesting." She looked around the room; everyone was looking in her direction, not only because it was a pleasant break from the previous often contentious discussion, but because she was easy to listen to.

"Let me tell you a little bit about how we put this research project together," she began. She very consciously avoided mentioning that the National Affiliated Hog Producers, of which National West Industries was a member, had financed the project. She didn't want to get into an argument about the pros and cons of an industry financing research that ultimately related to what that industry did.

She pushed a button on the projector's remote control, and a new slide appeared on the screen:

Survey Forms:
> One for Whistler County, Iowa
> One for Ames County, Wisconsin
> One for the Tamarack River Valley

We developed the first set of questions for Whistler County, Iowa, which has several large, confined hog operations. We developed a second set for

Ames County, Wisconsin, with a special subset for those living in the Tamarack River Valley. We didn't send the questionnaires to everyone, but rather to a randomly selected sample of the landowners. So you may not have gotten one of our forms. We asked several questions, but I believe the one of most interest to you is this one." She clicked the remote once more:

Whistler County, Iowa, Sample:
Do you approve of large, confined hog operations in your county?

"For Ames County and the subsample of folks living in the Tamarack River Valley, we asked—" She pushed the remote again:

Ames County, Wisconsin, and the Tamarack River Valley Sample:
Do you approve of a large, confined hog operation *coming* to Ames County?

"I'll bet you'd now like to see what we've learned? Right? So here goes." She once more clicked the remote.

Approval Percentages for Large, Confined Hog Operations in Whistler County, Iowa:
Yes—65 percent
No—30 percent
No opinion—5 percent

"Now let's move to Ames County."

Approval Percentages for Large, Confined Hog Operations Coming to Ames County, Wisconsin:
Yes—67 percent
No—20 percent
No opinion—13 percent

Approval Percentages for Large, Confined Hog Operations Coming to Tamarack River Valley:
   Yes—75 percent
   No—20 percent
   No opinion—5 percent

Once people had seen the numbers on the screen, some of them looked astonished that the numbers in favor were so high. Of course, this was the first time Randy had seen these preliminary figures, and he had a perplexed look on his face. The figures weren't close to what he would have guessed, but he remained quiet. He was kicking himself for not having insisted on seeing the numbers and how Emily had arrived at them.

Josh was also surprised. He had expected at best a fifty-fifty approval level for the entire county, with the Tamarack River Valley numbers falling and probably sixty-forty against. Remembering something about survey research from his college days, he held up his hand.

"Yes," Emily said.

"Can you tell us how accurate you believe these figures are?"

"I surely can. We have followed standard survey research protocols. The error rate is no more than plus or minus five percentage points. It's clear from our research that the people of Ames County, especially those living in the Tamarack River Valley, approve of large, confined hog operations."

"Thank you," Josh said.

"Any more questions?" asked Emily. She stood smiling, the picture of confidence.

Several more people asked questions about how they selected the people who received the forms and how confident she was that the results represented the "true" opinions of those living in Ames County and the Tamarack River Valley.

"I have every confidence in these results," Emily said.

After a few more questions, Cindy Jennings returned to the podium.

"Let's give this young woman and her professor a big round of applause for their hard work." The applause was muted. People were still shaking their heads, not believing that so many people in their county thought large, confined hog operations were a good thing.

Promptly at ten, Cindy declared the listening session closed. She thanked everyone for coming and informed them that the zoning committee would now move into closed session and hoped to have a decision yet this evening.

Back in their car, Randy and Emily, with Emily at the wheel, began their trip back to Madison.

"Well, that was quite a meeting," Emily said. "Nice bunch of folks up there in Ames County."

"Are you certain of those numbers? Those are the highest percentages in favor I've ever seen."

"Surprised me a little too," said Emily. "But statistics don't lie. Looks to me like the folks in Ames County, especially those in the Tamarack River Valley, want Nathan West to be one of their neighbors."

They drove on quietly through the cool April night, reaching Madison about 11:30. "How about stopping at my place for a nightcap?" asked Emily. She seemed not the least bit fatigued from their trip to Willow River and her presentation to a room full of people, many of them not happy about what they saw happening to their beloved valley.

"We should celebrate a little," she continued. "Most of the hard work of the research project is completed. The preliminary analysis is finished. We've given our first report to the public."

"Thank you, Emily. But I should be getting back to my place. I've got two committee meetings tomorrow, and you know how those can drag on."

"I owe you a lot, Professor Oakfield. You helped me every step of the way with this research project. Come on up to the apartment for a glass of wine. It's one small way I can say thank you."

"Oh, all right," said Randy.

Emily's apartment was in an older apartment building on Langdon Street, easy walking distance from the campus. Her apartment was on the second floor, its north-facing windows offering a glimpse of Lake Mendota. Emily unlocked the front door of the building. "Up these stairs," she said as she led the way to the hallway on the second floor and the door to her apartment. She opened the door, and they stepped inside. It was neat and tidy, not at all like some of the student apartments Randy had seen. It consisted of a moderate-sized living-dining room, a small kitchen, a bath, and, he assumed, one bedroom. A large painting of a farm scene hung over a new-looking leather sofa, and a stuffed Bucky Badger sat in a chair near the sofa. A wooden table with four chairs, they looked new, sat on one end of the living room, nearest the kitchen. A big-screen TV took up most of one wall in the living room. The apartment was considerably better furnished than any graduate student apartment Randy had ever seen.

"Would you like some merlot?"

"Sure," replied Randy. He didn't want to confess that he didn't know one wine from another.

"Take off your coat and relax. I'll be back in a minute."

Randy felt a bit uncomfortable. What if someone he knew, perhaps one of his students, had seen him enter the apartment with Emily? That would surely set tongues to wagging. He hadn't seen anyone on the street. Late Tuesday evenings were fairly quiet, even on Langdon Street.

Soon Emily returned. She had changed clothes and was carrying a bottle of wine and two glasses, plus some cheese and crackers. She wore a gray UW T-shirt and sweat pants.

She sat down at the table and poured the glasses half full.

"To our research project," she said.

They clinked their glasses.

"And a big thank you to my major professor," she said, raising her glass in a salute.

"Thank you," Randy said. He wondered how he could graciously leave without offending Emily, who had obviously earlier planned to have him stop by after their trip to Willow River.

Emily made sure Randy's glass remained filled, as they enjoyed cheese and crackers and chatted about the department, other research projects, and university life in general. Randy soon began to feel a little lightheaded— he had little experience with wine, or any other alcoholic beverage, for that matter.

As they talked, Emily put her hand on Randy's arm and told him again what a wonderful advisor he was, and what a great future he had in the department. Soon, her hand was on his, and he began to feel things he hadn't felt since he was in high school and had attended the junior prom with a blind date who, as it turned out, was looking for more than dancing. He could feel perspiration beading on his forehead.

An hour later, his head still spinning, Randy found himself in bed with Emily, and neither of them had on a stitch of clothing.

"We . . . we shouldn't have done this," he stammered.

"Why not," she said, smiling. Her long red hair lay mussed on a pillow.

"It's not . . . it's not right."

"I won't tell," Emily said. "Besides, wasn't it fun?" Emily giggled.

"I've . . . I've got to be going," Randy said as he began pulling on his clothes.

"See you tomorrow morning," Emily said. Smiling broadly and wrapped in a sheet, she walked him to the door.

Randy drove the couple of miles to his apartment on Mineral Point Road. His mind was a clutter of mixed thoughts.

Newspaper Demise

The morning after the listening session, Josh Wittmore was on the phone with Cindy Jennings, chair of the Ames County Zoning Committee.

"Did your committee vote last night?"

"We did. We voted four to one to approve the zoning change. The university research results took most of the wind out of the sails of those opposing the project. Didn't hurt that the company promised a pile of money to spiff up Tamarack Corners either," said Cindy, "but I was a little surprised at those research results."

"So was I. But the university wouldn't report erroneous figures. I've never known it to do that. Looks like Nathan West will have clear sailing from here on out," Josh said.

"It looks that way. Fellow from Nathan West called this morning too. Folks from the company will start building next week," said Cindy.

"I figured they would," said Josh. "They've already waited longer than they like for a decision."

"Democracy sometimes takes time," said Cindy.

"As it should," said Josh.

Josh turned on his computer and read an e-mail from the mysterious M.D. He checked for a return address and saw nothing but numbers and letters. The subject line read: "Something for Your Paper."

Sold Down the River

Sold down the river.
The vote was four to one.

Four people deciding.
Four people deciding the fate
Of the Tamarack River Valley.
Four people!
Can you believe it?
Democracy run amok.
Democracy at its worst.
Who wins: Big Business.
Who loses: We all do.
We are losing our beautiful
Tamarack River Valley.
What next?

Josh printed the e-mail and set it on the side of his desk. He'd show the piece to Bert and then find a place for it in the next edition of the paper, due out the end of the week. He wondered what he would write about the hearing at the library and the vote taken by the Ames County Zoning Committee. He took the M.D. piece and walked out into the hall and then to Bert's office. His door was closed—it was never closed. Josh knocked.

"Come in," a muffled voice said. It didn't sound like Bert. Josh wondered if his boss was sick. He opened the door and saw Bert with his head down on his desk.

"Are you all right?" Josh asked, surprised at what he saw.

"It's lost."

"What's lost?"

"Everything is lost, Josh. Everything is lost," said Bert as he lifted his head from the desk. His eyes were red. His gray hair was mussed. He put on his wire-rimmed glasses.

"What's lost, Bert?"

"Our paper. *Farm Country News* is gone. Gone forever."

"What happened?"

"Hector Cadwalader from the bank called about an hour ago. He said he couldn't lend me anymore money, that he'd given me too much already. He's pulled the plug on us, Josh. The paper is finished."

"What are we gonna do?"

"Nothing we can do. Everybody is out of work, myself included. Imagine, we've been in business since 1868; that's more than 140 years. More than a 140 years and now, just like that—poof. We're no more. Bank is gonna own us, what's left of us. Cadwalader said he would try to find a buyer. Who'd buy our rag? If we couldn't make it work, who does he think can?"

Bert looked like he was going to cry.

"I'm sorry," Josh said. "Just when we had a good story going too. I thought we'd turned the corner, that people were paying attention to us again."

"So did I," said Bert. "But paying attention doesn't pay the bills. Advertisements and subscriptions pay the bills, and, as you know, both have been disappearing the last couple years. Internet's done us in. People expect to get their news for free these days, right off their computers or their cell phones. And they read these goofy blogs that every Tom, Dick, and Jane write and they think they're getting the news. Or they listen to some horse's-ass radio guy shooting off his mouth about something that he hasn't bothered to research or think through. That's what people think is the news. Well, it isn't." Bert pounded his fist on the table. As he talked, his face got redder and redder.

Bert paused and then said, "Hector said the two of us should stay on to the end of the week, at least until we let everybody know that the paper is dead. He said we should do an inventory of what we have here in the office. He'd make sure we'd get paid until the end of the week."

"Want me to help you write letters to the bureaus to let them know what happened?" Josh interrupted, not knowing where Bert's tirade was going to take him.

"I would appreciate it if you'd do that. Draft the letters, and I'll sign them. Tell everyone how sorry I am that this happened and that I'd tried my best to keep the paper afloat and failed—use your own words. You're a better writer than I am."

Josh returned to his office, his mind in a muddle, He worried about Bert; he certainly wasn't taking the news well. He worried about his own career. What would he do? He had enough savings to last about four months, six on the outside, if he really skimped, and unemployment benefits would also help. He thought about Natalie and their relationship. He had even begun to think he might propose to her someday. But propose to someone when you don't have a job? She'd laugh at him, and he couldn't blame her.

He drafted a letter on his computer, taking the better part of an hour to do it. He knew Bert quite well, and he wanted to make sure that the letter sounded like his boss, not like him. He kept it simple, laying out the facts of the matter and explaining that everything possible had been done to keep the paper alive and well. He mentioned other newspapers that had folded and how journalism as a profession was suffering in the face of so much information available on the Internet, almost all of it free.

He printed a draft of the letter, knowing Bert would want to add some of his own phrases and perhaps leave out some of what Josh had written. Bert's office door was still closed. He knocked gently, then louder. But there was no answer. He opened the door and saw Bert, face-down on the desk; his glasses had twisted and broken when he'd fallen on them. His arms hung limp from his sides. Josh immediately called 911.

The next few days were a blur for Josh. In one day he had lost two dear friends: Bert had died of a heart attack, and the newspaper where he had worked since he graduated from college had folded. The people at the bank that now owned the defunct paper were reasonable. They turned the informing—termination letters to all the staff at the various bureaus—over to Josh. Josh preceded each letter with a phone call. He believed the staff members deserved to hear a real voice tell them what had happened and why they were losing their jobs.

Josh received a few e-mails with questions about what had happened. He was surprised to see an inquiry from the *Wall Street Journal* asking for details of the paper's closing, requesting a quotation about what he believed was happening in the newspaper world, even among newspapers such as *Farm Country News*, which had well-defined audiences.

Between business phone calls, Natalie called. "I'm so sorry to hear about Bert's death; he was one of the good guys," she said.

"He certainly was," said Josh. "I just can't believe he's gone. Just can't believe it. Bert took the demise of the newspaper pretty hard. He couldn't accept that the bank was closing down his life's work."

"What about you, Josh? You okay?" Natalie asked. She had genuine concern in her voice. "You want to stop by tonight? I'll fix you supper."

"I can't. I've got too much to do. The bank wants everything inventoried and organized by week's end. I'm only about half done, and I'm the only one here. Everyone's gone."

"Well, I'm thinking about you, Josh."

"Thank you," Josh said. He was thankful that Natalie didn't ask him what he was going to do with the rest of his life, now that he was out of work with no job prospects in mind. While he was inventorying newspaper archives, photo archives, computer equipment—a rather mindless job—he thought about his prospects. The more he thought about it, the more depressed he got. His job had been a rather specialized one, within a rather specialized area of journalism—agricultural reporter. The handful of other magazines and newspapers that focused on farming and agriculture also struggled to keep afloat. They surely weren't looking for any laid-off farm reporters.

New Journalism

Shortly after noon on Friday, Josh's phone rang. At least the bank hadn't disconnected the phone, not yet anyway.

"This is Josh Wittmore."

"This is Hector Cadwalader, over at the bank. Could you stop by my office this afternoon, say around 3:00?"

"Sure," Josh said. He thought that Cadwalader wanted the inventory reports he been working on all week and probably wanted to hear how the former staff members had taken the news about losing their jobs. He hurried to finish the last of the equipment inventory, gathered up the lists, and put them in a folder. At 2:58, he was in the lobby of the Ames County Bank and Trust. The bank building, one of the prominent structures on Main Street, had housed the bank since 1912. It was built of quarried rock, built the way many banks of its era were: banks needed to show strength and power and let people know at first glance that if they put their money there, it would be safe. The bank's lobby had been completely remodeled within the past year; it was as up to date as any new bank in the area. Josh stopped at the information desk, where a young woman worked at a computer.

"Can I help you?" She had a pleasant smile and a kind of welcome-to-our-living-room style of speaking.

"I'm Josh Wittmore. I have an appointment with Mr. Cadwalader."

"Yes, he's expecting you." She motioned toward an open office door on the right side of the lobby.

Josh approached the door where he saw a man with thick, graying hair sitting behind a huge, wooden desk. When he saw Josh at the door, he stepped from behind his desk and thrust out his hand. He was several inches taller than Josh and as thin as a fence post.

"I'm Hector," he said. "I don't think we've met, but I remember working with your dad some years ago. How's he doing?"

"Oh, Pa's hanging in there," Josh replied. "He and my mother are mostly retired now." Josh glanced around the office and for the first time saw another man sitting off to the side of the desk. The man was smiling as he stood up.

"Meet Lawrence Lexington," said Cadwalader.

Josh and Lexington shook hands. Josh noticed that Lexington's handshake was firm, but his hands were soft. He stood maybe five feet ten, a little shorter than Josh. He was nearly bald; Josh took him to be about fifty years old. Josh was now puzzled. He thought his meeting with Cadwalader would be about inventories and such.

"Mr. Lexington lives in New York, but he plans on moving to Ames County, he tells me."

"Ames County is a good place to live. I was born and raised here and moved back last year," offered Josh.

"Well, let's all sit down and see if we can figure something out," said Cadwalader.

"Mr. Lexington was an investment banker, and he is now looking for new opportunities, new challenges."

"That's right," said Lexington. "Besides, I've had it with New York City. Some people like that place. I'm not one of them. It's time to leave, make a career change. And it looks to me like the Midwest is a place where money can be made."

"Mr. Lexington—" began Cadwalader.

"Call me Lawrence; everybody calls me Lawrence."

"Lawrence," Cadwalader began again, "has expressed an interest in purchasing *Farm Country News.*"

"Really," said Josh. He was a little skeptical.

"Lawrence, tell Josh a little bit about your plans—and I must say, we here at the bank are selling at a good price. A bank doesn't want to be in the publishing business."

"Thank you, Hector. Josh, here's what I have in mind for *Farm Country News*, if I purchase it. First, we are going almost entirely electronic, with the exception of one monthly print edition during the transition time. We are doing away with deadlines and publishing dates. As news becomes available, we will put it up on the *Farm Country News* website. And there will be no advertising."

"No advertising?" Josh interrupted. "Decline in advertising revenues is what killed the paper."

"That's right, Josh. No advertising. We will try an entirely new model—one that, to the best of my knowledge, has never been tried before. We'll be trendsetters in the industry."

Cadwalader sat listening intently. Josh, always the skeptic, wondered what possible new funding model this fast-talking fellow from New York had in mind.

"Lots of people want to be published these days. Lots of them. Some have their own blogs and their own websites. They e-mail their stuff to every person they've ever met. But what they lack is a legitimate publisher. People are skeptical of these unedited, never-fact-checked pieces of writings. When you read something in the *Wall Street Journal* or the *New York Times*, or the *Atlantic Monthly*, you believe it. You know the piece, at least most of the time, has been well researched and carefully edited."

"So how do you make money with this model, if I could be so bold to ask?" said Josh.

"You charge writers to have their material printed in the paper. Doesn't matter if it's a letter to the editor, a story about a new agriculture business, a new idea on the farm—you charge to have it printed. They pay so much a word to see their stuff in print."

"What about the editing, the fact-checking? Keeping our journalistic integrity? Somehow, it doesn't seem right that people should pay to have a news story published. How is what you're saying different from selling and printing ads?

"Josh, this is the new journalism. The paper's staff will be responsible for making sure the material is accurate and well edited. It's a new way of making certain we have an income stream sufficient to make a profit. It's the future, Josh."

Josh wasn't quite sure he understood what he was hearing. He had many more questions.

"Something else," Lexington continued. "At the end of each month, we'll select the best pieces, the best stories we've run online, and put them in our print edition. We'll distribute the print edition free at all the feed stores, all the implement dealers, the banks—everywhere farmers and agriculture people gather."

"What about photographs?" asked Josh. "People expect photos these days."

"Same plan. Anybody wants to submit a photo for publication, he's welcome. The photographer will pay to have his or her photo published, of course."

"I don't know," said Josh. "What about those stories that need to be told, the ones that require digging and careful writing, the ones like our stories about Nathan West Industries? What about those kinds of stories?"

"The staff will research and write them, but we won't have as many of that kind of story. Journalism is changing, Josh. Changing as the world becomes electronic."

Lexington went on describing his ideas for a "modern" *Farm Country News*. "We'll have no bureaus," he explained. "Everything will take place at headquarters here in Willow River. By eliminating the bureaus and all those employees, we will reduce our overhead by at least 75 percent— salaries cut into profits. We all know that. I'm thinking of a staff of about five or six at the office here in Willow River: a managing editor, an assistant editor, a fact checker, a copyeditor, and a couple computer geeks to make sure everything gets online when it should. Of course, I will also plan to work in the office."

"Well and good," said Josh, still quite skeptical of the plan. "But why are you telling me all this?"

"I want you to be our managing editor," said Lexington. "I want you to run the paper. Make it work. Make it hum. And have it make money."

Josh sat speechless; he'd thought Cadwalader had invited him to the meeting to discuss inventories. He had no idea he'd be offered a job.

"I'll . . . I'll have to think about it," Josh finally said.

"Let me know by next week," said Lexington. He handed Josh his business card with e-mail addresses and phone numbers. "I doubt I'd be interested in buying the paper without having you at the helm. We need somebody who knows both agriculture and journalism. And you're the guy. No question about it. I read some of the stories you've written. You are definitely our guy."

The three men shook hands all around. Josh got into his pickup and drove to his apartment. He didn't notice that a warm southerly wind had moved into Ames County, bringing with it the rest of spring, which had been reluctant to show its face, for fear of another late snowstorm.

Fred and Oscar

*F*red Russo drove over to Oscar Anderson's farm for a visit. The two of them sat on Oscar's back porch, each in a rocking chair as the late April sun slipped behind the horizon and a warm breeze swept over them. Spring was in the air.

"You planning on plantin' a garden this year, Fred?" asked Oscar.

"Thinkin' about it. Always plant a garden. Never missed a year yet."

"It's a little late to put in potatoes—wanna get them in by mid-April so they get a good start before them damn potato bugs come around to feast on 'em."

"Still April ain't it, Oscar? Don't wanna hurry these things too much. Garden plantin' is not for hurryin'. It's for taking your time and enjoyin' it."

"Suit yourself, Fred. I don't much care when you plant your garden."

"Well don't get all het up about it. You got your potatoes in? You planted your spuds?"

"Yes, I have. I planted 'em yesterday. Got five rows of them in."

"Five rows! What in hell you gonna do with five rows of potatoes?" asked Fred, looking straight at his friend.

"I like potatoes. Eat 'em three times a day in the fall and winter. Potatoes are good for you. Keep you fit."

"Yeah, I guess they do," said Fred.

The two rocked for a few minutes without saying anything. "Squeak, squeak, squeak," the worn rocker runners ran over the uneven floor boards on the porch. A whip-poor-will called from the distance. Otherwise the evening was still, except for the little breeze that rustled the still-bare oak limbs of the tree in the yard and the sound of the rockers gently caressing old porch boards.

"Two things I wanna ask you about, Fred. Get your opinion."

"You already asked me one—asked about my potatoes—what's the second one?"

"I got two more things on my mind."

"Oscar, I didn't think your mind could handle all that at the same time. Didn't think you could keep three ideas straight."

"There's only two ideas. Two ideas, Fred."

"So, what's in your craw? What's roaming around in that big empty head of yours?"

"You hear about the zoning committee vote on Tuesday night?"

"Yup, I did. Heard it on the radio. I bet you were at the meeting."

"I was. You should have been there too."

"I had other things to do. I'm pretty busy these days," said Fred, smiling.

"Up until that cute redheaded chick from the university stood up and showed us her numbers, among other things, I thought the discussion was leaning toward opposing the big hog farm. But then she got everybody's attention with them numbers, showin' that most people are in favor of big hog farms—according to some kind of survey she and her young professor conducted."

"Hear the committee voted to rezone the land and give the pig people a big green light to build."

"That it did, and it's a dirty shame. We don't need no big hog farm here in the Tamarack River Valley. You mark my words, next year if we're sitting here on your porch we're not gonna be smelling spring; we're gonna be smelling hog manure."

"Expect that's the price of progress," Fred said. "The price of progress."

"The old Tamarack River Ghost's not gonna like the decision. Not gonna like it one bit."

"You still believe in that old ghost, don't you, Oscar? You still think that ghost is the real McCoy."

"Yup, I do. The ghost's still out there. He's out there, all right. And I'll bet he's concerned. More than a little concerned."

"How do you know that, Oscar? You talk to him?" Fred chuckled.

"No, I ain't talked to him. But I feel it. Feel it in my bones. I can feel what that old Tamarack River Ghost is thinkin'."

Fred shook his head but didn't say anything. Sometimes he wondered if his old friend was going off the deep end on this ghost thing.

The two men sat quietly for a time, gently rocking and enjoying the evening.

"Thought you had two ideas you wanted to talk about. Two besides potatoes."

"I do, but I didn't wanna spring 'em both on you too close together. Wanted you to have time to mull things over a little before I brought on another thought."

"Geez, Oscar, whaddya think, I'm stupid or something? Spit out what you got to say."

"It's about the newspaper. *Farm Country News*."

"Hey, that reminds me. It was supposed to come today. It didn't. Delivery guy must have missed me."

"The paper's dead, and so is its publisher. Bank took over the paper, and Bert Schmid had a heart attack and died."

"I hadn't heard. That newspaper's been coming to our place since I was a kid and even before that. I think I heard Pa say once that Grandpa subscribed to *Farm Country News*."

"Well, the paper's gone. It closed down. The bank's got it. Don't know what the bank's gonna do with it. Can't see the bank runnin' a newspaper."

"Oscar, how we gonna find out what's going on in farming? How we gonna find that out, with no farm newspaper coming every week?"

"I don't know, Fred. Don't know where everything is headed. Don't look good, Fred. Don't look good."

Different Results

The morning after the zoning committee meeting in Willow River, Emily Jordan punched in a phone number in Dubuque.

"Hello, Nathan West Industries, Robert Jordan."

"Uncle Bob, how are you?"

"I'm just fine, Emily. How'd the meeting go last night?

"It worked. My little number manipulation did the trick. Just heard on the radio that the zoning committee voted four to one to approve the zoning change. We can start building immediately."

"Good news, Emily. What a great idea to have you work undercover as a graduate student! Worked wonders in Ohio; working in Wisconsin, too."

"We may have a problem, though."

"What's that?" said Robert Jordan, some of the glee gone from his voice.

"This dorky assistant professor I'm working for wants to refigure everything. I'll try to stonewall it, but the guy will likely find out that I tampered with the data. My hope is he'll be too scared to tell anybody."

"Let him tell somebody. What difference does it make? The committee has voted."

"This will likely end my days as a graduate student."

"So, you'll be back in the head office a little sooner than we planned. Not a problem. We've got lots for you to do. Nobody knows you work for NWI, do they?"

"Not a soul. And I won't tell them either. I've got a wild story about why I changed the numbers if they push me, but nobody will find out about why I really did it."

"Good work, Emily. I knew we could count on you. This will probably earn you a promotion—certainly a bump in salary."

"Thank you, Uncle Bob. Always good to talk with you. Say hello to Aunt Mary for me."

*R*andy was in his office by 7:00 a.m. the morning following the meeting at Willow River and the little celebration in his graduate student's apartment. He tried to move that latter bit out of his mind, for he knew well the consequences of a professor sleeping with his student, especially a graduate assistant he supervised. If there was ever a reason for dismissal, it was just that. The university had strict rules about sexual harassment, and he had clearly violated one of the most serious ones. His only hope was that no one would find out.

Randy immediately looked for the returned questionnaires he and Emily had been working on. He had not had time to examine them and had left much of the early analysis to Emily. Now he wished he had said "no" to a couple of committee assignments so he could have had more time to work on the research project. Emily had come with such high recommendations for her research skills that he had trusted her to do the early analysis correctly. Still, the project was in his name, and he should have reviewed the preliminary results before she presented them. Perhaps Emily had made an error; there was always that possibility. He needed to go through the returns himself and check what he found against Emily's work. The university demanded accurate research, checked many times and often by several people.

He walked over to the administrative assistant's desk. "Do you know where Emily Jordan has filed the returned questionnaires from our research project?"

"Sorry, I don't," she said as she reached to answer the phone. It seemed the phone never stopped ringing at the main desk of the Department of Agribusiness Studies. So much for cell phones and text-messaging replacing all land lines.

He waited until she had hung up. "Do you know if Emily is expected in this morning?"

"I'll check her schedule—don't you have a copy in your office?"

"Probably, but you know my office." He smiled when he said it, because everyone knew that his office was not the most tidy and organized in the department.

"She should be in by nine this morning," the administrative assistant said, reaching to answer the phone again. "This one's for you," she said as she covered her hand over the mouthpiece.

Randy returned to his office and picked up the phone.

"This is Ben Wesley, county agent in Ames County. I was at the meeting in Willow River, and I've been getting lots of calls about the research report you and your graduate assistant shared last night. I have a question for you."

"Yes?" Randy tried to make his voice sound professional.

"About the numbers your assistant was sharing last night."

"Yes," Randy said again, but he could feel the color draining from his face.

"Do you stand by these numbers? I remember you saying they were preliminary."

"Yes, yes, we do." Randy knew his answer and tone of voice did not sound convincing. How could they be, when he, too, had some serious questions about the numbers' accuracy?

"Will you be providing a more complete report of the study in the near future?"

"Yes, we will."

"Do you have an idea of when that might be?"

"As soon as we've had a chance to analyze all the data. Final report should be ready in a couple months." Randy tried to remain calm.

"Could you make sure to send a copy to my office?"

"We certainly will." Randy was sweating. He wondered how many calls like this he would get. He wished he hadn't agreed to have Emily share anything about the research project until they had analyzed all of it, carefully thought about it, and had others check the report for accuracy.

The return rate for the questionnaire seemed a bit high for the Tamarack River Valley, but he knew these people were the most divided about a new hog facility coming into their community, so they would be more likely to respond.

But where were the returned questionnaires? He checked the area around Emily's desk; the forms would fill several file boxes, so they should be easy to spot. He looked in the machine room, where the department kept the copy machine, fax machine, and other such equipment. No boxes there. No boxes anywhere. Randy had been extremely busy with his courses and committee work the last couple of weeks. He had seen the pile of mail—the returned questionnaires coming in—and he had asked Emily to take care of logging each one in and filing it. But where? He was becoming frustrated. Just then Emily, her usual bubbly self, entered the main office.

"Good morning, Professor Oakfield," she said, a big smile on her face. She was the picture of radiance and positive attitude. Department Chair Evans had recently commented at a department meeting: "I wish all our graduate students had a personality like Emily. Always upbeat. Always optimistic. Some of our graduate students mope around like the end of the world is just around the corner."

"Emily, could you come into my office," Randy said.

"Sure, what's up?"

"Please close the door."

"This sounds serious."

"I've already gotten a call about the preliminary numbers from the research project that you reported last night in Willow River."

"A call about what?"

"The caller, he was polite about it, wanted a bit more information. He . . . he was questioning the accuracy of the numbers."

"The accuracy of the numbers? I checked everything twice. The numbers are accurate." She looked right at Randy when she spoke, her green eyes flashing.

"Where are the returned questionnaires? Do you have a spreadsheet on your computer? I'd like to spend some time with the results myself. We've got to be completely sure of our work before we make any more of it public."

"The questionnaires are at my apartment; that's where I've been doing the work the last several days. I'll bring them in tomorrow."

"Could you bring the questionnaires in this afternoon? I'll help you, or we can ask another graduate student to help."

"I believe I am capable of carrying four boxes of papers," Emily said curtly. "Is there anything else?"

"No, nothing else."

Emily got up, opened the door, and left. Randy, never one with much finesse in personal relationships, felt bad that he had so clumsily handled the simple request of bringing the survey materials to the office. He sensed that Emily believed that he was questioning her research and especially her data analysis skills.

When he returned from lunch, Randy found a big box of returned questionnaires on his desk with a little note: "Here's some of them. I'll bring in the rest tomorrow—I'm having a little trouble finding them."

Randy read the note. How could Emily have misplaced the rest of them? He shouldn't have allowed the returned questionnaires to leave the office. He remembered he'd said nothing about where they should be filed when they arrived. All that he remembered saying to Emily was that she should carefully log in each returned questionnaire, recording its number and date. He trusted her to take good care of the materials. Now he realized that "taking good care of the materials" should have included the stipulation that they not leave the office.

After two days and several more phone calls requesting more detailed information about the results of the research, he had all the returned questionnaires—at least, he hoped so. He divided them into three piles: Whistler County, Iowa; Ames County, Wisconsin; and the Tamarack River Valley. Randy knew they had mailed twelve hundred questionnaires: five hundred to the sample in Whistler County, another five hundred to rural landowners in Ames County, and a final two hundred to property owners living in the Tamarack River Valley. He remembered Emily sharing the return percentages with him—50 percent from Whistler County, 55 percent from Ames County, and 62 percent from the Tamarack River Valley.

He counted the questionnaires in each pile and noted the percentages: Whistler County = 250 (50 percent); Ames County = 275 (55 percent); Tamarack River Valley = 124 (62 percent). So far, Emily's numbers were accurate.

He started with the questionnaires for Ames County and on a tally sheet he'd developed began recording the answers to one question: "Do you approve of a large, confined hog operation coming to the Tamarack River Valley?" Although Emily reported just three categories—"yes," "no," and "no opinion," actually people responded in five categories: "strong yes," "yes," "no opinion," "no," and "strong no." For reporting purposes, especially for preliminary reports, the two positive categories and the two negative categories were often combined.

In a couple of hours he had the results:

Ames County (275 respondents):
>   Strong yes—15 percent
>   Yes—25 percent
>   No opinion—5 percent
>   No—30 percent
>   Strong no—25 percent

He added the two positive categories together as well as the two negative categories and compared his numbers to those Emily had reported at the Willow River meeting:

Ames County:

Oakfield	Jordan
Yes—40 percent	Yes—67 percent
No opinion—5 percent	No opinion—13 percent
No—55 percent	No—20 percent

Randy went over his figures one more time, trying to see where his graduate assistant had come up with her numbers. He simply couldn't do it, at least not for the Ames County figures. He began examining the returned questionnaires for the Tamarack River Valley and came up with the following, which he compared to Emily's numbers:

Tamarack River Valley (124 respondents):

Oakfield	Jordan
Yes—40 percent	Yes—75 percent
No opinion—5 percent	No opinion—5 percent
No—55 percent	No—20 percent

Finally, Randy turned to the returned questionnaires from Whistler County, Iowa, once more only tabulating the responses to the question about approval of confined hog operations in their county.

Whistler County (250 returns):

Oakfield	Jordan
Yes—55 percent	Yes—65 percent
No opinion—10 percent	No opinion—5 percent
No—35 percent	No—30 percent

Once more, Randy double-checked his figures for accuracy, then he thought, *Emily's got to have made a major error, or I have totally missed how she did her calculations.* He began to perspire. He was well aware that the numbers Emily shared at the zoning committee hearing had a considerable effect on the final decision to allow Nathan West to build in the Tamarack River Valley.

Randy hadn't even taken time to break for dinner; he worked until 9:00 p.m., figuring and refiguring and trying to determine how his assistant had come up with numbers so different from his. He didn't want to believe the unbelievable, that she had manipulated the numbers. If she had, she surely must have known that she would be found out, and she also must surely know the consequences of such action. Not only would she lose her research assistantship and the opportunity to work toward her doctorate degree at the University of Wisconsin, but, with this serious blemish on her record, she would likely never be accepted at another research institution.

But if, indeed, Emily had made an honest error—he must talk to her about all this before jumping to any more conclusions—his own career would be in serious jeopardy. If she had consciously manipulated the numbers and then reported them, not only was she responsible, but he, too, as the research project supervisor, the principle investigator, would be in serious trouble. Ultimately, he was responsible for every research report, small and large, that came out of his office. It was his duty to make sure that those under his watch were acting honestly, ethically, and with complete accuracy. He had trouble sleeping as these thoughts swirled in his mind.

Randy was in his office at 6:30 the following morning, once more checking over his calculations to make sure they were absolutely correct. He was not looking forward to the meeting he knew he must have with his graduate assistant. In the back of his mind, he had a glimmer of hope that her numbers were correct and that she had used a different strategy than he had for coming up with them. But he couldn't imagine what that would be.

Emily arrived at the office promptly at eight, greeting the office staff and saying hello to any of the professors who were already at work.

"Good morning, Professor Oakfield," she said when she saw him. "My, you have a glum look on your face this morning."

"Could you stop in my office as soon as you have a minute?" Randy said.

"Sure can," she said. "How about as soon as I get a cup of coffee?"

She appeared at Randy's office door with cup in hand. "Do I need a notepad?" she asked, smiling.

"No, just close the door and have a chair."

"Why the serious look?" Emily was the picture of innocence.

"We've got problems," Randy said. "Serious problems."

"How so?"

"I've spent the last two days going over our questionnaire returns, and something doesn't make sense to me."

"And what would that be?" Now Emily had a serious look on her face.

"Can you explain to me how you arrived at the numbers you presented at the Willow River meeting?"

"Sure, but what seems to be the problem?"

"First, tell me how you did the calculations."

"Well, let's see," Emily began. "As the questionnaires arrived in the office, I logged them in. Once we passed the deadline to receive them, I did a simple count and figured the return-rate percentages for each of our three samples."

"Here we agree completely. We came up with the same percentages," said Randy. "But then what did you do? At the moment I'm only interested in the question about positive or negative responses to confined hog operations in the three communities we surveyed. Let's start with Ames County, Wisconsin."

"Nothing fancy at all. I didn't do anything fancy. I simply recorded the responses from each person on a computer spreadsheet."

"Yes, I did the same thing, except I did it by hand. Then what did you do?"

Emily hesitated a moment before answering because she knew full well where the conversation was headed. "I added the 'strong yes' and 'yes' responses together for the entire group, and I did the same for the 'strong no' and 'no.'"

"I did the same thing," said Randy. "In fact, I added these numbers three times to make sure I was correct. Do you know what I found?"

"What?" asked Emily curtly. All appearances of pleasantness had drained from her face.

"I'll put it bluntly," Randy said. He tried to catch Emily's eyes but she was staring at her hands, which she held in her lap. "Your numbers are very different from mine. Let's take the Tamarack River Valley results, for instance. Your figures say that 75 percent of the respondents are in favor of confined hog operations. My figures show only 40 percent. How do you explain that?"

For a long moment, Emily continued looking at her hands and said nothing.

"I can't," she finally said quietly.

"You can't," said Randy, with an incredulous tone to his voice.

"That's right, I can't. And I don't want to." She raised her voice.

"You what?"

"You heard me. I can't explain my figures, and I don't want to." Her voice had changed from quiet research assistant to confrontational.

"So, what's going on?"

"What's going on? How naïve can you be? You young assistant professors are all the same. Dumb and naïve. I came up with the same figures you did, and then I changed them a little. Made it look like the people of Ames County, and especially those living in the Tamarack River Valley, really wanted to see a new industry come their way."

A different Emily than the one Randy had come to know was now speaking, and he was more than a little concerned about what he was hearing.

"But why? Why would you do that?"

"Because I believe the folks in the Tamarack River Valley deserve a boost to their economy. This big Nathan West operation will change everything for them, give them a glimpse into the future, a chance to change their outlooks. Don't you think this happens all the time? These people don't know what they want; how can they? Most of them have never left the valley. How could they know about a better life? Sometimes people need others to show them the way. Show them a better life in spite of themselves."

Randy couldn't believe what he was hearing; it didn't make sense. Surely she must have another reason for doctoring the data. But what would that be?

"Don't you know the risks you've taken in doing this, both for yourself and for me?" Randy asked.

"Risks, what risks? Do you see what I have here?" She reached into her purse and pulled out an iPad.

"Looks like an iPad to me."

"How right you are."

"So what's that got to do with what we're talking about?"

Emily used her index finger to unlock the device, then she touched the video icon on the screen, which opened up a folder. She selected one and opened it. "Here, have a look," she said as she passed the device to Randy.

"Where'd this come from . . . where'd you get this?" Randy blurted out. His face turned a bright red as he looked at a full-color video. It was dark and grainy, but he could quickly see that both he and his graduate student were easily recognizable and doing something he hoped no one else would see.

"I'm sure you remember what happened in my bed a few nights ago. Well, what you didn't know was that I recorded it all. I've got several copies, as well. That's why I'm not worried about what I did. You say one word about me changing numbers on the research report, and a DVD of this little event will appear mysteriously on our department chairman's desk."

"You wouldn't," said Randy. He could feel perspiration beading on his forehead.

"Try me. Just try me." Emily grabbed back her iPad and left the office.

Randy pounded his hand against his head. "What is going on?" he said aloud.

"Who is Emily Jordan? Surely not the person I've come to know."

34

Spring Snowstorm

Although May was right around the corner, the last Wednesday in April was unusually chilly, even for central Wisconsin. Only two days earlier, after many area farmers had their potato and oat crops planted and vegetable growers had their peas and early sweet corn in, it snowed two inches, destroying anybody's hopes that maybe this year spring would succeed in pushing winter aside before May. The snow stayed; it didn't melt as it fell. It accumulated and even threatened to make those who put away their shovels find them again. The April snow put everyone in a deep funk, including Fred and Oscar, who sat at their regular Wednesday-morning table in Christo's.

"So whaddya make of the snow, Oscar?" Fred asked.

"Not much. Don't think much of it at all. Kind of pretty, though. Kind of a pretty snow, all white and fluffy."

"Oscar, you are losin' it. This time of year, no damn snow is pretty. Not one little bit pretty. People are sick to death of snow. They want spring. People have had it with winter," said Fred.

"I suppose so," said Oscar. "I can sure tell you don't want no more winter."

"You sure got that right, Oscar."

With coffee refills, the two old men gazed out the window at the bright sun working hard to melt any last snow remnants from the restaurant's lawn that fronted the Tamarack River, now running full and fast.

"Say, Fred, did you get a copy of *Farm Country News* in the mail yesterday?"

"I did. Good to see them back in business. I need to read a farm paper every week, see what's going on. See what the farmers are gettin' for their milk, that sort of thing. Check on the price for live hogs."

"Did you read it?"

"Sure, skimmed right through it. Looked for stuff that's interesting to me. The way I always did. Not much to it, I must say. Read it all in about fifteen minutes. Didn't find what I kinda liked reading every week, though. Didn't find it."

"What was that?"

"That stuff this M.D. guy wrote almost every week. I like that guy's spunk. Lotta spunk there. Even liked his attempts at poetry. I liked the farm cartoons too. Guy who draws them is from Iowa—gave me a chuckle every week. Yes they did. Everybody needs a chuckle once in a while. At least once a week."

"So you really didn't read much of the farm news?"

"Didn't say that. Said I skimmed the farm news," said Fred.

"You wanna hear what the new owner has planned for the paper?"

"Do I have a choice? I know you're gonna tell me."

Oscar took a long drink of coffee. "First off, this is the last copy of *Farm Country News* you're gonna find in your mailbox."

"Last copy. I thought this was the first one under new ownership; I did glance at the part about new ownership."

"The paper is gonna be in electronic format, with only one print edition a month."

"In what kind of format?"

"Electronic, which means you will have to read it on your computer."

"I don't own no damn computer. Don't intend to buy one either."

"Then you'll see *Farm Country News* just once a month, and it won't come to your mailbox either. You'll have to pick it up at the feed store, or the John Deere dealer, or the bank. And it will be free."

"Free, huh? Sounds like that's what it will be worth."

"It's the wave of the future, Fred. The way newspapers in the country are headed."

"What about all us old timers who don't, and never will, have computers? What about us?"

"Guess you'll have to buy one, Fred."

"So I gotta buy a computer to read news about farmin', and I get to read the *Farm Country News* on a TV screen."

"Something like that, Fred."

"Where's it gonna end, Oscar? When's all this newfangled stuff gonna quit comin' at us? It's about to drive me just a little crazy."

"You sure it hasn't already, Fred?"

"You want a kick in the leg, Oscar?" Fred picked up his coffee cup and looked out the window at the Tamarack River.

"You got your fishin' license yet, Fred? Opening day for trout fishin' is coming up before you can say 'dig for some more worms.'"

"Don't you worry about me none; I'll have my license in plenty of time. Wouldn't want to miss opening day on the Willow River Millpond for anything."

"That old millpond sure attracts fishermen, just like flies to a cow pie. They come from all over: Oshkosh, Fond du Lac, Appleton, Madison, Milwaukee. Come from all over to try and catch one of those little native brook trout," said Oscar.

"Not something a person would want to miss, seein' all those folks trying to catch a fish. Something to see, for sure," said Fred as he set down his coffee cup and stood up.

"Where you goin'?"

"Home."

"Why?"

"'Cause that's where I live, and I've got stuff to do. I'm a busy guy, or haven't you noticed?"

"Nope, I haven't noticed," said Oscar, smiling. Both old men left the restaurant laughing.

35

Confession

*R*andy spent two sleepless nights after his office meeting with his graduate student. She admitted she had doctored the research results she had reported at the Willow River meeting. Even more disturbing, she had threatened that if he told anyone about her manipulation of research data, she would make sure the chair of the Department of Agribusiness Studies would get an incriminating DVD.

Her reasons for tampering with the data didn't make sense. Did she really believe she was helping the citizens of the Tamarack River Valley with her actions? What should he do? For three days, he rolled the alternatives around in his mind: not say anything to anyone about Emily's admission of changing research numbers, say that she had made an honest mistake and reveal the true numbers, or go to the department chair and tell the truth in all its gory detail.

He considered the ramifications of each. If he said nothing, the phone calls about the research data would keep coming in. He would need to have an answer for these callers, and he didn't have one.

He could make a case for the second alternative. He could say that in their haste to put together the numbers for the meeting, they had simply made some honest mistakes in analyzing the survey data. He would apologize, probably get a reprimand from the department chair, and the whole thing would blow over—he hoped. But Emily was still the un-known. What would she do? She had incriminating evidence against him and could, and probably would, hold it over his head throughout her PhD program. What if she ran into difficulty with a required course—say, advanced statistics? Would she come to him and say she would tell the world about their little roll in the hay if he didn't make the problem she was having go away?

The third alternative would be to go to Professor Evans and tell him what had happened, that his graduate student had manipulated the numbers—on purpose. That it was not an error. He wouldn't mention that he and Emily had slept together. That little error in judgment he would keep to himself, unless Emily filed a sexual harassment suit against him. Then everything would hit the fan. He knew the university's rules about sexual harassment; breaking them was grounds for dismissal. He would be looking for another job, and with this blemish on his record, finding another university research position would be difficult, if not impossible. Randy knew what he must do. He contacted the department administrator and set up a meeting for the following morning with the department chair.

*P*rofessor Evans sat behind his big wooden desk, with piles of paper on each side of it and on the chairs nearby and books stacked on the floor. He looked his dapper self, his signature bowtie standing out against his white shirt and his blue blazer hung behind the office door. With a corner office on the third floor of Agriculture Hall, he had a view of Lake Mendota to the north and campus buildings to the east.

He stood to shake Randy's hand.

"How are things going, Randy? The research project on track?" he asked.

Randy expected him to ask about the phone calls Evans had been receiving from the press and others asking about the numbers presented at the Willow River meeting.

"I know you've been getting phone calls about the Willow River meeting," Randy began.

"Yes, I have. Do you have some answers for me?"

"I do. That's why I'm here this morning." Randy opened his manila folder and pulled out Emily's computer spreadsheets and his own hand-tally sheets.

Evans pushed aside some of the clutter on his desk to make room for the papers.

"These are our tally sheets for the one question on our survey that asked if the communities supported large, confined hog operations."

Evans peered at the numbers and said "hmm" a couple of times.

"How do you account for the differences? Did Emily make some big mistakes along the way?"

"No, she didn't. I asked her about the numbers, and she said she first came up with the exact numbers that I did."

"What happened?"

"She manipulated them. Changed them."

"Why would she do that?" Evans had a perplexed look on his face.

"She said that the good people of Ames County, especially the Tamarack River Valley, needed an economic boost and this new hog facility would provide it. She correctly figured that our research findings would influence the decision-making, and it seems that they did."

"Randy, these are serious accusations. You realize that, of course. Do you have any proof beyond these tally sheets and what she told you?"

"I don't. But these sheets seem to speak for themselves."

"They do. But we don't have any evidence of intent. Do you believe the reasons she gave for changing the numbers?"

"She seemed sincere, seemed to believe she was doing the right thing. But I must say, I have my doubts about her reasons for changing the data."

"Hmm," Evans said. He rubbed his chin with his hand. "Hmm," he said again.

"Well, thank you, Randy, for sharing all this. You realize this casts a long shadow on your research supervision. It was your responsibility to make sure your numbers were accurate before they were presented to the public."

Randy could see Evans was clearly agitated, his normally smiling face frowning. He tapped a pencil on the desk.

"I know that. I know it's not an excuse, but we were in a hurry to have something ready for the meeting, and I didn't take time to check Emily's work."

"You should have found some time, or you should have cancelled your appearance there." Evans's voice was stern and a bit too loud for the setting.

"I know that now."

"Is Emily Jordan in this morning? I need to talk with her."

"She is. Do you want me to ask her to come in?"

"Please. And leave these tally sheets with me."

"Of course."

Emily was her usual upbeat self. To see and hear her around the department, you would not realize that she and her major professor faced serious problems.

"Emily," Randy said when he approached her desk. "Professor Evans would like a word with you."

"About what?" She had noticed that Randy had just come out of Evans's office.

"He's waiting to see you," Randy said.

Emily slowly got up from her chair, glared at Randy, and walked toward Professor Evans's open office door.

"Emily, good to see you," Evans said as he rose from his desk and shut the door behind her. "Appreciate that you could stop by."

"Glad to do it, Professor Evans. How can I help?"

"I've got a bit of a problem here, and I believe you can help me work my way through it." Evans had a rather clever way of getting at difficult issues without immediately putting people on the defensive.

"What's the problem?" Emily knew full well what it was, but she was interested in how Evans would handle it.

"I've been getting lots of phone calls about the accuracy of the numbers you and Randy presented at the Willow River meeting."

"I've heard that. Randy says he got several calls as well."

"Have you seen these?" Evans asked as he pushed the tally sheets to the front of his desk.

"Yes, I have," she said. "I did one of them, and Randy did the other."

"How do you account for the differences? Your results are very different from Randy's." Evans's voice turned from friendly to stern, even a bit confrontational.

"I know that. And I feel bad about it."

"How do you account for the differences?"

"Well, I hate to say it, but it was Randy's idea that I present false data at the Willow River meeting."

"Did he tell you to do it?" Evans asked, a surprised tone to his voice.

"Yes, he did. He told me that there would be serious consequences if I didn't change the numbers, and there would be even worse consequences if I told anyone."

"He said that?"

"Yes, he did."

"What reason did he give you for changing the numbers?"

"Well, . . ." Emily hesitated for a moment and lowered her voice. "He said the good people of Ames County and especially those living in the Tamarack River Valley deserved a boost in their economy. He said that if we presented favorable research results, that is, showed that the majority of the people agreed with having a large, confined hog operation in their community, the zoning committee would give approval to Nathan West to build. And they did."

"Hmm," Professor Evans said. "Kind of an unbelievable reason, I would say." He began tapping his pencil again.

"Well, thank you for stopping by and sharing all this. These are serious charges, you know. Manipulation of research findings is a serious offense. I've got to look into this further. This is a difficult matter." Evans continued tapping his pencil.

"I know that," Emily said. "I was very disappointed in Randy. I couldn't imagine him asking me to do this, but he did."

Once Emily had left his office, Evans walked to the locked file cabinet where he kept personnel files of all faculty members and graduate students. He pulled Emily Jordan's file and began reading her letters of recommendation.

After a few minutes, he turned to the Rolodex on his desk, found a telephone number, and punched the numbers into his phone. He heard the phone ring twice.

"This is George Adams."

"Bill Evans up in Madison. How's everything going in that great city of Columbus?"

"Oh, fine. Running the department is about as good as can be expected. But you should know. Being a department chair at Ohio State can't be a lot different than at UW," said Adams.

Evans laughed, as he knew being a department chair at a large state university had its challenges, no matter where.

"How're Susan and the kids? Let's see, you've got one in high school now?"

"I do. Our little Wyatt is no longer little. He's over six feet tall and playing varsity football. Susan's fine. She just got a part-time job at a little bookstore here in Columbus. Something she's always wanted to do. How can I help you, Bill?"

"Do you remember a grad student named Emily Jordan?"

"I surely do. Friendly personality. Full of enthusiasm. Most optimistic person I'd ever seen, especially among the crop of grad students we had when she was here. Sometimes they can be an unhappy bunch."

"What can you tell me about her, beyond what you just said and what you wrote in your letter of recommendation?"

"Well, she's a better than average student and a good researcher. She's good with details, and once she's working on something she sticks with it until it's done."

"I got all that from your letter. But anything you didn't put in the letter? Something I should know?"

Adams hesitated for a moment. "I'm guessing you have a good reason for asking."

"We've run into a little problem here. Emily's being accused of tampering with some research data—making it look quite different from what the results really show," said Evans.

There was more hesitation on the other end of the line.

"Well, as a matter of fact she had the same problem here. It was pretty clear that on one research project that involved some big agribusiness firms she may have doctored the data a little. But there was no evidence. No way of proving it."

"Well, well, well," said Evans. "Seems like she may be up to her old tricks."

"Appears that way, doesn't it. Shame, too. She's a good student and a good researcher, no need to mess around with the results. What usually happens is you get caught, one way or another," said Adams.

"George, thank you. I'll let you know how all this turns out. It's shaping up to be a real mess."

"Let me know if I can be of further help. Nobody wins in these situations, nobody. How well I know."

Bill Evans hung up the phone and sat back in his chair. Once the word got out that the preliminary data from a research project had been tampered with, everything would go south. He, as department chair, would be called on the carpet by the dean—why hadn't he more closely supervised his assistant professor's research projects? And the dean would be admonished by the chancellor, and so on up the pecking order of the university's bureaucracy. Tampering with research data was right up there with sexual harassment cases—they were always messy and ended up with splashy headlines in the newspapers. Evans was well aware of the many problems state universities faced these days, especially with legislators who decided university budgets. The least little bit of negative news became fodder for the budget cutters.

Evans knew what he must do. He thought for a fleeting moment that he would sit on the information, with the hope that it would all go away. But he knew better. He knew of a case or two in which a rule was broken and the person in charge tried to keep it quiet. It didn't happen. The information got out.

He turned to his phone and punched in some numbers.

A voice on the other end of the line said, "Dean's office."

36

Opening Day

Two days on the Wisconsin calendar take on near religious significance: in November, the opening day of deer season, and in May, the opening day of fishing season. Wisconsin sportsmen and sportswomen mark these dates on their new calendars every January. Absolutely nothing takes precedence over them—no clear-headed person would ever schedule a wedding, a birthday party, or even a funeral on these days—that is, if anyone were expected to attend. These were sacred days, revered year after year.

Opening day of fishing season took on circus proportions on the Willow River Millpond each year. Fishermen from as far away as Milwaukee and Madison gathered to try their luck at catching a native brook trout. They fished from shore, they fished from the dam that created the mill-pond, they fished from boats small and large (no motors of any kind were allowed, however). They drank beer, told stories, and partied as they waited for first light. They fished with fly rods and spinning rods, with cane rods and old-fashioned casting rods. They fished with fancy home-tied flies. They fished with spinners and assorted lures. They fished with earth-worms and minnows, little-finger-length, silver bait minnows, that for most fishermen worked best to lure a spring-hungry brook trout.

Some built campfires on the shore, where they huddled to keep warm on a chilly early May morning. They laughed and hooted—they woke up the neighbors, but nobody complained. These loud and rowdy fishermen brought much-needed money into Willow River.

On this particular opening day, Natalie was on duty, of course. She had invited Josh to accompany her; they had arrived at the millpond about midnight, and the parties were already in full swing. She didn't think much of the shenanigans that were a part of opening day. For her, trout-fishing meant sneaking along a quiet little stream with a fly rod, allowing a fishing fly to float over a likely hole where a trout lay dozing, and then, when the fish took the bait, set the hook and pull it in, all the while respecting the fish and its fight for survival. Once the fish was in your net, you admire it, perhaps take a photo of it, and then let it go. The folks on the Willow River Millpond today were fish eaters—nothing wrong with that, of course. It was their right. But the way they went about it galled Natalie.

Her job was to check fishing licenses and make sure nobody was taking home more than their limit—which was unlikely of course, because fishing competition was so heavy that anyone was lucky to catch one or two fish.

Natalie and Josh sat in her truck, watching the goings on and waiting for first light, when she would begin checking licenses and fish numbers. She had a big thermos of coffee, which the two of them shared as they talked. It was a cold morning, right around freezing, so she started the truck every half hour or so to take off some of the chill.

"How's the new job going?" Natalie asked. Josh hadn't talked much about it.

"I haven't gotten used to it; it's a new approach to journalism, I must say."

"People pay to have their news published?"

"That's right. You have a story you want published, say you want to report on some recent arrests, the DNR would have to pay to have it published."

"So what about the story that needs telling and nobody has money to pay to see it in print?"

"Well, according to my boss, the assistant editor and I are in charge of writing those stories."

"Sounds a little weird to me."

"My boss says it's the future, that it's the new model for the publishing industry that will both make money and get the news out. Online news does have some advantages; we can link to video; we can provide up-to-the-minute market reports. Even link to social networks."

Opening Day

"So do you think you'll keep reporting on the big hog operation that's coming into the valley?" Natalie asked.

"I hope so. That's the biggest story to come along in a while. Right now it looks like a done deal—I thought for a time that public opinion might sway the zoning committee to vote against it, but the university's research seemed to seal the deal for Nathan West."

"You think that research was accurate? Those numbers looked a little goofy to me," said Natalie.

"Looked that way to me, too. I'm doing some checking on that right now. But no matter what, looks like we'll have a big hog producer in the county."

"Are these big factory farms the future, Josh? Is the small, family farm dead?"

"Looks that way. Sure looks that way," said Josh.

Josh looked out over the millpond as early-morning darkness slowly slipped away, revealing a millpond covered with boats, sometimes only six or seven feet apart. Occasionally, he heard the thump of one boat slamming into another, then some loud words admonishing the culprit who had failed to anchor his boat properly.

"Well, it looks like time to go to work," Natalie said, taking a last sip of coffee. "You coming?"

"Sure, I'll tag along," said Josh. "Might find a story for the paper."

Natalie began checking fishing licenses; most folks were polite and dug into their pockets for the little slips of paper that gave them the right to fish. A few grumbled because they had to take off their gloves to dig out their billfolds. But everyone complied. Natalie knew full well that those fishermen who did not have licenses, and there were always a few, had quietly slipped away when they spotted the warden's truck.

"You like a beer?" one fisherman asked after he'd been checked and put his billfold away. His speech was slurred. From the pile of empty beer cans in front of the guy, it was obvious he had been drinking since he had arrived.

"No, thank you," said Natalie, smiling.

Today, she would only be checking those fishing from shore—they were not in short supply, as they stood almost shoulder to shoulder all

213

around the pond. Those in the boats she would check another day, when she launched her boat. She did not want to push her boat into a pond overcrowded with boats and noisy fishermen.

As the first glimpse of the sun appeared in the east, Natalie heard an enormous splash and a drunken yell, "Man overboard. Man overboard." Someone had fallen in. Several people on shore began chuckling, but it was not a laughing matter. The water was cold, as was the air, and hypothermia would quickly incapacitate the fellow if he weren't quickly fished out of the water. Several boats were immediately at the place where he had fallen in. He popped to the surface; the down jacket he wore helped him do so, but it would quickly become soaked and drag him under again, had not a couple of nearby fishermen grabbed him and hauled him into their boat, likely saving his life.

Natalie and Josh watched the entire episode; she was especially concerned because she didn't want to face a drowning on opening day of fishing season. "This is Warden Karlsen," she called out. "Bring the man to shore. Bring him here." She waved so the fisherman could spot her.

Soon the inebriated, thoroughly soaked fisherman stood on shore next to one of the several campfires. He was shivering uncontrollably, suffering the first stages of hypothermia.

"My . . . fishing rod . . . ," the man muttered. His teeth were chattering.

"What about your fishing rod?" Natalie asked.

"It fell . . . overboard with me. It's . . . on the bottom of the pond."

Natalie gave the man a perplexed look. He was worried more about his fishing rod than his own life.

"My wife . . . gave it to me for Christmas," the man said. He continued to shiver as someone helped him replace his thoroughly soaked jacket with a dry one.

"She'll . . . kill me," he said, near tears.

"You should have thought about that before you decided to drink while in a boat. And next time, remember to wear your life vest," Natalie said. She had no patience with boaters who drank and even less patience for those who refused to wear life vests. Even those in rowboats, as was the case for this thoroughly soaked fellow. He said nothing. With the warm jacket and the blazing campfire, his shivering had slowed. His dip in the pond had also sobered him up considerably. He stood now, lamenting the loss of his new fishing rod and thinking about the tongue-lashing he would receive from his wife when he returned home.

Josh thought about doing an article on boat safety, the perils of not wearing a life vest while boating, and the even greater risks of drinking while boating. He wondered if such an article would fit the editorial model his new boss had laid out for *Farm Country News*.

Natalie checked licenses and catches all around the pond, with Josh tagging along behind, observing but not saying anything. When they returned to her truck, she offered, "You ready for breakfast? I'm buying."

They drove to the Lone Pine and feasted on eggs and flapjacks and drank more coffee.

"Another opening morning of fishing season in the record book," said Natalie.

Electronic News

By late May, the online version of *Farm Country News*, with its new editorial approach, was humming along. So far there had been some, but not much, grumbling about paying to have something in the newspaper. Payment rates varied. If someone wanted something to appear on the home page, the cost was twenty-five cents per word. Everything else was a flat fifteen cents a word, with no limit on the number of words.

The paper was divided into several sections so people viewing could easily find material that interested them: "Front Page," "Latest Farm News," "New Ways for New Days," "Tales from an Earlier Time," "Market Reports," "Country Poetry."

Material poured in, a bit of a surprise for Josh, who was more than a little skeptical of how the former readers of the print version of *Farm Country News* would take to the electronic version. Josh was well aware that now, with the electronic version, people were reading their newspaper on a vast array of devices, from their cell phones, computers, iPads, and Kindles. The paper had received a dozen or so letters lamenting the loss of the print newspaper that had been a mainstay in rural homes for nearly 150 years. But it received an equal number of, if not even more, e-mail letters applauding it for "looking to the future and becoming a part of it," as one reader commented.

Of course, it didn't hurt that the newspaper was entirely free, both online and its monthly print versions. And further, at first glance it appeared that the paper included absolutely no advertising, not one display ad and no pages of classified ads. Some people didn't realize that the advertising in the paper was disguised as news stories. And none, except for those who read carefully, could at first glance tell the difference between a "real" story and a "story ad," as Josh began calling them. He had a serious problem with the approach; it clearly violated his sense of journalistic integrity—but for the time being, he chose not to bring the issue up with his boss.

Josh hired two new staff members; each had once been a member of either the *Capital Times* or the *Wisconsin State Journal* staffs in Madison. The masthead for *Farm Country News* read:

Publisher: Lawrence Lexington
Managing Editor: Josh Wittmore
Assistant Editor: Natasha Bruchs
Copyeditor: Jerry Kolka

Every article that appeared in the newspaper carried a byline, and with the many and varied contributions, it appeared at first glance that *Farm Country News* had an enormous staff. Few knew that the actual staff consisted of essentially only four people, plus a couple of additional persons who took care of the computer work.

It was Josh's idea to include a "Country Poetry" section. He was hoping that perhaps M.D. would see fit to submit some more material. He'd come to like this person's blunt, in-your-face take on matters. M.D. had no love for the big hog operation coming to Ames County, that was for sure. Josh wondered if he had anything more to say on the question.

Some poetry did arrive; at least those sending it in called it poetry. Because the writers had included checks and sometimes even cash, with word counts carefully calculated, he had no reason to turn anything down, no matter what its quality. Besides, he reasoned, who knows what makes good poetry, anyway? He'd always placed poetry in the same category as paintings. He knew what he liked, and he knew what he didn't; he believed the same held for poetry. During the first week, he included three poems, expecting to hear some word from his boss about such drivel, but he didn't. A dollar is a dollar, no matter whether wrapped around poor poetry or an important news story.

Farming

By George

Roses are red,
Violets are fine.
Farming is fun,
But not all the time.

Not much to it, but George had included the required fifteen cents a word, even counting "By George." From the nature of the handwriting, he suspected George must be an elementary school student. But the paper was wide open to submissions, no matter the writer's age. He suspected about the only reason he had for turning someone down was profanity—at least that was the guideline he was using.

A second poem was a bit more intriguing:

Spring

By JoAnn Clausen

When the warm winds from the south
Gently caress the newly turned soil.
And when the leaves of the oak are the size of a squirrel's ear
Farmers know to plant their corn.
It is not the calendar they watch for guidance,
It is the feel of the wind,
And the leaves of the oak tree.
These things they know to watch.

But when two ads disguised as stories arrived on his desk, he knew he must stand up for what he believed.

Fritz's hardware store in Willow River e-mailed in a story describing its new lawnmower. "We have just received a new battery-operated mower. One overnight charge is enough to mow a good-sized town lawn, with the muss and fuss of handling gasoline a memory left in the past, and there's no trouble at all in starting the machine. Push the 'on' button, and the machine comes to life with a silent purr that means business." The article went on at length, describing the virtues of the mower, making in-depth comparisons to the gasoline-powered machines that customers had long been accustomed to using.

John Deere sent a long story describing its new lineup of tractors for the smaller "hobby farmer." "No matter the size of your acreage, we have the tractor for you," the article concluded.

With copies of the two stories in hand, Josh walked down the hall to his boss's office, where the door was always closed. He knocked.

"Enter."

Josh opened the door and found Lexington staring at a computer screen, his big desk absolutely devoid of any paper.

"What can I do for you, Josh? Everything going okay? Lots of material pouring in, just as I predicted."

"Got these two items this morning," said Josh. He put them on Lexington's desk.

"Did the money come in with the stories?"

"It did."

"So, what's the problem?" asked Lexington.

Josh hesitated for a moment. "These are not stories; these are ads."

"So?"

"We shouldn't be disguising ads as news stories; it's just not right. It's deceiving, and it will tarnish our reputation."

"Whoa, there, Josh. Calm down. Haven't you been listening to me? This is the new journalism. People don't know the difference between an ad and a story, and, frankly, most of them don't care."

"It's our job to be honest with people. Not calling this sort of material advertising is dishonest."

"Are you finished?"

"I am."

"Then get back to work. We've got a newspaper to run."

Josh returned to his office, angry at the response he'd gotten from his boss and perplexed by how he should proceed. Lexington was challenging everything he had learned about ethics and responsible journalism. He knew the exchange he'd just had was likely the first of more such confrontations. He turned to some of the other materials the paper had been receiving.

He was surprised at the number of articles he received that fit within the "Tales from an Earlier Year" section of the paper. Every week, a half dozen or so stories would arrive from around the country, some by e-mail, some by regular mail. Just this week he'd gotten an e-mail submission from what appeared to be a retired farmer in Minnesota, recounting what farm life was like when he was a boy and how bears would regularly raid the hog pen at night. In considerable detail, the farmer told how he would sit up all night with a 12-gauge shotgun in his lap, waiting for a marauding bear to come by.

A farmwoman from Iowa wrote about May baskets and how they made the small paper baskets, filled with spring flowers—violets and dandelions mostly—at the country school, then would walk through the neighborhood with them on warm May nights and quietly hang them on friends' doorknobs and yell "May basket!" Their friends were then supposed to chase after the basket-giver, trying to catch her.

A farmer from Portage County, Wisconsin, sent in a story about how when he was a kid his family planted up to twenty acres of potatoes with a hand-operated potato planter. He wrote how he would drop a piece of seed potato into the top of the device; push the planter into the soft ground; push it forward so the seed potato would escape into the hole; and then pull the planter out of the ground, making a "clop" sound when the bottom closed. "There was a rhythm to potato planting, a melodic sound made when a couple of men planted potatoes side by side, working their way across the potato field, following the long marks etched in the soft soil, which were earlier made by a horse-drawn marker. On a quiet day, the sound of the 'clop,' 'clop,' when the planter closed, could be heard for some considerable distance."

Lawrence Lexington (never Larry, always Lawrence) was elated at the new venture's success. The paper staff met each day to discuss what it would include on the home page and what stories seemed to merit inclusion in the monthly print edition—so far they had published just one print edition; all the rest had been online. The issue of what was an ad and what was a news story did not come up.

At one of these staff meetings, Josh asked, "Shouldn't we be including more photos? Shouldn't we include photos that go beyond what a company sends us with its story—photos of new tractors, pictures of new lawn mowers, those kinds of photos?"

"What'd you have in mind?"

"Well, let's say I do a story about something I find interesting—a feature story about a farm family, for example. Photos would make the story come alive; I could even include some video."

"Sure. I suggest you take your camera along when you're doing a story like that. Snap some photos and include them with your story. But another point: I'm sure you realize we don't want to include many of these 'feature stories,' as you call them. We don't make any money on them. Not a nickel. And besides, they take up some of your valuable time, Josh. I'm sure you understand that."

Josh didn't respond. He wanted to ask what Lexington thought about another story on the new hog facility being built in the Tamarack River Valley, a story that he, Josh, would write following his best journalist instincts, but he thought this was not the time to ask. And he thought, *Why should I ask, anyway? After all, I am the managing editor; shouldn't I be able to make decisions about stories like this without having to check with the publisher?*

The following Monday, Josh grabbed his point-and-shoot digital camera, tape recorder, and notepad and headed out to the former golf course destined to become one of Ames County's largest agricultural enterprises, if not the largest. He had a meeting set up with Ed Clark, Nathan West's regional representative, who agreed to give him a tour of the facility. They had agreed to meet at one of the former condo buildings that NWI had converted into offices.

As Josh drove west from Willow River, through the vegetable-growing area of Ames County where many hundreds of acres of potatoes had already been planted, and where farmers were hustling to get their seed corn into the ground, he thought about all that had happened in the past few weeks. He hadn't yet figured out his new boss; he was surely not at all like Bert Schmid. "Look for the story behind the story" was how Bert described good journalism. Josh missed Bert, missed him more than he thought he would. Bert had been Josh's mentor, and even though he'd gotten a good basic education in journalism at the University of Wisconsin, he had learned many of the nuances of writing from Bert—not a great writer himself, but he knew great writing when he saw it and pushed his reporters to go the extra mile with their stories.

Josh was beginning to strongly question whether this new model of journalism, with no advertising and everyone, individuals and corporations, paying by the word to see their material in print, was the future. He had to admit that the paper—they had to come up with new language for what they were doing, as little paper was used, only one print edition a month, which didn't amount to much—was making a profit. Of course, there was little overhead, a tiny staff, and few press and paper costs. Josh, still feeling a lot of Bert's influence, wondered why people seemed to enjoy seeing their words on an electronic screen. Josh still liked to hold a newspaper with two hands and see black words on white paper, without batteries or an electrical cord.

But most important, he worried whether *Farm Country News* could maintain its reputation as the hard-hitting, get-at-the-facts-and-tell-the-story paper that it had been. So far, in Josh's estimation, the new paper had mostly published "soft" material, feature stories, a little poetry, and advertising that was supposed to be hidden in a story. Nothing that would approach in-depth journalism. Josh had agreed with Bert that Nathan West could be such a story, which was why he had driven out to the Tamarack River Valley on this warm May morning.

As a good journalist, Josh wanted to present all sides of the story, even though earth was being moved, buildings were being built, and soon thousands of pigs would be housed in what had been a tranquil river valley. Josh knew that many people were not at all pleased with what was happening; they liked the valley as it had been and weren't pleased with the idea of thousands of smelly pigs as their neighbors.

As Josh drove along, his pickup window open to allow in the warm spring air, his mind turned to Natalie. Did they have a future together? Could a newspaperman and a conservation warden have a long-term relationship? He surely hoped so. Today, with his new job as managing editor and a considerable bump in salary from his old position, he believed it was possible. But what did Natalie think about it? She was so busy during these early days of the fishing season that they had no time at all for each other. And with all of his new responsibilities at *Farm Country News*, he had little time for a social life either.

Surprise Present

Fred and Oscar arrived at Christo's about the same time on this warm late-May morning. They found their way to their reserved table that looked out on the Tamarack River, now back to its normal flow after the spring breakup and the rush of melt-water coming down from the snow pack in the north.

So far, neither had said anything, not even so much as a "good morning" to the waitress. After sipping his coffee, Oscar finally broke the silence.

"Little ornery this morning, I see."

"Who's ornery?"

"You are, Fred. You're ornery this morning."

"What about yourself? I don't hear much happiness coming out of you."

"It's a nice day. Nice May day."

"Well, at least we got that going for us," said Fred as he sipped coffee and looked off toward the river.

"Always good to have nice weather in May. It lets farmers get their corn in the ground in a timely fashion."

"Timely fashion. Where in hell did you come onto those words? Those are pretty fancy words for an old farmer like yourself."

"Heard the county agent on the radio this morning. Ben Wesley said farmers were planting their corn in a timely fashion," said Oscar.

"Oh," said Fred.

"Yup, I always listen to the county agent's radio program. You don't have to pay one cent for it, and besides that there's none of that goofy advertising that clutters up most newspapers, such as the *Ames County Argus* and the old *Farm Country News*."

"I sure miss *Farm Country News*," said Fred. "Just like my old dog, Rex, that newspaper had become a member of the family."

"Geez, Fred, no damn old newspaper can be the member of a family. The thing ain't alive. Ain't alive like a person, or a horse or a dog. The thing is just ground-up trees made into paper. That's all it is. Just ground up wood."

"Trees were once alive," muttered Fred.

Oscar shook his head and held out his near-empty cup of coffee for the waitress to fill when she walked by.

"Bought myself a present," Oscar said after a long pause.

"Ain't your birthday. Ain't Christmas either. Why'd you do that?

"Just thought I would. Seemed like the right thing to do."

"You gonna tell me what it is? What present you bought?"

"Nope, I ain't."

"You're not gonna tell me."

"Nope." Oscar took a long sip of his coffee and smiled. "But if you stop by my place on your way home, I'll show it to you. You'll be the first person outside of myself to see what I bought. You got time to stop by on your way home?"

"Might be able to work it into my schedule. Pretty busy these days. Got my garden to plant, got strawberries to hoe, gotta put away my ice-fishing gear. Got lots to do. Busy time. May's a busy time."

"You think you'd be able to work a visit at my place into your schedule?"

"Might be able to do that. Might be able to put off some of these jobs that are demanding my attention. Kinda curious, I must say. Kinda curious about what present you bought for yourself. Especially knowing that you squeeze every nickel before you spend it." Fred grinned when he said it.

A short time later, the two old men were standing in Oscar's kitchen, where a little table had been pushed next to the wall. Oscar's new present stood on the table.

"So where's that new present you bought for yourself—that big mystery present?" asked Fred.

"You blind, Fred? There she is, sitting right in front of you."

"You mean that TV sittin' on that little table? You broke up my morning's busy schedule to look at a damn TV?"

"Fred, look a little closer, that ain't no TV. Looks like a TV, but it's a lot more than a TV. Does a lot more than a TV does."

"You didn't go off and buy a computer, did you? You showin' me a computer?"

"Yup, that's what I did. Bought myself a new computer. Fellow delivered it yesterday. Set it up for me and started me usin' it."

"Oscar, I thought you was one of them who said that it'd be over your dead body before a computer ever found its way into this house. You're lookin' mostly alive to me."

"Changed my mind. Decided it was time I joined the twenty-first century."

"Well, you gonna show me how she works? About the only computers I see are the ones at the library in Willow River—I didn't pay much attention, but it did look like ordinary people were workin' 'em."

"Nothin' much to it. Here, I'll show you." Oscar flipped a couple of switches, and the screen glowed and a little box standing on the floor began humming. Oscar typed a couple of letters on the keyboard, and the *Farm Country News* logo appeared on the screen after a brief wait.

"That's the new *Farm Country News*," Oscar said. "Read it right on the computer screen. Read it anywhere in the world."

"So, you're going on a trip?" Fred asked.

"No, I ain't going on no trip. I just said that now you can read *Farm Country News* wherever there's a computer. Slick as can be."

"I'd rather hold the newspaper in my hands, have it right in front of me when I sit by the stove on a cold winter day. Don't like the idea of sitting in front of one these damn glowing screens. Staring at that thing will give you a headache, Oscar."

"Fred, it's the future. These days, if you ain't got yourself a computer, you're gonna be left behind in the sands of time."

"There you go again, sounding all fluffy. 'Sands of time.' Never heard you use them words before."

"Those are poet's words, Fred. Poet's words. *Farm Country News*, besides everything else it contains, has a poetry section. A section just on country poetry. Think I'll send something in. I just type up a poem and e-mail it in. Don't even need an envelope or a stamp. Easy as can be."

"Oscar, you ain't no poet. Never have been. Never will be. You didn't even graduate from high school. Poets need to know lots of words. Need to string 'em together in special ways."

"I'm gonna send one of my poems in—you don't know that I got a whole drawer full of 'em; been scratching poems down for more than twenty years. Been doing it a long time. Paper's got a new system since it's gone electronic—easy to get my stuff published. Just send in the poem, along with my credit card number."

"Your credit card number?"

"Well, you don't think they'd run my poems for free, do you? Gotta pay to have 'em printed. Just like everybody else. You want something in the paper, you pay to have it there. It's a new world, Fred. A new world."

"I think I liked the old way better, Oscar. I guess I'll just have to be content wallowing around in the sands of time."

Fred didn't say anything for a time as Oscar fumbled with the computer mouse and brought up another screen of *Farm Country News* material.

"Wonder what the Tamarack River Ghost thinks about computers?" asked Fred as he stared at the screen. He was smiling.

"How'd you happen to think about the ghost just now?"

"Staring at that screen did it. Looking at those words coming up on that screen seems kind of mysterious to me. Kind of like the old river ghost sneaking around in the mists at night. Kind of like that."

"Maybe so. Maybe so," said Oscar. "Wouldn't that be something, Fred, if right out of the blue words would come up on this screen and they'd be writ by the old ghost? Wouldn't that be something? Make people sit up and pay attention. Make 'em believers."

"Wonder what the ghost thinks of that big hog house going up on the old golf course? Wonder what the ghost would have to say about that?" asked Fred.

"I guess we'll see soon enough," said Oscar. "I can't believe the Tamarack River Ghost can be too happy about all that activity going on so near to his empty grave."

New Hog House

As Josh followed the road into the former golf course, he saw bulldozers working, moving huge piles of soil in preparation for the buildings. A big concrete truck grumbled ahead of him, its enormous red body slowly turning, diesel fumes spurting from its silver exhaust pipe. As he topped a little rise, he could see the Tamarack River in the distance, a blue ribbon contrasting with the browns of construction, moving quietly as enormous equipment loudly tore up the landscape. As he approached the now abandoned condominium development, he spotted a small sign, "Nathan West Office," with an arrow pointing toward the end unit. He parked his pickup, got out, walked to the door marked "office," and stepped inside.

"Good to see you again," said Ed Clark, emerging from a back room. He extended his hand to Josh.

"How's it going?" asked Josh.

"See for yourself," said Clark, motioning his arm toward all the building activity visible through the open door.

"Mind if I record our conversation and snap some photos?"

"Don't mind at all," said Clark, smiling. Together they walked toward an enormous building that appeared nearly completed.

"Tell me about this building," said Josh. "How big is it? What will it house?"

"This building is 82 feet wide and 740 feet long. It's where we'll house our bred sows."

"How many?"

"About three thousand is its capacity."

"Not many buildings this big in Ames County," said Josh as he snapped several photos.

"Want a look inside?"

"Sure do."

The inside of the windowless building was gleaming white—the ceiling, the walls, the dividing gates. Everything smelled new: the freshly painted walls, the poured concrete floors in the aisles, the new wooden slated floors in the pens. Banks of lights in the ceiling made the building brighter than daylight. As far as Josh could see were pens, designed to hold about fifteen sows each. Josh remembered the visit to the Nathan West facility in Iowa, one almost identical to this one. He once more noticed the automatic feeding stations, shiny and new, with their computerized systems that recorded how much feed each sow ate. He noticed the automatic watering systems as well.

"Everything is controlled by computers," Clark pointed out. "This will be the most up-to-date, most state-of-the-art hog facility in the United States, likely in the world. We're quite proud of what we're able to do here."

Josh snapped several pictures before he returned outside.

As he pointed to a yellow Caterpillar bulldozer working a few hundred yards from where they were standing, Clark explained, "Over there will be our farrowing house, where the little pigs are born and where they will stay for eighteen to twenty days."

"What else is on the drawing board?" asked Josh.

"We've just begun working on our nursery building, where the little pigs grow to about forty-five pounds. Once they reach that weight, we move them into our finishing houses, yet to be constructed. By the time they are six months old they'll weigh about 260 to 280 pounds and will be ready for our processing plant in Dubuque."

"Impressive," said Josh as he continued snapping photos.

"We've got lots to do before we bring in our first sows. But if everything goes according to plan, and the weather stays decent, we should have our first hogs on site by early fall."

"Mind if I wander around a bit and take some more photos?" asked Josh.

"Wander away; if you have any questions I'll be in my office. Thanks for coming out." Josh shook hands with Clark and thanked him for the tour, then climbed back in his truck and followed the winding road through the golf course toward the river. He hadn't realized how beautiful a site this was, with the slightly rolling hills of the former golf course, now returning to the grassy prairie it had once been, with the river flowing peacefully along one side. Josh found his way to the little cemetery, located on the top of a little rise overlooking the river and surrounded by a woven wire fence, a little wire gate on one side. There, Josh could see the new construction in one direction and the Tamarack River in the other. He parked his truck, pulled open the gate, and stepped inside. Green grass and dandelions greeted him, growing between the gravestones. One large gravestone had the word "Dunn" etched into it. Smaller tombstones read "Amelia Dunn, 1867–1932," and "Albert Dunn, 1890–1893." There were gravestones for other Dunns as well.

To the left of Albert's tombstone, a slightly larger one read:

Mortimer Dunn
Father, Log Driver, Farmer, Woodcarver
May 15, 1865
April 15, 1900

This was the first time Josh had seen the grave of the legendary Mortimer Dunn, the Tamarack River Ghost. Josh felt a shiver down his back as he stood quietly looking at the gravestone with the river flowing gently along a few dozen yards away. It was a clear and sunny May day, yet Josh felt something strange, like someone was nearby, although he could clearly see that no one was there. He briefly thought he'd caught a whiff of tobacco smoke, and in the distance the sound of a little bell. He remembered the many stories he'd heard about the ghost and how it came in the night, searching for its grave. He recalled how many people thought the former golf course had failed because an early condo buyer claimed to have heard the ghost the first night he was there and left immediately. Josh's scientific training and his journalistic, objective mind told him that ghosts didn't exist, that there was no such thing. But now, after what he had just experienced at the gravesite, he wondered if there might be some truth to the many tales he'd heard about the Tamarack River Ghost.

He returned to his truck and drove slowly back to Willow River, thinking about his experience. *I wonder what the Tamarack River Ghost thinks about this hog farm?* He chuckled. He said aloud, "There are no ghosts. There is no Tamarack River Ghost."

Back in his Willow River office, Josh checked his e-mail. There was one from the University of Wisconsin's Department of Agribusiness Studies:

We regret that the results of one of our department's research projects were prematurely released at a meeting held in Willow River, Wisconsin, in April. As a result, some of the data presented were incorrect. We regret this and apologize if the incorrect information inconvenienced anyone in any way.

William Willard Evans, PhD
Department Chair

Josh read the e-mail a second time. It was a bit ironic, especially the statement about inconveniencing anyone. He wondered what the accurate research results showed. His guess was that the percentage of those approving building the new hog facility in the Tamarack River Valley was much smaller than reported; indeed the results likely would have shown a majority opposing the plan.

Josh immediately picked up the phone and punched in the numbers for the Department of Agribusiness Studies. In a minute, he was talking to his old professor.

"Josh, it's good to hear from you again. How can I help?"

"I'm calling about the e-mail I just received from you, the one saying some of the early research results of the Tamarack River Valley survey were in error."

"Unfortunate. Very unfortunate. Shouldn't have happened."

"Can you tell me what the results really showed? I assume you now have the correct information."

"We do—thankfully none of the preliminary findings were published, only presented at the meeting in Willow River. Give me a minute, and I'll find the correct information."

Soon Evans was back on the phone; Josh figured he would be receiving many calls like his and would have the information handy.

"What would you like to know? I've got the accurate data in front of me."

"For now, I'd like to know what percentage of the people sampled in the Tamarack River Valley approved of a big hog operation coming into their neighborhood."

"Okay, I've got it right here, both the numbers of the preliminary report and the accurate numbers. The preliminary numbers for the Tamarack River Valley respondents were: *Yes—75 percent, No—20 percent, No opinion—5 percent*. These were the ones that were inaccurate."

"Yes, I know," said Josh. "I wrote them down when your graduate student shared them at the meeting."

"The accurate numbers are: *Yes—40 percent, No—55 percent, No opinion—5 percent*."

"So 55 percent of the Tamarack folks disagree with the hog operation coming to their community?" Josh raised his voice a bit.

"That's what the correct figures show."

"The preliminary figures said 75 percent were in favor—that's quite a difference in numbers, wouldn't you say? Quite an error?" Josh asked. His voice had an edge to it.

"Clearly an error—unfortunately, a big one. The preliminary numbers should not have been presented."

"Thank you, Professor Evans. Thank you for being candid," Josh said. "As soon as you have the complete report ready, make sure I get a copy."

"You're on the list."

Josh hung up and sat back in his chair. He could tell by Evans's tone of voice that he was embarrassed about what happened. Josh, knowing something about university departments, also knew that a department's reputation was extremely important, especially when it came to attracting outstanding students, and it was even more important for obtaining research grants.

The department, nearly a hundred years old, had carried out outstanding research that had assisted the agriculture community in untold important ways. But it had surely muffed reporting its most recent research findings. He decided to run the e-mail as he had received it, as a sidebar to the story he was writing about Nathan West's progress in building its new facility, and he decided to run the corrected preliminary figures. He would wait for the complete report to write a longer piece about the research.

40

Outrage

Josh wrote a lengthy article, complete with photos, of the progress Nathan West was making with its new hog production facility. He worked hard on the piece, which included quotations from Ed Clark. It was an objective piece; it included lots of facts and no opinions about either the positive or negative features of a large-scale confined hog operation.

In addition to the sidebar with the e-mail he'd received with the corrected survey results, he included another sidebar, one recounting some history of the Tamarack River Ghost with a photo of Mortimer Dunn's gravestone.

He sent the piece over to the paper's copyeditor for proofing, and an hour later he punched a button on his computer keyboard and the story appeared on the website.

Two minutes later, Josh's phone rang.

"Could you step into my office, please?" It was Lexington. His office was two doors from Josh's. Josh wondered why he hadn't just walked the few feet and talked with him face to face.

Josh walked down the hall, knocked on the door, and heard "Enter."

Lexington sat at his desk, staring at a computer screen. His black-rimmed glasses hung on the end of his nose and his nearly bald head shone.

"Just read your piece on the progress Nathan West is making. Good piece, a little long, but a good piece. You could have written something about what an asset the big hog operation will be to the county and the valley—something that would praise its efforts a bit more. We'd likely get more stories from NWI, stories the corporation would pay for, if you did that."

"I wanted to keep the piece objective," said Josh.

"Objective is yesterday's way of doing things. Today people take positions, say what they think, share their opinions. It's the new journalism."

Josh stood quietly, not saying anything. He knew what good journalism was, and he also knew the difference between an opinion piece and a good piece of objective writing.

"Something else. Why in the world did you include the sidebar about the university's correction of its early research report? All that will do is stir up people. And it'll stir up Nathan West as well; the company won't like it, you can bet on that. Once the company reads this, we'll hear."

Josh remained standing silently, thinking but not expressing his thoughts.

"And one final thing. What's with this ghost? It's not Halloween. Why are you writing about ghosts, tombstones, and cemeteries, for heaven's sake?" It was obvious from the question that he had done little digging into the community's history.

Josh opened his mouth to respond but thought better of it. He wanted to explain what journalism was all about, how it was important to try to remain objective when writing about something. And, as far as the sidebar e-mail of the agribusiness studies department confessing an error in its preliminary research report—well, that was news and must be reported, no matter who might be offended or might take issue with it.

But he said nothing, deciding this was not the time or the place. He could see that his boss was upset with him—no sense in fanning the flames.

"That's all," Lexington said, waving Josh away.

Josh returned to his office, not sure what he should do about the exchange—it really wasn't an exchange, as the conversation was a one-sided dressing down. How should he help his new boss understand what the newspaper business was about, what *Farm Country News* had been doing for so long? He wondered if a confrontation was the answer. It might get him fired before he'd given the second reason for why he wrote the Nathan West story the way he did.

Before he'd had more than five minutes to think about a strategy, the e-mails began arriving.

To the Editor:

I knew something was phony about those university research results. I just knew it. My take was the majority of the people here in the valley wanted nothing to do with Nathan West and their truckloads of stinkin' hogs.

J. Anderson
Tamarack River Valley

To the Editor:

What next? People who are against lower taxes are doing it again—now they say the majority of the people living here don't want Nathan West to build. Well, Nathan West is building, whether 55 percent of the people like it or not.

F. Summerville
Tamarack River Valley

Thirty e-mails arrived within the first hour of the piece's appearance on the paper's website. The percentage for and against the new hog farm broke down almost identically to the survey results—more than 50 percent were against the idea. Josh wrote back to all of them, asking if they wanted their message to appear in the paper and explaining that the cost to do so would be 15 cents a word.

If hitting a hornets' nest would stir up the wrath of hornets, the idea that readers should have to pay to submit a letter to the editor was like smashing into the largest hornets' nest in existence. To a person, those for the new hog facility and those against were united in opposition to *Farm Country News*'s policy for charging people for their submissions. They were livid. Several wrote that they would immediately cancel their subscriptions to the paper, not realizing that the paper was free and that they no longer had subscriptions.

People didn't seem to mind paying for advertising-type stories, or stories that fit into the "Remembering an Early Time," "New Ways for New Days," or any other section of the paper. But the idea of paying for a letter to the editor struck them the wrong way. Some readers reminded Josh that protest letters of the type they had sent were as old as the country.

One wrote:

> This country was built on the premise that people have certain unalienable rights, that they have basic freedoms, and one of those is the right to express themselves—to state their opinions on something they feel strongly about. The newspaper, whatever form it might take, and it has changed considerably from the days of Benjamin Franklin, has a responsibility to share these diverse perspectives. It is an outrage that we must pay to have our opinions appear in print, even if it is only fifteen cents a word.

Josh showed this last response to his boss, who quickly read through it and then snarled, "Write back and tell this guy that freedom is not free. It costs money."

Josh snatched the e-mail from Lexington's desk without a word. He went back to his own desk, not knowing what to do. The writer surely had a point. Josh agreed with him, but how could he convince his boss of a newspaper's responsibilities, in whatever form it took—paper or electronic?

41

Department Decisions

*I*n a series of meetings in the Department of Agribusiness Studies and in the College of Agricultural and Life Sciences as a whole—deadly serious meetings held without fanfare or publicity—the "Randy case," as it was called, was discussed at length. Randy appeared at each of these meetings to share his side of the story. Emily also appeared at each. For a time, the meetings seemed a series of "he said, she said" conflicts, with the attendants having difficulty knowing where to place blame. Ultimately, the information Department Chair Evans shared about Emily's actions at Ohio State University swayed the committee toward accusing her of tampering with data. However, they did not let Randy off the hook. He was, after all, responsible for the research project and for supervising his graduate student, both of which he had failed to adequately do.

Emily turned on all her charm at these meetings, but crotchety professors worrying about their department and their college's reputation are not easily charmed. She thought carefully about the appropriate time to share the video she had made. Ultimately, she decided it would probably weaken her case. She decided to pack it away—*Another day, another time*, she thought.

The day after the semester ended, Evans called Randy into his office. Randy had a good idea of what was coming; he hadn't slept for many nights, worrying about his future, concerned about how he hadn't properly supervised his graduate student who had presented tampered research results to the public. More than anything else, he worried about Emily's video. No matter what, he knew his career was in serious jeopardy, if not entirely derailed.

"Have a chair, Randy," Professor Evans said, motioning to the only chair in the office that did not have something piled on it. "I suspect you know why I wanted to see you."

"Yes, I believe I do," said Randy. His face felt hot and his stomach was churning.

"Well, I'll get right to it. As a better than average researcher, I believe you know how serious it is when data are tampered with," said Evans.

"Yes, I do."

"It's one thing to make a mistake; we all do that from time to time, but to alter data, that is unforgivable."

"I know that," said Randy. He could feel a bead of perspiration trickling down the side of his face. He brushed it away.

"After several meetings and considerable discussion, we are convinced that Emily Jordan was responsible."

"Yes, she admitted it to me."

"You probably know that she never admitted it to me or to the ethics committee, but she said you did the tampering and at the Willow River meeting she only did what you told her to do."

"I wasn't aware of that," said Randy angrily.

"You probably also didn't know that she did something like this when she was studying at Ohio State. They couldn't prove anything, but they asked her to leave, nonetheless."

"Really? I wish I had known." Randy sighed and slumped back in his chair.

"We all wish we had known," said Professor Evans. "But even though she did the actual tampering, you, Randy, were responsible for the project, supervising her work, and making sure what was reported was as accurate as possible."

"I know that," said Randy. He looked down at his hands.

"So, here's what we've decided to do. First, we have discontinued Emily Jordan's research assistantship, as of the end of this semester. She will be leaving the University of Wisconsin and will likely not be pursuing a PhD at any major research university, at least in this country."

"Yes." It was all Randy could think to say, because he knew that the other shoe was about to drop, and that shoe would land squarely on him. He also thought of Emily's dreaded video and wondered why she hadn't already shared it with Evans when he discussed canceling her assistantship. Or was something else going on, something that no one yet knew about Emily's real reason for tampering with the data?

"The department's personnel committee has decided not to renew your contract. You may teach here for one more year as you look for other employment. I will write you a letter of recommendation, provided you seek a teaching job without any research responsibilities."

"Thank you," Randy said. He knew he had the right to appeal the decision, but he also knew he would probably lose. Even though he did not alter any research, he was still responsible.

"I'm sorry, Randy. You had lots of promise, the potential to become one of our top researchers."

"I'm sorry I let you down," said Randy. He had tears in his eyes, and his voice broke when he spoke. He got up from his chair and left the office, his shoulders slumped and his head down. It was one small consolation that Emily apparently hadn't shared the video of the two of them.

Fourth of Seventh-Month

*I*t was the Fourth of July, and Josh sat at his desk at *Farm Country News*. With the paper putting several new pieces online every day, he was busier than ever. He and Assistant Editor Natasha Bruchs read the submitted material, searching for obvious factual errors and confused writing. Jerry Kolka, copyeditor, carefully read and corrected obvious spelling and grammatical errors before they put it online. Josh divided the responsibilities so that he worked on the front page and the "Latest Farm News" and "Market Reports" sections. Natasha was responsible for "New Ways for New Days," "Tales from an Earlier Time," and "Country Poetry."

Lawrence Lexington insisted that something new be posted every day, holidays included, thus the staff members were all at their desks that Fourth of July morning.

Natasha stuck her head into Josh's office.

"A word?" she said. She was clutching some papers. Natasha, in her early thirties, had short black hair. She was tall and willowy—and smart. A journalism major from the University of Wisconsin, she had worked for several newspapers as a reporter and features writer. She came to the *Farm Country News* with a couple of years' experience as an assistant editor at the *Capital Times* in Madison.

"Sure, come on in. Have a chair. Celebrate the Fourth of July with me," Josh said, smiling.

"This came in the mail yesterday—I think it's supposed to be a poem— by someone with the initials 'M.D.' Do we want to publish something like this?" Natasha asked.

"We received several pieces from M.D. before, when we were a print paper," said Josh. "Let me have a look."

Natasha handed Josh the single sheet of white paper, with the following words neatly typed across the page:

Tamarack River Valley Changed Forever

Been by the old golf course lately?
Have you seen the earth movers?
Have you smelled the diesel-powered machines tearing up the soil?
Have you seen the enormous building standing tall and long,
    with more buildings to come?
Is this what we want in the valley?
Doesn't matter.
This is what we got.
But can we live with it?
Will all these hogs be good neighbors?

              M.D.

"Was there a check for payment enclosed?" asked Josh.

"Nope, but there was eleven dollars in cash. It's paid for. Should we run it?"

"Sure, let's run it in the poetry section. Might get some reaction."

Natasha returned to her office and Josh continued working on a two-thousand-word piece from Nathan West Industries headquarters in Dubuque, to be put on the paper's front page. It came with a $500 payment (25 cents per word). Figuring it was written by some public relations person at Nathan West, Josh quickly decided it was wordy and at times repetitious and boring. He cut the piece to fifteen hundred words and refunded Nathan West the $125 for the words that he removed. As soon as it was copyedited, he put the piece online. It was noon. He sat back in his chair, his hands behind his head. The morning had been productive. The phone rang.

"This is Josh Wittmore. How can I help you?"

"Well, Mr. Wittmore, you can help me by agreeing to celebrate the fourth of Seventh-month with me," said Natalie.

"What in heaven's name is the 'fourth of Seventh-month'?" said Josh, recognizing Natalie's voice.

"Haven't you read *Leaves of Grass*? Walt Whitman calls the Fourth of July the 'fourth of Seventh-month.'"

"Oh," was all Josh could think to say. It had been a very long time since he had turned the pages of Walt Whitman's work.

"Are you planning to work all day?" Natalie asked.

"I should, but what do you have in mind?"

"How about I pick you up at your apartment at about four, and we can drive down to Link Lake, see their displays, and take in the fireworks at night."

"Sounds like a plan—and let me add one more thing. How about I take you out for dinner before the fireworks, at the Lake Edge Supper Club?" said Josh.

Josh left his office around three and drove to his apartment, his mind filled with thoughts of Natalie; the challenges and problems at the newspaper pushed into the background. It was a warm, sunny afternoon, typical for July.

Promptly at four, Natalie, driving her Civic, pulled up in front of Josh's apartment. She was wearing a red dress, which showed off her blonde hair, which today she allowed to hang loose.

"Don't you look nice," Josh said by way of greeting.

"You don't look so bad yourself," she said, smiling broadly.

They followed Highway 22 toward Link Lake, chatting about the weather and how nice it was and talking about the last fireworks displays they had seen; neither had seen one for several years. They had an unspoken agreement these days: that neither of them mentioned anything about their jobs—about the number of arrests Natalie had made earlier in the day or the rift developing between Josh and his boss.

When they arrived in Link Lake, they found a place to park and then walked down Main Street, which had been closed to traffic. Tents and display tables lined both sides of the street. They stopped briefly at the Ames County Woodcarvers' table, where three men sat whittling and talking with people about their work. They had an assortment of completed items for sale, ranging from ducks to robins, from Santa Clauses to old farmers with pitchforks on their backs.

"Wish I could do that," said Josh.

"I bet you'd cut your finger," Natalie said. They both laughed, as did the men whittling—one held up a finger with a strip of white tape wrapped around it.

They walked past the Ames County Farm Bureau tent and, a few feet further on, a table promoting the Ames County Farmer's Union. They stopped briefly at the Ames County Fruit and Vegetable Growers Cooperative's display, where Josh chatted briefly with Curt Nale, whom he had met at the previous winter's informational meeting about the Nathan West proposal.

Then they stopped at the Link Lake Rod and Gun Club display.

"You're Natalie Karlsen, our conservation warden, aren't you?" one of the members asked.

"I am," said Natalie.

"Almost didn't recognize you in a dress," he said, then looked like he wished he hadn't.

"Oh, I wear a dress once in a while," Natalie said. She smiled.

They chatted for a bit about the good things the rod and gun club was doing for the fish and game populations in the county before she and Josh moved on.

At the Link Lake Historical Society display, Natalie picked up a copy of a pamphlet titled "Link Lake: A History." She read the first paragraph and then gave it to Josh:

Preacher Increase Joseph Link moved to Wisconsin from New York State in 1852 with a small band of followers, called the Standalone Fellowship. This group established the village of Link Lake in the year of its arrival, built the Standalone church, ministered to the community, and challenged those who misused the land.

"Do you know this history, Josh? Do know about this preacher?"

"A little. My dad talked about the Standalone Church. Apparently, the members were a little on the unusual side."

244

"The part about 'challenging those who misused the land' sounds interesting. I wonder what that was about—sounds like they were environmentalists."

"I guess they were probably the first people in Wisconsin to really care about the land beyond trying to make a living off of it. Aside from the Native Americans, of course," said Josh.

They walked to the *Ames County Argus* booth and stopped to chat with Billy Baxter, editor.

"How's it going, Billy?" Natalie asked. They had known each other since Natalie had first taken the DNR warden job.

"Oh, we're still making it. Still keeping our heads above water."

"You know Josh Wittmore, from *Farm Country News*?"

"Josh, how're you doing? All of us small-town newspaper guys are watching what you're doing at *Farm Country News*. How's the pay-to-say program going?"

"We're working out the kinks," Josh said. "Seems to be working, though, lots of folks sending in material. And because it's all free to the readers, we've got thousands of people looking at our website everyday—from all over the country." He wanted to sound upbeat, but he worried his misgivings might be obvious from the tone of his voice.

"I've been doing some thinking," said Baxter. "I want to do more with our website at the *Argus*. Right now it's pretty primitive, needs work. Haven't really figured out how to handle the advertising online. I know most people hate seeing ads when they're on the Internet—but news is not free, no matter how you put it out there. Along the way, somebody's got to pay."

"That's right. People don't seem to realize that. On the Internet, there's also the problem of what is news, what is opinion, and, frankly, what is rumor," said Josh.

"You've hit the nail on the head," said Baxter. "All this stuff on TV and the Internet that's supposed to sound like news but really isn't."

"Okay, enough shop talk, you guys," said Natalie, pulling on Josh's arm. "This is supposed to be a day off—a day to celebrate."

"You ready for dinner? If we go now, we can beat the rush," said Josh.

"Sure, all the talk about newspapers has given me an appetite."

"Glad it didn't have the opposite effect."

They walked the couple of blocks to the Lake Edge Supper Club, where they were promptly seated at a table by a window overlooking Link Lake. Water-skiers were skimming by, and across the lake, in a little cove. Josh could make out a cluster of boats, fishing boats, he assumed.

"How're the water-skiers and the fishermen getting along these days?" asked Josh.

"Not well. They basically hate each other. Best we've been able to do is have the lake associations enact no-wake zones for the early morning and the early evening."

Soon Natalie and Josh were feasting on fresh walleye, the special at Lake Edge that day, along with glasses of New Glarus Spotted Cow beer. The view from the window was about as good as it gets, with the cool, clear water of Link Lake providing a backdrop to the white and red pines that grew along its shore, along with the occasional birch or aspen, plus several weeping willow trees. It was the first time Josh had felt relaxed since he took over as managing editor of *Farm Country News*.

"Thank you for thinking of this," said Josh, taking Natalie's hand in his and looking into her brown eyes. "Thank you so much."

"The dinner was your idea," she reminded him.

"I know, but I would still be sitting in front of my computer if you hadn't called."

"I've got the same problem. I could be out there checking on fishing and boat licenses—I did that this morning from the crack of dawn. We all need some downtime."

"Indeed we do."

Neither said anything for a time, as they sat holding hands and looking out over the lake.

With dinner finished and a couple of hours before dark and the start of the fireworks, Josh and Natalie sat on a park bench by the lake—a few others had already gathered for a front-row view of the fireworks show over the lake.

Natalie jumped when the first "KA-BOOM" of an aerial bomb exploded high over the lake.

"Sorry," she said. "Those noises remind me of my army days."

"You don't talk about your time in the army—why not?" asked Josh.

Natalie didn't reply but tucked her hand into Josh's as she continued looking out over the lake, now a dark shadow in the early evening. They sat quietly, enjoying being together. As darkness crept over the lake, the first rocket shot into the blackening sky with a boom and a sizzle, opening with a loud "pop" sending red, yellow, and blue streamers downward into the lake. A collective "ah" went up from the crowd. The show went on for a half hour, with bright colors exploding into a black sky and then cascading into the dark waters of Link Lake. For the grand finale, multiple rockets lit up the sky like daylight, so much so that the street lights, on light sensors, blinked off, sending the town into total darkness.

"Well, what do you think of that?" said Natalie.

"Typical Link Lake," said Josh. "Never know what'll happen next around here. Remember the place was that way when I was a kid."

Through the darkness, they fumbled their way along Main Street and then to the lot where Natalie had parked her car. She invited Josh out to her cabin for a nightcap.

At 8:09 the next morning, Josh was at his desk; he had just begun to read his e-mail when he heard, "Wittmore, get your ass in here, and right now." It was Lexington, yelling louder than Josh had ever heard him. He jumped at the command; no one had ever talked to him this way before. He walked into the publisher's office and stood in front of his desk. Lexington's face was as red as a newly ripened tomato; the veins in his neck pulsed.

"Did you read this e-mail from Nathan West?" yelled Lexington.

"I've just started going through my e-mail," answered Josh in a quiet, unemotional voice.

"Well, let me read it to you. 'We were astonished to see what your editorial staff did to the news article we sent you for *Farm Country News*. Your editors rearranged and cut a substantial number of words from the copy prepared by our public relations staff. I must say that we are more than a little disappointed. Returning some of the publishing fee based on the new word count does not make up for the hatchet job you did to our article. Emory Perkins, Communications Manager, Nathan West Industries.'"

"I did a bit of editing to the piece. It was wordy, and some of it made little sense," explained Josh.

"Well, who in hell gave you permission to tamper with a customer's writing? Who in hell gave you permission? Answer me that!" yelled Lexington. His face was even redder than before.

"I believe it is part of my job to edit the material that's submitted; that's what an editor is supposed to do. That's what I've been trained to do."

"Josh." Lexington's voice returned to a more normal level. "This is not an old-time newspaper. This is a new approach, a new idea, the future. You can't use yesterday's tools on tomorrow's products."

"Good editing is good editing. Readable and accurate writing ought to be our goal, no matter whether the material is on paper or on a screen," Josh said quietly but firmly.

"Josh, Josh, Josh . . . You are not listening to me. When a customer sends us a story along with the money to publish it, we publish it. The only editing we should do is to make sure there is no profanity and the customer hasn't said something over which they or we might get sued. Other than that, everything goes—as long as they pay their money. Understood?"

"I hear you, but the reputation of *Farm Country News* depends on the quality of the material we publish."

"Reputation be damned. I'm interested in the paper making a profit. Period," said Lexington. "Now I've got to write to Nathan West and offer to republish what they originally sent us for free—and we'll lose money on the deal."

"Is that all?" said Josh quietly.

"One more thing. Don't you ever send money back to a customer. What in hell were you thinking? Once we have the money, it's ours. You got that?"

"I've got it," Josh said, trying not to allow his disgust to show in his voice.

Truce

The remaining summer months flew by. Submissions continued to flow into the offices of *Farm Country News*. Articles from John Deere and Case IH, material from Archer Daniels Midland, a long piece from Monsanto, a story from Tyson Foods, another from Cargill, and a two-thousand-word piece from Land O'Lakes. Nothing from Nathan West headquarters in Dubuque—the folks there were obviously still angry about the editing Josh had done to their long article.

For days on end, Josh sat at his computer, reviewing the stories that came in and doing some minor, usually very minor, editing. He bit his tongue when he allowed some of the material to appear on the paper's website—in his mind too much of it was poorly written or at best sounded like an info-ad, which, indeed, most of the material was. As long as the money followed the stories, he had no reason to turn them down; his boss had made that abundantly clear.

Josh stopped out at the Nathan West building site in late July and again in late August and after each visit wrote a brief piece, including photos. His boss reminded him that he should allow Nathan West to write the stories and take the photos—that the paper would benefit in at least two ways. Josh wouldn't waste his time traveling, writing stories, and taking photos; and, of course, Nathan West would pay for everything that it submitted.

After each of Josh's stories appeared, the usual set of letters to the editor came flying in—some actual letters and most of them e-mails. Almost none included the required payment, so they were never published.

Dear Editor:

I drove by the building site for those new Nathan West hog houses. What a blight on the countryside. A stick in Mother Nature's eye, that's what they are.

Jamey House
Tamarack River Valley

Dear Editor:
    Mark my word. Something's gonna happen to them big hog houses. Something bad. We don't want them in our valley. Simple as that.

                                                                M.D.

The last letter came in an envelope with no return address; the post-mark was Plainfield. Josh stared at the signature. He had printed several items that M.D. had written, all of them quite critical of the Nathan West project, but none sounded the least bit threatening. Was M.D. going off in a new, more violent direction? He stared at the letter again; it was hand-written. All of the other M.D. pieces had arrived neatly typed. Could this be a different M.D.? Perhaps some kind of prank? Josh didn't know what to make of the letter, except that it clearly sounded like a threat. He called Natalie. As a trained law-enforcement officer, she would have had experience with these kinds of threats, if indeed it was a threat.

"Natalie, Josh. Got a question for you. What does it take for a threatening letter to become a threatening letter?"

"What?"

"What does it take for a threatening letter to become a threatening letter?"

"I heard you the first time. What's going on?"

Josh read the letter aloud.

"Who signed it?"

"This is the part that troubles me. It's signed "M.D." As you know from reading the paper, we get the occasional submission from an M.D., but we have never gotten a letter to the editor. I can't believe this is the same person, but you never know."

There was a pause on the other end of the line.

"Are you still there?" Josh asked.

"I'm still here. I don't think the letter reaches the threat level. The person didn't say he was going to harm the Nathan West buildings but merely said something might happen to them."

"True, but aren't you splitting hairs?"

"Maybe, but it sounds like a spoof, with the writer using 'M.D.' to stand for Mortimer Dunn, that old drowned lumberjack."

"I was thinking the same thing. Hey, Dunn may be dead, but his ghost is still around. People swear that his ghost is out there, searching for his grave on dark nights and trying to protect the valley. "

Natalie laughed. "You don't believe in all that ghost stuff, do you?"

"Well, I've been getting this poetry from somebody who uses the initials 'M.D.' I'm beginning to wonder if the old ghost isn't writing the stuff and sending it to me."

"Oh, Josh, what's happening to you? Where's that trained journalist who wants only to deal with the facts? Whatever happened to him?"

Now Josh laughed. "Just pulling your chain a little, Natalie. But I really do wonder who M.D. is. I also think I better give the folks over at Nathan West a call, just in case the threat is real and someone is planning to do something stupid."

"Sounds like a good idea. How about coming to my cabin for dinner on Saturday? I'll bake a chocolate cake."

"I'll be there with bells on," Josh said.

"You can leave the bells home—I don't think you'll need them." Natalie chuckled as she hung up the phone.

Immediately, Josh called Ed Clark at Nathan West's building site.

"Ed, it's Josh Wittmore at *Farm Country News*."

"How you doing?" answered Clark, who, unlike his superiors at Nathan Clark headquarters in Dubuque, had come to like Josh and his interest in and writings about their new hog operation.

"Say, I want to give you a heads-up. There may be nothing to it, but after the last piece I wrote about the progress you guys are making with your buildings, I got a rather nasty letter in the mail. I'll read it to you." Josh read him the letter.

"Who is this M.D.?" asked Clark.

"Probably stands for Mortimer Dunn, the Tamarack River Ghost."

"Him again?"

"Yup, lots of ghost believers around. This may be simply a prank. I wanted to let you know, though, just in case there is something to it."

"We've gotten this kind of stuff more times than I can count. We don't put much stock in these tirades. They come at us from all directions. But thanks for letting me know," said Clark.

*F*or weeks on end, Josh and his boss scarcely talked. They had obviously reached some kind of truce. Josh came to work each morning, put in his eight hours, and returned to his apartment. His heart was just not in his work anymore. He felt like a phony; he wanted to be a journalist, dig out important stories, interview people, find different points of view on a controversial topic, but now his hands were tied. He believed a high school dropout could do the work he was doing; his position certainly didn't require a trained journalist.

The electronic *Farm Country News* was making a profit. *It should,* thought Josh. The paper's fixed costs were minimal. It had a tiny full-time staff and almost no newsprint and press charges, as it printed only a thin broadsheet once a month. Posting material on the paper's website cost the paper little.

Josh had hoped people would begin to see that the printed articles, especially those that were supposed to be news, were not news at all but advertising pieces for the companies submitting them. A few people figured it out and let the paper know in no uncertain terms that they were opposed to what it was doing. A recent e-mail Josh received made the point:

Dear Editor:

What do you think your readers are? A bunch of idiots? I subscribed to
Farm Country News for more than twenty years. In its print format, I
found it interesting, informative and well edited. Now, with your new
online format, you've completely lost your direction, and, I might add,
you've lost my support. I'd like to say that I am canceling my subscription,
but alas, all I can do is no longer go to your website. (I am telling my
friends to avoid your website as well.) You claim that people want their
news free and unencumbered by ads and other moneymaking schemes.
Well, remember the old adage: there is no such thing as a free lunch. A
free newspaper without advertising falls into the "free lunch" category.
And perhaps, even worse, it is a major deception, coming right close to
being a scam. Some people actually believe they are reading news when
they are reading yet another advertisement presented to look like news.
You are doing a great disservice to the public, whether you are aware of it
or not. If I could think of a way of shutting you down, I would do it.

John Frederick
Ames, Iowa

Josh forwarded the e-mail to his boss, hoping that one day soon
Lexington might see his idea was failing and that if the paper was to
continue it must develop a new strategy. But he heard not a whisper from
his boss. Not one word.

Disaster

Some things never change, thought Natalie as she sat in her Ford F-150, parked on a little knoll that overlooked a considerable portion of the Tamarack River Valley. It was late September, and she was on poacher duty. As surely as the first frost arrives in the fall, the calls come in complaining about game poaching and wondering why she wasn't stopping all the illegal hunting. She wanted to tell these callers that rounding up game poachers wasn't nearly as easy as it sounded, especially those who poached deer at night—which was when most of them operated.

She remembered so well the previous fall when she had been certain that she had the goods on Dan Burman but then had been embarrassed when she and the sheriff trekked out to his farm only to find a pair of dressed goats hanging in his barn. Natalie was convinced at the time that Burman was guilty and that he had cleverly replaced the deer carcasses with goat carcasses. If he chose to do some poaching this year, she would nail his skin to the wall.

With the driver's-side window of her pickup open, she was listening to the early evening sounds and smelling the pungent aroma of fall. Even though she lost a lot of sleep on these watches, she also enjoyed the quiet. From time to time, she flicked on her Mag-Lite and scratched a few things in her ever-present journal. Writing helped to pass the time as she waited for the sound of a gunshot or the sight of a bright light sweeping across one of the open fields in the distance.

She allowed her mind to wander. Thoughts of Josh Wittmore and the good times they'd had together this past year quickly crowded out anything else. Was he the one? Should she say "yes" if he proposed marriage? A year ago marriage was the farthest thing from her mind as she worked hard to establish herself as a female warden in a county that believed only men should hold such positions. She believed, with substantial evidence, that she had garnered considerable respect in the county, especially from other law-enforcement people, environmental groups, and fish and wild-life organizations interested in sensible management of the county's fish and game resources. Even those she arrested begrudgingly admitted that she was tough but fair—she treated everyone the same. She chuckled when she recalled the time she cited the mayor of Link Lake for having in his boat a largemouth bass one inch short of the lawful length. At the time, she didn't know who he was, but it wouldn't have mattered. She would have cited anyone—the law was the law. The incident was a considerable embarrassment to the mayor when his name appeared in the *Ames County Argus*'s citation list. Most of the people in Link Lake found the incident hilarious and never ceased kidding their mayor. Several even mailed him rulers with instructions on how to use them.

Would a marriage work? A law enforcement officer married to a journalist? She knew Josh was a good journalist, but he had a job that he hated. She had lately become his sounding board. When they got together, whether over a cup of coffee or for a night at her cabin, he always got around to sharing his unhappiness over what had become of *Farm Country News*. "It's just not right what our paper is doing," he often said.

A near full moon, orange and bright, hung low in the night sky as Natalie continued to look and listen. She inhaled deeply. The cool night air was refreshing, and it helped keep her alert, but soon she smelled something different. Just a hint of wood smoke. She wondered if the evening breeze had pushed the smoke from a neighbor's chimney her way. She knew that many people in the valley continued to warm their homes, at least some of the time, with woodstoves. Heating a home this way was considerably less expensive than using propane, especially when most folks had their own woodlots.

She sat back and relaxed, pushing the new smell aside. She watched and listened, scanning the fields to the south, listening for a pickup, for the report of a rifle, for voices that carried some distance on quiet nights. Her eyes fixed on a faint red glow in the sky she hadn't noticed before. She picked up her binoculars. It was brighter, but she still couldn't make out what it was. Then she caught an even stronger whiff of wood smoke. She decided to check it out—could this be a forest fire? She fired up her pickup, drove out on the road, and headed toward the red glow.

As she got closer, the smoke smell became even stronger. Soon she saw what it was; the big new hog house at Nathan West was on fire, flames shooting into the air. She immediately got on her radio and called in the fire, alerting the local volunteer fire departments and letting the sheriff's office know.

She parked a safe distance away, grabbed her bag, which contained her cell phone, and ran around to the back of the building. Through the single window, she thought she saw movement inside, but she couldn't be sure. She was clearly the first person to arrive at the scene. Could someone be trapped inside? One entire end of the building was on fire, smoke and flames everywhere. She forced open a door and entered the burning building, which was filled with thick, acrid smoke.

"Anybody in here?" she yelled. "Anybody in here?"

No response. She yelled again, "Anybody in here?" Then she heard what sounded like the tinkling of a bell, coming from deep within the building. The smoke was so thick that even with her flashlight she could see only a few feet in front of her. She was finding it increasingly difficult to breathe. She decided to return to the outside, but in the thick smoke she couldn't find the door, couldn't see anything, couldn't breathe. She was on her knees, gasping for breath, the dense smoke curling around her. Then everything went black.

Oscar Anderson smelled smoke and saw flames lighting the night sky of the Tamarack River Valley. He hopped into his pickup and drove to the former golf course. He arrived the same time as Fred Russo. By this point, a half dozen fire trucks were spraying water on the fire, which still blazed out of control. On the way, Oscar met an ambulance, its red lights flashing and siren wailing.

"Geez," said Fred when Oscar told him about seeing the ambulance. "Wonder what that's all about?"

"Somebody must have gotten hurt in the fire," said Oscar. "Wonder who?"

The sheriff's deputies strung up yellow tape to keep a growing number of spectators a safe distance from the fire.

"What happened?" Oscar asked one of them.

"I don't know; when I got here, the whole thing was on fire. Terrible fire," said the deputy.

"I just met the ambulance; did somebody get hurt?" asked Oscar.

"The game warden, Natalie Karlsen. Dan Burman found her just inside the door of the burning building. He must have gotten to the fire right after the warden and seen her go inside. He went in and dragged her out. I heard she was alive, but just barely. Smoke inhalation can be a killer. Burman's a hero," said the deputy.

"Imagine that, Dan Burman a hero," said Oscar. Oscar had known Burman since he was a kid but never thought much of him. Burman had a reputation for hating the DNR. "Imagine him saving the game warden. Hard to believe."

"Wonder how the fire got started?" asked Fred. By now the building had nearly burned to the ground.

"I bet it was the Tamarack River Ghost," answered Oscar.

"You're kidding, aren't you?" said Fred.

"Nope, I'm not. The ghost didn't want all these buildings and thousands of smelly pigs messing up his valley. The ghost takes care of this valley. Protects it."

"Oscar, you are losing it. The old-timer's disease has got you by the collar."

"Scoff away, Fred. Make fun of me. Snicker away. But mark my word; the Tamarack River Ghost has got to be reckoned with."

"Well I've got some other suspects in mind."

"Like who?"

"Like some animal rights organization. They could've done it. Remember how that woman shot off her mouth at the meeting last winter?"

"They could have. But they didn't. The Tamarack River Ghost started this fire."

Josh was asleep when the ringing phone awakened him. He glanced at his watch; it was 10:30 p.m. He picked up the phone and mumbled, "Hello."

"Is this Josh Wittmore?"

"Yes," answered Josh. He didn't recognize the voice.

"This is Sheriff Bliss, and I'm afraid I've got bad news for you."

"Yes?" was all Josh could think to say. He was now fully awake.

"You are good friends with Warden Natalie Karlsen?"

"Yes, yes I am. Has something happened to Natalie?"

"She's in the Willow River Hospital. She got caught in a big fire out here at the Nathan West hog operation."

"A big fire at Nathan West? What burned? Will Natalie be okay?"

"The new hog house burned to the ground, and I don't know how Natalie Karlsen is doing. But I wanted you to know."

"Thank you," Josh said.

For the past several weeks, Josh had turned off his scanner when he came home from work, something he had previously never done. When he learned that his new boss at *Farm Country News* really didn't want him covering stories, he decided not to bother listening to his scanner. Still, had it been on, he would have known about the fire and would have hurried out to the golf course to get the story. But now he quickly pulled on his clothes and drove to the hospital, only a short distance from his apartment. After parking, he sprinted to the hospital door, a revolving affair that seemed to take forever to go around. He hurried to the information desk.

"Could you tell me Natalie Karlsen's room number, please?"

The person on duty scanned a computer screen in front of her. "Room 325," she said.

Josh ran to the elevator, punched the up button several times, and waited and waited for the elevator door to open. When it did arrive, he pushed "3" and soon was on the third floor, standing in front of the nurse's station.

"Can I help you?" the nurse on duty asked.

"I'm here to see Natalie Karlsen," Josh blurted out. "I believe she's in room 325."

"Yes, she is. But she may be sleeping. She had a close call today."

Josh knocked gently on the door before entering. Natalie's eyes were closed, and her nose and mouth were covered with a plastic mask. Tubes were stuck in her arms.

Josh touched her on the arm and said quietly, "It's Josh, Natalie."

Her eyes flickered open, and she smiled. Josh took her hand in his. She gently squeezed it.

"I love you," Josh said. He had tears in his eyes. Natalie squeezed his hand again.

"You'd better get some sleep," said Josh. "I'll wait around for a while before I go home."

Josh saw Natalie's bag on the chair next to him. It looked as if some of the loose sheets of paper stuffed in it might fall out if someone moved it so Josh decided to fold the papers and push them further into the bag.

He glanced at the first sheet—it appeared to be a poem, and the byline was "M.D." *How did Natalie get one of M.D.'s poems?* he wondered. He held the sheet of smudged paper in his hand for a moment. And then it hit him. Natalie was M.D. The mysterious writer of poetry—this possibility had never occurred to him. As well as he had come to know her, she had never once let on that she wrote poetry or had ever submitted anything to his or any other publication. He was both surprised and angry. Why had she not shared with him what she'd been writing? After all, he was the one who decided to publish it.

But then a darker thought crossed his mind. Did Natalie write the possibly threatening letter about Nathan West? And did she have something to do with starting the fire? His reporter's instincts kicked in. He would have to find the answers to these troubling questions. He glanced over at Natalie, sleeping peacefully. The answers would have to wait.

45

Blame

*J*osh slept fitfully. His mind was on Natalie, the identity of M.D., and the huge fire that had completely destroyed one of Nathan West's main buildings. Was it possible that Natalie, the woman he loved, was an arsonist? Was she someone with such an overzealous concern for the environment that she would burn a building to make a point?

He had a vivid dream of a wild-eyed blonde woman, splashing gasoline on the new hog house and then touching a match to the liquid, and watching, laughing wildly, as the flames quickly spread up its side. Through an enormous cloud of black smoke, he heard the woman yelling in a high-pitched, eerie voice, "The Tamarack River Ghost doesn't want you here. The valley doesn't want you here. Leave, and don't ever come back." Then she walked into the burning building and disappeared as the flames shot ever higher into the air and the smoke became blacker and denser. As he watched the building burn, a strange apparition appeared above it—a white ghostlike creature emerging from the fire without seeming to be harmed by it. A faceless blonde joined the apparition, which embraced her. Then the two merged into one ghostly figure that floated off toward the river, away from the fire. He heard singing as the apparition slowly moved away:

> Ho Ho, Ho Hay, keep the logs a-going
> Keep 'em rolling and twisting.

He sat up in bed, wide awake. Had he really heard the song? Was it in his room, or was it just a dream, a bad dream? He glanced at his bedside clock—4:00 a.m. He walked into the kitchen and started a pot of coffee.

He knew there would be no more sleep this night. The memory of the dream played over and over again, as he sat at his little kitchen table, drank coffee, and tried to sort out his feelings toward Natalie.

At 8:00 a.m., he drove to the hospital. He went directly to Natalie's room, where he found her sitting up, looking mostly like her old self. The oxygen mask had been removed from her face, as had the tubes from her arms. She was eating breakfast.

"Good morning, Josh," she said, smiling. "Do you want a cup of coffee? I can order one for you."

"No thanks."

"You are looking terribly glum on this fine morning, and rather tired, too, I might add."

"I didn't sleep well."

"How come? I hope you weren't worried about me. I just got a little too much smoke last night. Doctor said I could go home this morning and that I'm fine."

"We've got to talk," Josh said.

"You are the serious one this morning. You look like you've lost your best friend."

"Maybe I have," said Josh quietly.

"So, what do you want to talk about?" Natalie sipped on her coffee.

"Last night when I was here, some papers were falling out of your bag, which was over on that chair."

He pointed to a chair next to the wall on the far side of the room where her bag still sat.

"I saw some poetry written by M.D. You are M.D., aren't you?" asked Josh, frowning.

"You've finally found me out." Natalie held up her hands. "Yes, I'm the mysterious M.D. I wouldn't dare have used my real name, being the county conservation warden."

"But . . . but you could have told me. I wouldn't have told anyone. I know how to keep a secret!" Josh hesitated for moment before continuing. "Did you . . . did you write that rather threatening letter I shared with you on the phone?"

"Of course not. Somebody else was trying to remind us of Mortimer Dunn—the letter was not mine."

The room filled with silence.

"What?" Natalie asked, raising her voice.

"About the fire—" Josh stammered.

More silence filled the room as the young couple stared at each other.

"You think that I . . . You think that I started that fire that almost killed me?"

"I . . . I didn't say that."

"You're thinking it, aren't you? You're thinking I did it."

Now the room was filled with thick, emotional silence.

"Well, Mr. Josh Wittmore, you just turn around and leave this room right now. Leave me alone, you hear."

"But, but—"

"Just leave," Natalie said as she burst into tears.

Josh turned and left the room, then drove toward his office. He felt like someone had just kicked him in the stomach. He couldn't remember when he had felt more awful.

As he passed by the counter outside his office, he picked up the morning copy of the *Milwaukee Journal Sentinel*. He tossed the paper on his desk and turned on his computer and waited for it to boot up.

"Wittmore, did I hear you come in?" his boss yelled from the office next door.

"I'm here."

"Well, get your ass in my office. Right now."

Josh dragged himself out of his chair and walked into the office next door.

"You look like hell," his boss said, by way of greeting.

"I didn't sleep too well last night."

"Have you seen this? Have you read this?" Lexington was waving a copy of the *Milwaukee Journal Sentinel*.

"Not yet—I just picked up my copy."

"Well, let me tell you what's here. Let me tell you about the biggest story of the year and how you missed it. Completely missed it."

Josh almost blurted out, "What story?" But he remained silent.

"See this?" Lexington was waving a copy of the newspaper again.

"Did you know that one of Nathan West's big hog barns burned last night? Burned to the ground. Did you know that?" Lexington yelled.

"Yes, I heard about that."

"Well, why weren't you out there, taking pictures, interviewing people, putting together a story? Where the hell were you?" Josh chose not to admit that he'd turned off his scanner and hadn't heard about the fire until the sheriff called him.

"I was at the hospital with my friend, Natalie, who was caught in that fire. I think I have my priorities straight, which is more than I can say for you," Josh blurted out, his face red with anger. "Besides, you told me not to cover stories like this."

"Are you challenging me? Are you questioning my priorities?" Lexington asked, the veins in his neck bulging.

"You just don't get it, do you, Lexington?" Josh said. This was the first time he called his boss by his last name. "You have no idea what good journalism is all about. All you're interested in is the almighty dollar, journalism be damned."

"You . . . you impertinent bastard. Where do you get off, talking to me like this?" shouted Lexington.

"It's about time somebody stood up to you and all the rest of those hiding behind journalism, trying to make money by being deceptive. This thing you call a newspaper—it's no newspaper. It's just a bunch of poorly written ads with some paid-for freelance material tossed in to make it look legitimate. Well, it's not legitimate, not by a long shot."

"Are you finished? You done with your little tirade?"

"For the moment, yes," Josh said quietly.

"Well I have one more thing to say to you. You are fired. I don't want to see your sorry ass around here ever again," Lexington said.

"Thank you," Josh said, with a bit of sarcasm in his voice. "I was about to quit anyway."

Josh returned to his office, found a box, and gathered up his camera, laptop computer, a photo of Natalie, and a few other items and carried them to his truck. He tossed the morning *Journal Sentinel* in with his other things. As he slowly drove back to his apartment, his mind was in a fog. He felt relieved and concerned at the same time. Relieved that he didn't have to work at a job that went against all his principles. Concerned because he now was without an income—and without a girlfriend. He did not see the brilliant yellow aspen leaves or the maples that were in full fall splendor. He did not hear the long skeins of Canada geese winging their way south from their summer nesting sites deep in Canada. He saw nothing of autumn's beauty that was once more visiting central Wisconsin.

He parked his pickup and climbed the stairs to his apartment, carrying his box of office possessions. He put the box on the table, the photo of Natalie that he'd taken last winter when they were cross-country skiing on top. He stared at it. Natalie was smiling, obviously enjoying the day. Could she possibly have had anything to do with the fire at Nathan West's big operation? Now that he knew she was really M.D., at least the M.D. that contributed poetry to the paper, he was both relieved and furious. He thought he knew this woman, thought he knew her well. But she had secrets, obviously lots of them. Why hadn't she told him that she wrote the M.D. poems? He wouldn't have told anyone.

He put the photo facedown on the table and sighed deeply. In a matter of twenty-four hours, he had lost both his job and his girlfriend. He slumped deep into the chair and rubbed his eyes. He could feel a headache coming, one of the throbbing head-busters that started just above his eyes and then moved around to his neck. The kind that aspirins barely touch, that wouldn't stop until it ran its course, which sometimes took more than twelve hours.

Josh walked to the bathroom, turned on the cold water, opened the medicine cabinet, and dumped three aspirins in his hand. Maybe three would help stop the pain. He went to his bedroom and sprawled out on the bed, not even bothering to take off his shoes. What would he do now? What could he do? Since he had graduated from college, he had always had a job—when *Farm Country News* was flourishing, even a good job and a good boss. How he missed Bert Schmid. He could talk to Bert, share his problems with him. His new boss—former boss, he reminded himself—was a money-obsessed tyrant. All that Lawrence Lexington had on his mind was money and how he could make more of it, newspaper be damned. The newspaper's employees were merely cogs in his moneymaking machine.

When Josh awakened, the room was nearly dark. He glanced at his clock. He had slept all day. He went to the kitchen and started a pot of coffee—his head felt better, but the sickening feeling of loss was still overwhelming. He saw the *Journal Sentinel* sticking out of the box of his office possessions. He looked at the photo on the front page—the Nathan West building with smoke billowing from its roof—and then he began reading.

Tamarack River Valley, Ames County, Wisconsin

Dan Burman, a farmer in the Tamarack River Valley, became a hero last night. He is credited with saving the life of Natalie Karlsen, Ames County conservation warden. Burman arrived at the disastrous fire at the Nathan West holdings in the valley shortly after Karlsen. He found her inside the building and pulled her to safety.

Burman said, "I saw the smoke and fire and jumped in my truck to see what was going on. It had to be a big fire. A really big fire, from the smoke I saw. And it weren't no forest fire either. I could tell by the smoke. The smoke I was seein' was black, really black.

"When I turned into the Nathan West property, I noticed the lady warden's truck a ways ahead of me. I don't believe she saw me. The warden jumped out of her truck, and I saw her go into the flaming building—the end where she went in wasn't burning. I suspect she was checking to see if anyone was trapped in there. I parked my truck and waited for a bit, not quite knowing what to do. I heard sirens in the distance, so I knew help was comin'. She must have radioed in.

"The warden didn't come out of the building. So I went inside myself. It was so smoky I couldn't breathe, so I got down on my hands and knees and started crawlin'. I had only crawled a few feet from the door when I bumped into something. It was the lady warden. I pulled her outside and away from the building. She seemed to be breathin', but she didn't look too good. Just then, the first fire truck and an EMT unit arrived and took over. That was about it."

By the time the firefighters arrived, the building was beyond saving. The smoke and flames from the inferno could be seen for miles around. One of the neighbors of the new hog operation, when asked about the fire, said, "Good riddance. Nobody wanted all these pigs here anyway." She would not give her name.

As of late last night the warden was in the Willow River Hospital and reported to be doing well, thanks to Dan Burman. Ed Clark, regional representative for Nathan West, one of the country's leading hog producers, said, "This new production unit, with the most up-to-date technology for raising hogs, is a complete loss." When asked if the company planned to rebuild, Clark said, "I don't know. That will be a corporate decision."

The company recently purchased the former Tamarack River Golf Course in western Ames County. After some considerable debate with many people opposed to the construction, Nathan West eventually gained approval and the necessary permits to build. They had planned to produce more than 75,000 hogs a year on this site.

Josh read the article a second time. *What a fool I have been*, he thought. *What a fool.* He immediately went to the phone and called Natalie's number. No answer. When her voicemail kicked in, he said, "It's Josh, Natalie. I've made a fool of myself. A complete fool. Can I come over? I have lots of explaining to do."

He slumped back into his chair, remembering when he and Natalie first met and she had accused him of tipping off Dan Burman, whom she suspected of game poaching. Now he had done the same thing, but much worse. He had suspected Natalie had something to do with starting the fire at Nathan West, and the truth was she arrived first on the scene afterward, prepared to rescue anyone who might have been trapped in the flames. He had the story completely backward. No wonder she was so angry with him. She had every right.

Blame

Rather than wait for her to call—he feared that she probably wouldn't—he pulled on his jacket and ran down the stairs and out to his truck. He stopped at the Willow River Bakery and bought a chocolate cake, then drove to the liquor store, where he bought two bottles of wine. He headed toward Natalie's cabin. He was feeling better, much better. He saw smoke coming from the cabin's chimney. She had a fire going in the fireplace. He parked his truck. Carrying his peace offerings, he walked up to the cabin door. He knocked. Knocked again. Then knocked a third time. Finally, Natalie, her eyes red from crying, answered the door. She had heard the phone message and couldn't help but smile when she saw a very contrite Josh standing at her door, holding two bottles of wine and a chocolate cake.

46

A New Beginning

*T*he following morning, after Natalie had driven off to work, Josh returned to his apartment. He felt better than he had for days, but he still worried about finding a job. He was well aware of the limited demand for agricultural reporters. One of his other worries had been ill-founded—Natalie didn't care that he had lost his job; in fact, she was pleased that he no longer worked for what she called "that scumbag phony newspaper."

They also had a long discussion about why she had kept secret that she was really M.D., the person submitting anti–factory farm material to his newspaper. She had tried to explain that she thought it best not to tell anyone that she was M.D. If someone found out that the conservation warden had picked sides against large-scale agriculture, she'd have lots of difficulty doing her job. She thought, once they had gotten better acquainted, that she'd tell Josh—but she hadn't, fearing that as a good writer he'd see her attempts as amateurish.

"Amateurish they are not," said Josh. "Good poetry? That, I don't know. But what you wrote surely had an edge to it, and it came from the heart. That's what good writing is all about, no matter what label you put on it."

*J*osh had just gotten out of the shower when the phone rang. "This is Billy Baxter, over at the *Argus*."

"How you doing, Billy?"

"I'm fine. I was wondering if you'd have time to join me for a cup of coffee at the Lone Pine this morning, say around ten?"

"Sure, meet you there," said Josh. He wondered what Billy wanted—he was quite sure that few people knew that he had lost his job at *Farm Country News.*

When he arrived at the Lone Pine, Billy was already there, sitting in a booth off to the side, away from the old timers clustered together for their morning coffee discussions. He already had a cup of coffee in front of him.

"Slide in, Josh," Billy said as he waved at Mazy to bring over another cup. "That was some fire over at the river—put the kibosh on that big hog outfit, at least for a while. Heard that your game warden friend got hurt. How's she doing?"

"Oh, she's doing fine. Got a little too much smoke."

"Glad to hear that she's okay. So how are you and *Farm Country News* getting along these days?"

"Not too good. Lexington fired me."

"Really. Well, I'm not surprised. I could see it coming. You didn't fit with what that Lexington guy is trying to do. I saw that right from the beginning. I've been reading your work for years—good stuff. It's not like what *Farm Country* is publishing these days."

"You're right, Billy. Lexington has no idea what good journalism is; his ideas are all green—and I'm talking about money."

Billy laughed. "It's a bit ironic that I'm talking to you this morning."

"How's that?"

"I've wanted to lure you away from *Farm Country News* ever since Lawrence Lexington took over—see if I could convince you to join our staff—for probably less money than you've been earning," Billy said, smiling.

"Well, as of yesterday, my income is zero. So I'm all ears."

"Remember a while back, when I mentioned I wanted to improve our paper's website?"

"I do remember you mentioning it."

"Well, I'm ready to move ahead, and I'd like you to take charge of doing it. In fact, I'd like you to be our new online editor."

A New Beginning

"Really?" A smile spread across Josh's face.

"Not only that, I'd like you to develop an online agricultural section that we'll market throughout the Midwest. Something like what the old *Farm Country News* was doing with its print edition."

Josh couldn't believe what he was hearing—to be employed again and doing something he believed in!

"When do I start?" Josh asked, smiling broadly.

"Right now, if you want. I'll find a desk for you at the *Argus* office, and you'll be good to go. Stop by after lunch—give me time to organize an office for you—and we'll get you started."

They talked a bit more about details—salary and benefits (same as he had received at the old *Farm Country News*), expectations (an online agriculture section up and running in a couple of weeks), and a general discussion about what possible stories to include. They talked generally about the important role the press must play, no matter whether a local, regional, or national paper.

"The press is the watchdog for our society, has been, and will always be," said Billy. "What goes on in society needs watching, especially so in agriculture. These big-time farming operations like Nathan West need somebody to keep an eye on them. That's one of the reasons I hired you, Josh. Because you know agriculture and you also know journalism."

Josh listened to his new boss's speech; it sounded nearly identical to one Bert Schmid used to give. He was pleased to hear someone saying what he had long believed and because of Lawrence Lexington's new approach had found himself straying from.

They also discussed online advertising, which they agreed could be a problem, but Billy said the *Argus*'s advertising department was prepared for and even looking forward to the challenge.

Promptly after lunch, Josh drove to the *Argus* offices, got a quick tour of the facilities, met the staff, and found his desk and computer.

Anxious to get to work, he got on the phone with Ed Clark at the Nathan West site, told him about his new position with the *Argus*, and arranged for a meeting. He wanted to do a follow-up on the big fire. He left word with the receptionist and was soon driving toward Tamarack Corners.

He drove slowly, taking time to see the beauty of the fall colors, the brilliant yellows of the aspens, the deep reds of maples contrasting with the golden cornfields waiting to be harvested. He noticed the clear blue, cloudless sky and the green pastures with Holsteins grazing here and there. He couldn't remember when he had enjoyed this trip more than today—the only thing that would have made it even more perfect would be Natalie sitting beside him, enjoying the day with him.

Soon he arrived at the Nathan West building site; the remains of the hog barn were a tangled mess of burned wood and twisted metal. He drove past the destruction to the farm office, where Ed Clark was waiting for him.

After shaking hands, Josh thanked Ed for agreeing to meet with him.

"I know you've probably got lots to do, so I won't take up much of your time," said Josh.

"Matter of fact, I've got lots of time," Ed said. "I resigned from my job with Nathan West this morning."

Surprised, Josh blurted out, "Why?" As soon as he said it, he thought it was none of his business and he shouldn't have asked.

"I just couldn't stomach the company's ethics anymore. I gave them two weeks' notice."

"Really, what happened?" He could sense a good story in the making.

"Remember the meeting where Emily Jordan presented the tampered research data?"

"How could I forget? Her report swayed the zoning committee's vote."

"Did you know what was really going on?" Clark asked. "With Emily Jordan, I mean? Do you know why she changed the numbers?"

"I heard she wanted to help Tamarack Corners by bringing new jobs to the area."

"Ha. That was just a smokescreen. I'll bet you didn't know that cute little Emily was working for Nathan West the whole time. She was a plant. Sure, she was a graduate student—but she also was on the payroll of Nathan West with one important job—help convince communities to accept Nathan West's big hog operations. One of the vice presidents at Nathan West is her uncle."

Josh was dumbfounded by what he was hearing.

"You mean the whole thing was a setup, with Nathan West duping the university as well as Tamarack Corners and Ames County?" said Josh.

"That it was, and that's the main reason I resigned. I just couldn't take this stuff anymore. Emily did the same thing in Ohio, except the Ohio State University people couldn't prove it."

"This is all on the record?"

"Print whatever you want, and you can quote me too. There was a day when Nathan West was an honest, respectable company. But they got too big, and too greedy, and too willing to cut corners to get what they wanted. You can quote me on that, too."

All the while, Josh was furiously taking notes. He realized that he had a story that would make national news.

Epilogue

Natalie Karlsen and Josh Wittmore were married on June 18, 2011. They share the cabin on Copperhead Lake, which they have purchased. On special occasions, they enjoy chocolate cake with a bottle of wine. Natalie continues as the Ames County conservation warden. She makes certain the game and conservation laws of Ames County are strictly enforced. But since the fire at Nathan West, and her close call with death, she spends less time searching for game poachers in the Tamarack River Valley. After the fire, Natalie penned a personal note to Dan Burman, thanking him for his heroic act and wishing him and his family all the best. She didn't mention her concern about his game poaching. Natalie continues writing but has promised Josh that she will do no more "ghost writing." "No need for it," she told him, chuckling.

Josh Wittmore's story "When Factory Farming Loses Its Way," published in the *Ames County Argus* in both its online and print editions, was nominated for a Pulitzer. Josh is well on his way to becoming one of the leading voices for agriculture in the Midwest. With his leadership, the *Argus* created a section titled "Farming Yesterday and Today," which is available on the *Argus* website and has already won an award for regional agricultural reporting. Several freelance reporters in the upper midwestern states regularly contribute to the section. Many freelance submissions arrive every week from farmers wanting to share their stories about what farming was like when they were kids. The *Argus*'s website edition, with its regional agricultural section, has taken up much of the slack created when the electronic version of *Farm Country News* went off the track, as Josh explains it.

Epilogue

The electronic *Farm Country News* is still in business, but barely. Its staff now consists of just three people, and Lawrence Lexington stubbornly promotes his everyone-pays-to-publish model. Lexington has already missed one loan payment to the bank; the future of *Farm Country News* appears bleak.

The University of Wisconsin–Madison's Department of Agribusiness Studies continues as a national leader in both its undergraduate and graduate training programs, and especially in its cutting-edge research on large-scale farming operations. Assistant Professor Randy Oakfield left the department at the end of the spring semester. He began a new teaching assignment in a small community college in south Texas that September. He has not maintained any contact with the University of Wisconsin–Madison. The week before he moved from Wisconsin, a small package arrived in his mailbox. It had no return address. When he opened it, he discovered a DVD and a note: "Here is the only copy of this DVD; I destroyed the other copies and removed the file from my iPad. Have a good life. Emily Jordan."

Emily Jordan continues as a consumer researcher with Nathan West Industries in Dubuque, Iowa. She has not sought entry into any university graduate program.

*E*d Clark now works as a sales representative for Ames County Feed and Supply. He and Josh have become close friends and regularly have coffee at the Lone Pine, where they discuss farming and agricultural issues.

Marcella Happsit, president of the Tamarack Corners Historical Society, reported at the society's meeting after the fire that she had received a note from Nathan West, canceling all of its promises to give money to the community. All except the full-sized statue of Mortimer Dunn and his dog, which had been completed at the time of the fire. Today the statue stands in front of the Tamarack Corners Museum. "At least we got one good thing out of the company," Marcella said.

Nathan West Industries sent several fire inspectors to the site of its destroyed building. They found nothing definitive as to its cause, other than evidence that the fire started at one end of the building, where electricians had been working on a special new computerized feeding system earlier on the day of the fire. The workers claimed they turned off all the electricity when they left that day.

A couple of weeks after the fire, bulldozers leveled the site of the burned building, and all work stopped on additional buildings. An announcement from Nathan West Industries in Dubuque stated: "Nathan West officials are reviewing all options as to whether we will rebuild this site or abandon." At this time, no decision has been made.

Fred Russo and Oscar Anderson still meet regularly for coffee. At one of their meetings they discussed the possible cause of the fire. Oscar was convinced that the Tamarack River Ghost set it.

"Remember what the fire inspectors said," offered Oscar. "They couldn't find a cause. It's got to be the Tamarack River Ghost, no question about it. Know what else? I was over at the Dunn cemetery the other day. Just looking around. Know what I found?"

"You're gonna tell me no matter what, aren't you?"

"I found one of Mortimer Dunn's wood carvings. It was a wooden spoon, all nicely decorated. Found it on top of his wife's grave. Looked like it was just put there, no grass growing over it or anything. It was old looking, all faded. I picked it up, and you know what it said on the back, carved with little letters?"

"Okay, what'd it say?"

"It said, 'For Amelia, from Mort. 1900.'"

"I know what you're thinkin'. You think the ghost put the spoon there."

"He did. No doubt about it."

Since the fire, several people who live in the Tamarack River Valley or have visited there in the evening swear they have heard the ghost, especially on nights when the wind is down and the moon is up. They smell pipe tobacco smoke, hear the clear sound of the ghost dog's little bell, and hear his song, sometimes faintly, other times more distinctly:

Epilogue

Ho Ho, Ho Hay, keep the logs a-going.
Keep 'em rolling and twisting.
Keep 'em moving, keep 'em straight.
On the way to the lake called Poygan.
Ho Ho, Ho Hay,
What a day, what a day.